A Piece of Time

A Piece of Time

VICTORIA FIELDING

Sunshine ~
You are that! Here's
to families, &
being with them eternally!
Victoria

LIGHT SOJOURN PUBLISHING

A PIECE OF TIME

First Printing
ISBN 978-0-9837052-0-8

LIGHT SOJOURN PUBLISHING

Please send E-mail correspondence to:
thelightcameon@gmail.com
For speaking engagements, please call (801) 652-5820
Cover Design and Graphics by Emily Webb, emsflower@msn.com
Printed in USA

READERS' REVIEWS

"This book lifted me to a place of forgiveness, peace, and love; it then brought me back to a place of understanding what really matters in my life."

—S. Noyce

"Our heroine experiences time in a new dimension . . . a chance to change."

—E. Webb

"A Piece of Time is an extraordinary depiction of love, acceptance and forgiveness presented in a most unusual and thought-provoking manner. You will be compelled to keep reading. Fielding masterfully presents scenarios that will stimulate your own imagination and tug at your heart strings."

—M. Neumann

"Victoria Fielding gives the reader a glimpse into eternity."

—J. Bowen

"Captivating! This book captured my interest in the first chapter and I couldn't put it down until I had enjoyed its surprising end. It is one of those feel good books that really touches your heart. You will want to put it on your shelf and read it over and over again."

—D. Godfrey

"You will remember—when you arrive in Heaven and it feels familiar to you—that you read about it in her book. Victoria Fielding, our tour guide, will put knots in your belly, a lump in your throat, and leave an impression on your heart. An adventurous ride with some heavenly detours."

—E. Marlowe

"I LOVED this. My eyes are now open to unknown possibilities. I didn't just read this book; I felt it, too. I am so glad this novel came my way.

—A. Arntsen

DEDICATION

To the children; the precious, precious children.

ACKNOWLEDGEMENTS

Oh, the comfort —
The inexpressible comfort of feeling
safe with a person,
Having neither to weigh thoughts,
Nor measure words — but pouring them
All right out — just as they are —
Chaff and grain together —
Certain that a faithful hand will
Take and sift them —
Keep what is worth keeping —
and with the breath of kindness
Blow the rest away.

— *Dinah Maria Craik*

Many, many thanks to all my friends for the support, encouragement, and investment of their time:

To my sister, Jan, who showed me we must forgive everyone; to JoAnn Bowen, who provides me continual strength and perspective when my reserve dries up; to Marv Neumann, perhaps my most enthusiastic cheerleader, and an intense grammarian who lets me get away with very little; to Steve Draper, my proud-to-know Viet Nam hero, who helped me to understand just how bad war is from the eyes of a soldier; to Susan Christensen, for sharing her medical background and making sure I got it right; to Hayley-bug, whose heaven-sent message from her grandmother graces these pages.

To Michael Ramsdell, for being my mentor and friend; to Emily Webb whose limitless artistic talents grace the cover of this book; to my alpha-readers—Gail, Karlee, Elise, Aroura, Shelby, Laurie, Shaun, Michelle, Dean, Marchelle, Les, Lisa, and twenty-five more--whose comments and insights were invaluable; to Leslie Householder and Marnie Pherson whose perspective on the Seven Laws and teaching me how to incorporate them has made a real difference in pursuing my dream; to Fanny Crosby (1860) and William B. Bradbury (1867) who wrote and composed a favorite childhood song, Give Said the Little Stream.

To my own precious children and my wonderful sisters, for all their support and belief in me; to my family members who have gone before—Sarah, Thomas, Nephi, Lillie, Anna, Amy, Mae—thank you for showing me the way. Lastly, to my parents who gave me life and those experiences to best help me grow. Our lives truly are "By Design".

— Victoria Fielding

INTRODUCTION

At one point in A Piece of Time, Lilly—the main character—exclaims: "And then the lights went out!"

What lights?
When?
Why?

The simple truth is that, sooner or later, the lights are going to go out for each of us. Death is inevitable, and almost as certain as death is our curiosity about it. But this book is not so much about death as it is about life: Your life, my life, ticking away on this sphere called

Earth. Putting religious skepticism, agnostic beliefs, or other concerns aside, we are all occupants on this planet, and this book has been written for us, the living.

For every religion out there--Christianity, Buddhism, Islam, Hinduism, Judaism, Sikhism-- there is a different belief about what awaits us when we exit this planet and walk behind that dark curtain. Even among Christian religions there are varying beliefs as to what Heaven holds for us. Within these pages is my personal take of what awaits us. I may have it wrong, but—if so--I am in good company. I have read about countless near-death experiences (NDEs) of individuals who have stepped over that threshold, through that curtain, and then returned. None of these people are quacks; they are ordinary people who have had extra-ordinary experiences. And all of those who stepped over that threshold—just to return--valued their lives more, desired to live their lives more fully.

As I studied, I made a list of the many similarities in their descriptions of where they were, who they met, what they did there, and why they needed to return to their life here. The majority of the similarities are within these pages. I so very much appreciate the up- close and personal experiences these various authors shared with me. Reading their life stories simply confirmed what I have always sensed: Our death will be just a continuation of our life. And, for good or bad, we take ourselves with us. The circumstances may be different as to how we step over that threshold, but it IS just one step over.

Death is inevitable, as is that intense pain we struggle to carry when we lose a loved one. For many, the death of someone close compels us to think about an after-life. It does not matter if one is a believer or a non-believer; the loss of a loved one puts us all on the same playing field. We lost a part of us, and—for a piece of time--where that loved one went, we cannot go.

In the past twenty years the interest to know something, anything about a possible after-life has grown, More people are asking, "What if?" Several TV shows and movies have addressed making contact with the dead. What was once considered total quackery (and there IS still that element), has now been accepted by the mainstream as having some validity.

Are there ghosts? Unequivocally! But I prefer to call a ghost for what he or she is: A real-life individual whose spirit has passed on to the other side. Being able to come and go, our loved ones--in spirit--are among us. They protect us from harm; they give us direction; they help us feel their love and assurance. Obviously, someday you and I will be spirits too, for death is inevitable.

Are there negative, angry, confused spirits here on Earth as well? Absolutely! No doubt we have all felt them around us or others when we sense a dark, depressing energy. They are the ones who tend to linger here; nevertheless, we can learn how to protect ourselves from their influence.

Ultimately, you may agree–or not–with any of this. You may be thinking "get real", as your beliefs may be radically different. No problem there. But truth is truth wherever we may find it, whether it be in our studies or within our hearts. And, once we have bumped up against truth, we need to be responsible for what reveals itself to be true.

As friends and acquaintances have read the manuscript, I have been asked, "Is any of this true?" Much of it is true; however, I have changed the names to protect the innocent and the not-so-much. Just like you, my own life has taught me that it is through struggle that we grow; it is through disappointment that forgiveness is refined. In this life, we can feel sustaining peace.

I have no doubt that loved ones from the other side have assisted me with this story. I would vacillate for days over how best to present a particular concept. Then, at dawn, while in that thin place between the edges of sleep and full consciousness, the insights would come; even the parable Jesse shares with Lilly; even the title for this book.

Yes, death is inevitable. The simple truth is that, sooner or later, the lights are going to go out for each of us. Or are they? What if, instead, the light comes on?

Whatever conclusion you may come to, I hope that conclusion will serve to help you value your life, in the here and now, that much more. We can thrive in this life; we can know joy here. And that is what I wish for you; that is what I wish for all of us.

Victoria Fielding

There will come a time when you believe

Everything is finished;

That will be the beginning.

— Louis L'Amour

CHAPTER ONE

What an ugly three weeks. Not that it should really surprise me. After all, it was 'my' life I was describing. My friends were excluding me, plain and simple. I'd walk up to them in the halls, and they'd quit talking. They were obviously talking about me. My best friend, Skylar, had even become elusive, saying she was too busy to go shopping, too busy to hang out. I chalked it up to her exerting even more pressure on me to end my four-month relationship with my boyfriend, Alex.

I'll dump Alex when Hell freezes over," I mumbled to myself.

It seemed the harder I tried to make plans for my 18th birthday, the busier my friends got! 'Dang, Lilly, I'd love to hang out with you, but I'm studying for a test I'm taking in three weeks."

"Go to a movie with you? Wish I could, but my mom needs me home in case the pest control guys come."

As my misfortune would have it, my birthday–January 1– was coma day for everyone under the age of twenty-nine. So, I always celebrated my birthday on the Friday before. But, oh no, not this Friday. With Alex working and all my friends conveniently occupied elsewhere, I dragged home from my dance lesson fully resigned to sequestering myself in my room for the entire night. Two hours into my self-imposed exile, Mom knocked at my door, bribing me into letting her and Creepy Carl, her loser-boyfriend, take me to dinner.

"Archibalds is your favorite restaurant, after all, and we do have to eat dinner, and we could stop at a video store afterward and you could pick out some DVDs." Mom paused, breathless, waiting for my response.

She had rattled off my options so fast that I had to wonder why it mattered to her so very much that I tag along. I caved only because my other option was to drown myself in my own tub. I gave my dogs, Major and Minor, their very own hugs, told them to hide all sharp objects while I was gone and dragged my sorry butt to the car.

How lame was this? My 18th birthday and I was freezing to death in the backseat of a car driven by a guy who made me want to retch, while Mom rambled on nonstop about how pretty the snow was. Blah. Blah. Blah.

"Forget it, Mom," I said under my breath. Nothing was going to make me lighten up!

"Hey, Carl, could you send some heat back here, please?"

Where was Alex? Snuggling up to him could keep me from freezing to death! Another snowstorm was hitting the valley, reducing our speed to a mere crawl. I pulled my jacket tightly around me and looked out the window, watching the thick snowflakes hit the glass and dissolve into a cold rain, blurring the cars in the next lane.

At least next winter I would be in New York and not in Missoula, Montana. I suppose that was one reason to smile. I had been awarded one of three grants by the Avery School to enroll in their certificate program. Avery was to dance as Julliard was to music. Mom had maxed out her Visa to get me to Chicago for auditions. I had always been told that I had talent oozing from my pores, so I was not prepared for the competition I faced there. After watching the hordes of incredible dancers, I didn't think I had a chance. But the letter came, and not only had I been accepted, but I was awarded a grant. Mom had been standing behind me, whispering the words under her breath. Then she burst into tears.

'You did it, Lilly. You did it. All those lessons, all those endless practices! And, YOU did it!'

Pulling into the parking lot at Archibalds brought me back to the present. I slipped and slid in my bare-toed heels into the front entrance, just to be told that the main dining room was full and to follow the maitre-d' upstairs.

I trailed behind my mother and Carl into a separate dining room, to see there several long tables full of food, with forty plus chairs around the perimeter of the dance floor. The chairs were filled by all my friends. It was a bizarre moment. I tried to wrap my mind around whose party I had stumbled onto where everyone –and I mean everyone—had been invited but me.

"SURPRISE!" everyone yelled. Singing at the top of their lungs, they began:

"Happy Birthday to you, happy birthday to you!
Happy birthday, Dear Lilly, happy birthday to you.
Annddd Mannny Morrre, on Channellllll Four;
And Look At Youuuuuuuuuuu on Channel
Twooooooooooo!"

Alex was at my side in an instant. He picked me up, swung me around. "Hi, gorgeous! happy birthday!" He planted a hard kiss squarely on my mouth. The D.J. started playing Black Eyed Peas' ALIVE. Alex pulled me onto the dance floor and wrapped me tight in his arms.

I curled my fingers in his thick black hair and pulled his face down to mine, whispering in his ear. "So, I guess this is what it feels like to die and go to heaven."

Alex just smiled and pulled me closer. Alex was six foot, slender, and wore his hair long and tucked behind his ears. His olive skin accentuated his big brown eyes. That description alone would appeal to some girls, but when one added a gorgeous smile, perfect white teeth, great clothes, and an outrageous sense of humor, he would appeal to most females. But, I wasn't done. For the cherry on top, let's throw in his red Toyota Tacoma pick-up , four-door, long bed with 4" lift and 20" tires, and his reputation for spending money on his women, and now we have a guy who appeals to anything in a skirt.

Well, okay, he didn't appeal to Sky, but she had zero tolerance for drugs. It wasn't like he was a stoner or anything. And even though Alex knew he could get any girl in town, he had backed off from pressuring me to sleep with him. It was like he was finally SEEING me, falling for me, rather than following his usual agenda with the glut of girls he dated.

As the dance ended, we both saw Skylar approaching. Knowing they could not occupy the same space at the same time, Alex whispered in my car, "You'll get your birthday gift from me later tonight. I'm outta here." He melted into the dancers.

Before I could yell 'W-A-I-T!', Skylar was hugging me. "How sick was this, Lilly! We sooooo got ya!" Skylar yelled above the music.

As I looked around it was apparent that this was no last-minute ditch effort to throw a party. There wasn't a detail left out, right down to the ridiculous party hats and streamers. Skylar was obviously the official party planner, but it could have only been Mom who had sprung for all the expenses. At this very second, Mom was gyrating on the dance floor with Jerk Face, but one quick glance at her confirmed that she had indeed funded the fun. She was smiling like the Cheshire cat, while Carl—Mr. Personality—was looking over her head, no doubt undressing all my girlfriends in his twisted mind. The extravagance was the biggest surprise of all, because we had no money. Really, truly, no money. Dad's drinking had pretty much lost us most of the ranch. What money we did have went with him when he left us. Mom's teaching job left little extra to support a home, my dance classes, and the two of us.

Thinking back to the three previous Hell Weeks, if I had stopped to be rational, I would have known that Skylar would never turn on me. Skylar and I had been connected at the elbow since we were two. We were both officers in Missoula High's Dance Club, we lived at each other's house, wore each other's clothes, and we both loved dancing and literature. I envied Skylar. Skylar knew who she was. Unlike me, Skylar was unphased by peer pressure. Her confidence, over-the-top energy, and wicked sense of humor drew everyone to her. Only Sky could pull off two-inch spikes of purple and blond hair all over her head, making her look taller than her five feet. Her quirkiness—like wearing snow boots, striped orange and black tights and a heavy Army coat tonight — made her cute. Definitely, I might be the best dancer on the Dance Team, but Skylar was way more popular.

I wrapped my arms around her. "You so got me! This is so awesome!"

The D.J. started playing "Shake It Like A Polaroid." Feeling a tug on my arm, I turned to see who was dragging me onto the dance floor.

"Hey, Lilly, let's dance." Luke, home from college for the holidays, seemed oblivious to Alex fuming on the sidelines. I looked at Alex, shrugged my shoulders, and turned back to Luke.

"You are your usual brazen self."

"Hey, I don't see a ring on your finger, Lilly. And since when can't 'Two Doors Down' ask you to dance?"

I had to smile. Luke had lived two-doors down from me my whole life. Luke was yelling in my ear. "Do you have plans for New Year's Eve?" I looked at him incredulously. He knew Alex and I were exclusive.

I shouted over the music, "Of course I do, duh." The music switched to Kanye West's "Heartless" and Luke—being a decent dancer—held his own with his B Boy skills.

I was puzzled that Luke looked so crestfallen. Since when did he care to hang out with someone who was more like his little sister? I had been walking in his front door without knocking since I was six. Often I would stay and eat dinner with his Bubble Family.

"Hey, Mom, I am going over to the Bubbles," I used to announce, and that would always make Mom laugh. Luke's last name was Hartman, but the Bubbles label was so fitting as Luke's house was noisy, busy, and bubbly. Even though Luke's little brother, Landry, had been born with cerebral palsy, and Luke and his parents had to do absolutely everything for Landry, they were happy. His family was functional, so of course Jason, Sky and I flocked there. Due to Dad's drinking, dysfunction didn't run in my family; it galloped. Luke's parents loved each other. Mine did not. Luke actually enjoyed doing things for and with Landry. I was an only child. Luke's mother stayed home, so at dinner time the aroma of home-made bread and cookies baking often wafted from their windows and across the field to our house. Because my mother was always at work, the microwave and I had become intimate friends. My house had absorbed Mom's and my quiet sadness into its walls.

Luke shrugged his shoulders in defeat, and then teasing, rebounded with, "You only get me for one more week, babe, and then 'poof', I am heading back to college."

I looked around at the dancing crowd. Jason's absence left the usual huge void. Jason had lived right next to Luke, three-doors down from me. Jason was my wanna-be older brother, childhood protector, my best buddy. He, along with Luke and Skylar, made up my world. It had been two years now, and I still felt a sharp stab to my heart whenever I thought of Jason. Time hadn't lessened the hurt at all.

But I was ecstatic to see so many of my favorite people. There were only two people on the floor I wished I could kick to the curb: Carl, obviously, who was this very minute full-on French kissing my mother right in my line of vision. I caught Luke's eye and gestured toward Carl, yelling above the music.

"That is soooo disgusting!"

Carl was alive only because it was illegal to kill him. Somehow, some way I would get him out of Mom's life. Our Lives.

The second person I wished would disappear was the tall, yes—admittedly—gorgeous redhead bumping and grinding directly in front of Alex. My arch enemy from clear back in sixth grade: Helena!

Helena's mean girl syndrome had always targeted me.

She had moved from California to Missoula when she was twelve. As my luck would have it, she was assigned to my classroom. She treated me okay until Mom, one of the room mothers, started helping out in the classroom, brought goodies for us, and occasionally went along on field trips. Maybe Helena didn't like my Mom's baking; who knows. But for whatever reason, she was so rude to Mom at times, and I became her target all the time. It was typical for everyone to be invited to her outrageous birthday parties, except me. In junior high, a gazillion girls would be invited to her cabin for the weekend, except me. Helena upped the ante in high school. She bribed another girl, Kayla, to take a picture of me showering after P.E. class. Then Kayla—not the sharpest tool in the shed–sent it to everyone's phone. Of course, Kayla was expelled. And Helena? As always, untouched. Whenever I would gripe to Mom about her, I would get one of Mom's pearls: 'Remember, Lilly, we are expected to forgive seventy times seven.'

W h a t – e v e r!

Skylar knew I could barely tolerate Helena, so why was she invited to my party? Of course, I knew that answer. Helena had everything, except close friends, and Sky felt sorry for her. No doubt Helena was jealous of Sky and my friendship, and she was determined to push me out.

Even though Skylar was embarrassed to admit it, she did benefit from the rivalry. Helena had invited Skylar to Disney World with her family, a vacation I couldn't afford until I was at least graduated from the Avery School and finally making my own money. Helena let Skylar borrow her Mini Cooper on a regular basis. She gave Skylar clothes that Ms. Fashionista no longer wanted; after-all, they had been worn once. Even though I had always been No. 1 on Helena's hit list, others had made it on the list, as well. Everyone but Sky.

Not having the money to buy friends, the only way I could strike back was by out-dancing Helena in every dance competition west of the Mississippi. Outscoring Helena for the umpteenth time at the last one did not bode well for me, as she had really pushed the envelope in the past month. She came on to Alex whenever the opportunity presented itself. I could now add that line item to my long list of why I barely tolerated her.

But why try to steal Sky's friendship NOW? Did she have an uncanny ability to sense how precarious my mental state currently was? Did evil people simply prey on the weakest? I had been so worried that Sky was going over to the Dark Side and that I was losing my best friend!

"Oh, please! What a slut!" I turned Luke so he, too, could watch the exhibition. Helena must have confused Alex for a stripping pole because she faced him, full on, and after crouching down, slowly raised back up, running her hand up his thigh, his torso and to his face. Alex had been innocent enough, patiently waiting for me to quit placating Luke, but I could see that Helena now had Alex's, and several other guys', full attention.

"I've got to go, Luke," I yelled, and left him standing there in my haste to get to Alex. I grabbed Alex's hand and pulled him onto the floor.

In spite of Helena's obnoxious presence, the night rocked on. My most memorable feeling was one of total relief that I still had my friends. What I thought was slow but sure rejection by everyone important to me was actually subtle subterfuge as they planned and anticipated an unforgettable night. But as awesome as it all was, the look on Helena's face when Alex and I left the party arm-in-arm was the best birthday gift of all!

The little things that happen are tucked into your mind,

And come again to greet you (or most of them, you'll find)

Through many little doorways of which you keep the keys

They crowd into your thinking –

We call them memories.

But some stay ever near you; you'll find they never rove—

The keys are always shining – those are the things you love.

— *Marjorie Wilson*

CHAPTER TWO

It felt delicious to sleep in. I awoke to feel the winter sun spilling in the window and spreading across my bed. I kicked off my covers and, sinking back into my pillow, broke into a smile. The party had been magical. It would take me years to thank Sky and Mom sufficiently, and I was sure it would take Mom years to pay for it.

"This is the highlight of my life."

I reached to my neck and fondled the silver heart put there by Alex the night before. Alex must love me because he really showed his marshmallow side last night.

I smiled a slow smile as I remembered his declaration: 'I've never felt this way towards any other girl, Lil! I want you in my life forever.' Hearing that, being in his arms and his kissing me, was all total heaven. The last few years I had wondered how anybody could love me. After all, if my own dad didn't love me, who could? But now, my life was picking up, definitely picking up.

Hopping out of bed, I grabbed an afghan and curled up on my window seat to survey the stark December landscape outside my bedroom window. I had to admit that when I moved to New York, I would miss our ranch.

Great Grandpa Teancum had traveled from Colorado to Missoula, Montana with $16 in his pocket. He had homesteaded a thousand acres, which—over time—became a very successful ranch. When the homestead was passed down to my grandpa, Benjamin, the ranch did not do as well, and with Dad, not at all. Most of the original acreage had been sold off to sustain what was left, as the ranch became a money pit. Dad resorted to selling insurance just to hang onto the ranch, and keep us fed and clothed.

Out my window, to the left, was the barn Teancum had built. The whole thing was now listing precariously to the right, having yielded long ago to the stiff winter winds of the Montana plains. I had spent countless hours in the loft of that barn. The loft was packed with all kinds of ancient stuff: Oil lanterns, leather harnesses, a treadle sewing machine–its cabinet full of weird looking buttons and thread on wooden spools–and in one corner an old metal trunk.

***

The winter wind was picking up, swirling snow across the barren fields, and I wrapped the afghan tighter round me, pressing my forehead against the window to check out our horses in the corral below. Poor Raven and Duke. There they stood, Dad's horse and mine, bracing with their backs against the icy wind, their breath visible in the bitter cold.

My walk down memory lane was ruined by hearing the back door slam.

"Jen, honey, where are you?" Creepy Carl was making another appearance.

"Crap," I muttered under my breath. It was so strange how uniquely adapted he was to repulsing everyone but my mother. Hopping off the window seat, I grabbed my robe, wrapping it tightly around me.

Mom quickly knocked and peeked around my door. "Good morning, Merry Sunshine! What makes you wake so soon! You used to wake at 10 o'clock, and now you wake at Noon!"

"Mom, didn't I outgrow your little jingle when I was three?"

"Come down for pancakes, Lilly! Carl is here. Let's eat."

"Oh, goody," I said dryly. "Why is he always here for our Saturday breakfasts? That was always family day, Mom. Remember Dad's luscious specialty waffles with the . . ."

Mom interrupted me. "Why don't you like him, Lilly?"

"How long do you have, Mom? Won't the pancakes get cold?"

At that, Mom yelled over the banister, "Carl, we'll be down in a minute. Heat up the syrup, please and help yourself." Closing the door, she continued, "I'm dead serious, Lil. Your sarcasm is getting really old."

She was waiting for my response but it was taking me a long time to know how to begin to explain why I held him in such contempt.

Should I start with his evasiveness about his past before he moved to Missoula? I could continue by reminding Mom of all his empty promises to help financially so we could keep the ranch. Strange how his big deals never quite came through, leaving him always borrowing money from her!

And I could finish with how he looked at me when Mom wasn't around. He made my skin crawl. I had told Luke about Carl and how Mom had really underestimated his creepiness. I had been surprised at Luke's reaction.

"I swear, Lil, if that ass ever lays a finger on you, tell me

ASAP!"

I had never seen that side of Luke. With his wrestling skills, he was capable of doing some serious harm.

I used the first thing that came to mind, desperate though it was. "Mom, Major and Minor don't even like him! What does that tell you? Do you know that animals can sense evil?"

Ignoring my comment, Mom continued, "He's given up trying to have a relationship with you, Lilly, because it takes two making an effort."

"Mom," I pleaded, "you could do so much better. You're only 40, you're pretty, you're a great teacher and. . ." This I added to take the heat off of me, "Skylar says you've fallen into the Bad Boy Syndrome."

Mom was lightning quick with her comeback. "As though you haven't, Lilly? Didn't Skylar say you were dating your dad? I thought that observation was very wise of her. But it won't be alcohol that will kill Alex; it will be drugs." Mom looked at me with tired, defeated eyes. I couldn't fight with her, not after all she had done for me last night.

Retracting my talons, I conceded, at least for this round. "I'm sorry, Mom. I'll try to do better." I was out the door and half way down the stairs.

"Hi, Carl, I'm so happy you could join us for breakfast."

"Sure you are, Lilly; sure you are," Carl responded flatly.

***

I hated sitting at our little wooden kitchen table with him. Of course, he sat where Dad used to sit, putting him directly across from me. I pulled my chair out, plopped myself down–with attitude–bumping the table in the process. Orange juice from our glasses sloshed onto the vinyl table cloth.

"Lilly, watch it!"

Mom gave me one of her 'don't you dare make a scene' looks, and got up to grab a rag.

We ate our breakfast in silence, the tension around the table palpable. I stared down at my plate, not caring that the gloom inside me spread over the whole kitchen. Outside the wind continued to howl, and I looked to the kitchen window where the branches of the pussy willow bush scraped furiously against the window pane.

Buried long ago at the base of that willow bush, under the snow, were two make-shift caskets. One was a shoe box and the other an apple box; both certainly now reclaimed by the earth. The shoe box had contained Tweetie Bird, my little blue Parakeet. Tweetie had died a violent death. Mom had been cleaning his cage and Tweetie seized the opportunity of an open cage door to make a daring break for freedom. Taking flight, he swept into the living room, heading for a plate glass window. It only took a nano-second for Sophie, my precious terrier, to seize an opportunity as well. I was coloring on the couch, and was the only witness to the attack. I looked up to see Sophie leap into the air, clamp her tiny jaws around Tweetie, and come back to earth. Sophie seemed as stunned as I with her success at hunting. Blue feathers poofed out each side of Sophie's mouth, creating a disturbing sight. I started bellowing, Mom shrieked, and Tweetie was laid to rest soon after.

It was only six months later that death came calling for my unrepentant Sophie. Sophie had been Mom and Dad's baby until I was born, and had finally died of old age. As a toddler, I drooled on her, probably teethed on her, and tripped over her when learning to walk. Sophie tolerated my putting her in my doll's dresses–she wore pink well. However, she was not above retaliation. She knew full well that my bed was only twin-size. Yet, mornings would find me teetering on the edge, while Sophie slept perpendicular to me, her tail–and tongue–stretched out to the max.

As sad as I was at Sophie's death, Mom was inconsolable. Soon after laying Sophie to rest, Dad brought home two adorable yellow lab puppies, Major and Minor. Mom refused to let them eat out of Sophie's dish; they had to have their own.

"Smack. Smack. Smack."

Carl's chewing pulled me back to the present. The way he ate drove me stark raving mad! He didn't know what a napkin was. Jam dribbled down his chin, his fingers were greasy from the bacon, and he was oblivious to my looks of disgust.

"You're a pig, Carl! A pig," I screamed inside my head. I couldn't stand to watch him, and once again turned to the window.

Mom had made Dad and me participate in a moment of silence at that Pussy Willow bush every Memorial Day for the next three years.

Mom and Dad loved each other back then. Dad loved me back then. His drinking hadn't totally annihilated our happiness yet.

"Jen, honey, do you have any more of that great coffee of yours?"

"Of course, sweetie."

Mom jumped up to get the coffee pot. Why was she serving him! Couldn't he get his own stupid coffee?

Inwardly, though, I had to concede that Mom had waited on me, too. As Dad became more lost in his own blurry world, it was Mom who kept my world going. Without her, there would've been no birthday celebrations. Christmases would have come and gone, accomplishments in school would have been unacknowledged, prom dresses would have gone unnoticed.

Mom always gave more than she got. Major and Minor were Dad's last gifts to Mom, and they now occupied Dad's side of the bed.

And here was Carl, occupying Dad's place at our table.

Dad. Daddy. I forcibly held back tears that sprang unbidden from somewhere very deep. I would not miss him. I would NOT.

Looking up from my plate, still full of cold soggy pancakes, I stared daggers at Carl. How soon before Major and Minor would be given the boot? How soon before Carl would be occupying Dad's side of the bed?

Obtuse Carl finally caught my gaze, and there was a thirty-second stare down before he broke my gaze. He was no match for me!

"Go ahead and hate me, Lilly! Hell, nothing I can do about that, but . . ."

He leaned back in his chair, and crossed his leg over the other, exposing a glob of cow manure frozen to the sole of his boot. He nonchalantly reached for a toothpick, giving me one of his leering grins.

". . .I ain't goin nowhere!"

And then he winked at me.

Throwing down my fork, I stood up abruptly, knocking over the wooden chair. Mom looked like she could go for my throat.

"Lilly! What IS your problem!"

"I don't have a problem, Mom!" Sending another black look Carl's way, I hurled another insult over my shoulder as I left the kitchen, "But you do! You sure as hell do!"

"I am no devil, for there is none"

Nephi –

CHAPTER THREE

My bedroom was dark when I finally pulled my covers back and swung my legs over the side. Sleep had become my favorite form of escape a few years back, but recently I had honed it to a fine skill. Reaching for my phone, I flipped it open to check the time. 6 p.m. Not bad. A seven-hour nap. Not a new record, but close. Peering around the corner of my bedroom door, I listened closely for any sound coming from downstairs.

"Mom, are you still here? Mom?"

Not a sound. She must have already left with slimeball for the night. Tying my robe tight around my waist, I bounded down the stairs. There stood my faithful sentries, Major and Minor, wagging their tails furiously.

"Whatsamatter? Am I late getting you your dinner?"

Following me into the kitchen, I reached for their bowls: Red bowl for Major, yellow bowl for Minor. Dumping a cup of dog food into each, I gave them hugs.

"Dog food for you and a pan of boiling water for me."

I turned the stove plate on high, splashed water into a pan and set it on the plate. I looked at my babies smugly.

"Hey, you guys, you know the drill. No ratting me out."

Having inhaled their food, M and M followed me into the living room. I headed toward the Christmas tree.

Under the tree was the only present not opened on Christmas day. It was the pits having a birthday so close after Christmas. Any hope of making a haul on my Big Day was always snuffed out by the expense of 'doing' Christmas.

'You are not wearing those until your birthday,' Mom had declared. 'You have to have something to open on that day.'

And I, of course, knew what the gift was because I had picked them out. Mom gave up trying to buy clothes for me the day I turned twelve. I wouldn't be caught dead in clothes she thought looked 'just so-o-o cute' on me.

I grabbed the box, carefully wrapped in last year's Christmas wrap, and headed for the kitchen. The boiling water trick always worked. Mom never seemed to suspect as I was quite proficient at re-wrapping every gift. I held the box directly over the steam. Gently pulling on the tape, it gave way without taking any of the gift wrap with it.

"Voila."

Turning off the stove, I bolted up the stairs two at a time, with box in hand. Alex told me to be ready by eight as a bunch of us were hanging out at Diego's house. We were doubling with the new guy in town, Trevor, and his date.

Hmmm. Trevor. I didn't know much at all about him. His family had recently moved to Missoula from North Carolina. Trevor's father was the new minister at the Baptist church in town. Trevor didn't seem like the kind of guy Alex would hang out with. Oh well, maybe Alex was just trying to be nice.

After my shower I took my time picking out what to wear. I wanted to look fabulous for Alex. Looking in the full-length mirror, I viewed myself from all angles. Admittedly, I struggled with my looks. I had a 'butter face' as in, 'everything's great but her face.' It was true; my face was barely on the good side of plain. But, somehow, once past my face, God had smiled upon me. My black hair was thick enough for three people, and fell to just past my shoulders in length; my height–5'7"–helped with my dancing. And, lastly, Alex was always telling me what a great butt I had. My skinny jeans and my knee high boots didn't look too bad. Yeah, they were last year's style, but hey, the price was right. 'Beggars can't be choosers,' as Mom was always saying.

***

Major and Minor's barking announced Alex's arrival. I opened the door to a long wolf whistle.

"Well, if you don't look mighty fine," Alex said with a sly grin. "Mmmm, hmmm."

"You don't look too bad yourself," came my response. That was an understatement. It was impossible for Alex to look bad. I had never lusted over any guy. Until Alex.

"Hold down the fort, men," I instructed Major and Minor. Locking the door, we headed for Alex's truck in the pitch black.

"I HATE winter!"

The icy wind whipped my words away before Alex could hear them. He gripped my arm tightly, struggling to keep me upright as we plowed through the deep drifts.

I tried again, raising my voice above the howling wind and blowing snow. "Oh, you brought your dad's Escalade?"

"Yeah, we kind of have a crowd. Sorry."

"Why are you sorry?"

"Because you're not going to be too excited seeing who's in the backseat."

"Why, who is Trevor's date?"

"Helena."

"C R A P."

Reaching the passenger side, Alex gripped the door, hastily hefted me in and slammed the door.

I turned to see my arch-rival sitting in the backseat next to Trevor.

"Hi, guys." That was all the acknowledgement Helena was going to get from me. I faced forward and talked to Alex all the way.

***

Diego opened his front door.

"Follow me upstairs. Parents gone. I've got food and drinks in my room, and the board all set up, ready to go."

Diego's ranch house was even older than ours. The stairwell was narrow and dark, yellowed wallpaper torn and peeling from the walls. The stair boards creaked under our weight, the wood of some stairs actually split. I could see into a dark closet underneath the stairs.

"Hey, dude, are these stairs going to hold us?" Alex asked.

"Yeah, step more to the sides of the stairs; straddle the middle."

Reaching the landing, I rounded the corner into a large attic, Diego's pad. There was Diego's girlfriend, Zena. Good. Zena couldn't stand Helena either.

On Diego's old iron bed were four boxes of extra large pizzas, on the floor a blue cooler filled with ice, sodas and beer. Sitting in the middle of the room was an old card table, metal chairs sitting around it. On top of the table sat a Ouija board.

Mom's words sprang to my mind. 'Never, ever fool around with a Ouija board, Lilly. You have no idea what you're playing with.'

"Oh, Mom," came my retort. "You can't be serious; believing in devils is so passé, so archaic."

She had looked at me then, shaking her head. 'Mark my words, Lil; you're playing with fire.'

I pulled myself back into the present.

"Wow, this should be fun," I said, almost too cheerfully. I looked around. No one seemed bothered about tonight's activity, no one but Trevor. The new kid hung back, biting his lip, obviously something on his mind.

Everyone loaded up their plates with pizza, chips and dip. Diego popped open cans of Coke and Coors.

"Your choice, guys. Let's get this party started."

Alex reached for a beer, hesitated, looking at me.

Trevor spoke up. "Hey, I'll be the designated driver, if you don't mind my driving your dad's car."

Alex reached into his pocket, pulled out the keys and tossed them to Trevor. "You're on, dude," Alex said, smiling. He downed a large swallow of beer.

"You don't mind, do ya, Lil?" He held me tightly next to him.

"Of course not," I lied. So that was why he invited Trevor. Alex wouldn't have been able to find one of his friends willing to forfeit a night of drinking. I hated to admit it to myself, but I couldn't stand the smell of beer on his breath. It brought back too many lousy memories.

"Shake it off, Lilly," I counseled myself inwardly. "Act like you're at a party."

Trevor handed me a Coke, and took one for him. Dropping his voice, he asked me, "Do you play the board often?"

"No, I've never played it. I think it's dumb. Why?"

"I don't think this is such a good idea," he whispered.

Alex and I sat together on the edge of Diego's creaky, iron bed, the table pushed up close to us.

Diego took charge. Rubbing the palms of his hands together, he looked around the room smiling. "Okay, guys, what do we want to ask it?"

Alex spoke up. "Let's ask if our team will make the state finals."

"We can't all put our fingers on the planchette, guys," Trevor said. "How about Lilly, Zena, and I just watch?"

I looked at Trevor. What was he picking up from me? I wasn't scared to play the board.

Helena, Diego, and Alex put their finger tips on the planchette and waited. A minute passed. Two. Nothing. I couldn't help it. I laughed.

"You don't actually think you're going to get an answer, do you?" I asked incredulously.

"Lil, we always get an answer! Not always the answer we want, but we get one." Alex hugged me and reached across my lap for another beer.

"Hey, guys, we gotta focus. No talking or laughing. It won't respond if it doesn't know we're all serious." Wow, Diego was really into this.

I saluted him. "Yesssss, Sir."

Outside the wind howled around the corner of Diego's house. The ancient structure barely seemed to be holding its own against nature's forces. I looked at the small rectangular window behind Diego's head to see more horizontal snow hurling past. A cold draft blew in from underneath the old window casing, swaying the faded cotton curtains and giving me a chill. I shuddered.

"You cold, babe?" Draping his arm around my shoulder, Alex pulled me closer to him.

Still nothing was forthcoming from the board.

"Oooooooooh, ooooooooooooh." Helena gave out a ghostly wail. We all laughed then.

"Okay, Okay. Sorry, Diego, we'll be serious," she said. "Quiet everyone."

Not a sound but our breathing.

Again Diego intoned, "Will our basketball team make it to state finals this year?"

The planchette started moving, ever so slightly. I looked at the participants' faces.

"Yeah, right," I thought. "Who's the wise guy pushing it?" It certainly wasn't Helena. Her eyes were wide as saucers. Picking up speed, the planchette moved to the corner, and stopped.

NO.

"Damn," Alex said. "I thought we had a shot at it this year."

I stared at Alex. "You can't be serious," I laughed. "Which one of you is sliding it? Expose yourself!"

"Geez, Lil, I thought you'd never ask," Alex retorted.

"Funny." I socked his arm. "I'm serious here!"

"Well, I sure as hell wasn't moving it, Lil!" Alex looked at me and grinned.

"Not me," Diego responded, shrugging his shoulders.

"Nor me," Helena said. "This could make a believer out of me."

Diego offered up an idea. "Let's have Lilly play it alone.

You can see for yourself, Lil."

"Here, you put your fingers on it, Lil." Helena quickly pushed the planchette over to me, obviously relieved to be out of the game.

I placed my finger tips on the planchette. I felt like an idiot. I wasn't about to give into peer pressure and push the stupid thing under my own manpower just because they wanted so badly to believe in the boogy man.

"Okay, guys. What else do you want to know?" Diego asked.

Helena spoke up. "I know! Ask if my dad is going to give in and give me his Porsche."

I rolled my eyes and spit out a response. "Oh, yes, we a-l-l-l-l-l want to know that! It must be awful driving around in your very own mini-Cooper."

Alex's knee nudged mine. He knew how hard it was for me to practice restraint around Helena.

Zena lightened the moment. "Come on, ladies, we've got a séance to finish."

Helena gave me a death stare.

I capitulated and begrudgingly asked, "Is Helena's dad going to give her his Porsche?"

They waited. I waited. My fingers were barely making contact with the planchette.

"Holy crap! IT MOVED!"

I jerked my fingers off the planchette. I hadn't moved

the stupid thing. But SOMEONE had!

"Ah, Hah!" Diego laughed. "Now who's feeling stupid?"

I wanted answers. "If none of you are moving it, then who or what is the 'it' that IS?"

Zena waded in. "Isn't it our spiritual guides? I read in a book once that it's our dead relatives that come to communicate with us and to help us."

"But how do we know for sure, guys?" Trevor looked around. "The after life has got to be as populated as it is here. There's all kinds of low lifes that walk around here; why not there, too?"

I looked at Trevor. He actually believed this stuff. Just like Mom. Was Zena right? Was the Ouija board being controlled by good guys. . . or . . . bad guys? I pictured our old radio, passed down from Grandpa Benjamin, sitting on a shelf in our kitchen. Mom had to turn the knob slowly, getting far-away signals and a lot of static before she would finally hit on her station.

"Yeah, you guys. Maybe it's like a radio. Maybe a lot of dead people are trying to make contact. So how do we know for sure who we've got on the other end?"

I looked at it. There it sat, waiting.

"Well," I said, looking around, "I want to know WHO we are talking to!"

Trevor shifted nervously in his chair, looking like he was going to offer up something. He was cut off by Diego's enthusiasm.

"Well, ask! Lil, put your fingers back on the planchette," Diego directed, reaching for his fourth piece of pizza.

I reluctantly obeyed. "WHO is this?"

Silence. Nothing. It took all I had to stifle a nervous giggle. Diego would physically remove me from the room if I disrupted the mood again.

And then, with certainty, with no hesitation, the glass moved toward the alphabet, selecting one letter at a time: V L A D.

"Vlad? What's a vlad?" Alex, reaching for another beer, looked around the room at the rest of us.

Trevor had said little to this point. He cleared his throat. "The only Vlad I know is Prince Vlad. He reigned in the 1400's in a small war state called Wallachia, by Hungary. He is believed to be the guy from whom the character of Dracula originated."

"How so?" Zena squeaked.

"He didn't know who was for him or against him, so he assembled all the nobles to a great feast and had them killed; thousands of his own people even. He was called the 'impaler'."

"The IMPALER?" I took my hands off the glass. My throat was a little dry, my hands clammy.

"To discourage an approaching hostile army at his borders, he had 23,000 of his perceived enemies impaled on sticks—a forest of corpses. He set up his dinner table among them. Can you imagine the stench? And, oh yeah, he drank their blood. He was one evil dude. Hence, Dracula."

"Great; thanks, Trevor. I could have gone for years without knowing all those details," Helena looked a little sickish and set her drink down.

"Okay, guys, I'm scared. I don't want to do this anymore." Zena stood up, reaching for her coat off the bed.

"Zena, sit down," Diego whined. "This isn't THAT Vlad. There's got to be more than one Vlad."

"Let's ask him why he's here with us tonight," Alex offered up.

Diego looked at me. "You're working the planchette. You ask."

I looked around at the five expectant faces. Trevor's eyes drilled silently into mine. Almost imperceptibly, he shook his head. A chill went through me. How had I become the lone player on the board? I cleared my throat and put my fingertips back on the planchette.

"Why are you here tonight?"

Helena spoke softly under her breath. "I've come for pizza, and it better be pepperoni or off with your head!"

Diego flashed her a warning look.

"Sorry," she mouthed.

None of us moved. The winter wind outside had picked

up speed, forcing the old house to sway and groan around us.

With a feather touch my fingers rested on the planchette's surface. Slowly, and then more quickly, it slid forward, moving to several letters in the alphabet:

YOU OPENED THE GATE.

"If it would help you,

And if it were possible,

I would go down with you into Hell.

But, you cannot bring Hell into me."

-- C.S. Lewis

CHAPTER FOUR

"The gate?" Alex repeated, giving us all a clueless look.

"The gates of Hell," Trevor answered quietly.

We all turned to see if he was joking. He wasn't.

Alex, screwing up his face, looked over at Trevor. "Yeah, right! You don't believe in all that heaven/hell religion crap do you?"

I looked sideways at Trevor. Was this new, skinny kid going to argue with the coolest guy at school?

"Do you believe in Heaven?" Trevor asked us all.

Zena spoke up. "I do."

Diego added a bit too sarcastically. "Yeah, me too; you can't be a good Catholic and not believe in Heaven."

Helena countered. "Used to. Not any more. No one's ever answered my prayers."

I said nothing. Did I? I wasn't so sure anymore.

"Well, if there is a Heaven, then there must be a Hell." Trevor expected this group to understand that. They didn't.

Thinking back to a Sunday school lesson eons ago, I remembered Mrs. Wagoner explaining about opposites.

"If there's hot," I paused. "Then the opposite is. . .," I waited.

"Cold," came the simultaneous response from all of them.

"Rich?"

"Poor."

"Pretty?"

"Ugly."

"Good?"

"Evil."

And there it was.

"So, yeah, logically, Trevor's right," I acknowledged. "If there is a Heaven, then there's got to be a hell."

Alex offered up his take on things. "Who really cares?

Eat, drink, and be merry for tomorrow we die is what I say!" He reached over and planted a kiss on my mouth. "And when I'm with this fine specimen of a woman, I'm merry!"

I glanced at Helena. If looks could kill, I would most assuredly be dead.

With this group it was really showing a lot of chutzpah, but Trevor waded in, actually pulling some scripture out of his head:

" *'For it must needs be that there is an opposition in all things. If no good, then no bad; if no happiness, then no misery. If no evil, then no righteousness; if no Satan, then no God; and if no God, then we are not.'* "

"Okay," Diego challenged, "I don't remember any scriptures saying anything about the gates of hell?"

Not backing down, Trevor replied dryly. "Really? Well, try this: *'May the gates of hell be shut continually before me. Oh, Lord, will thou make a way for mine escape before mine enemies.'* So, once again, about THOSE gates."

"Well, alrighty then," I said, starting to stand up. "I think that's all for now." I was trying to be funny, trying to deflect the fear building inside my chest, trying to ignore Mom's warning playing in my head.

Alex pulled me back down, spilling some of his beer on me and him.

"Oops, sorry, babe."

Suddenly, all eyes shifted to the board. On its own, the planchette was moving fast, and then fiercely, again pointing to specific letters of the alphabet.

"Holy Shit!" Diego slid his chair away. "I've never seen it do that before!"

We were all standing now, backing up from the board, trying to get away from the table. But the table had a mind of its own. It raised several inches off the ground and slammed down, spilling our drinks, sending pizza to the floor.

"Whoever's doing this, it isn't funny!" Zena screeched, looking at each of us accusingly. Tears were rolling down her cheeks.

The card table was again off the ground, tilted crazily in the air. The Oujia board and planchette were sent flying into space. All hell broke loose, screams and expletives filling the room.

Alex yelled, "Let's get out of here." He headed toward the narrow door leading out of Diego's room.

I screamed, "Wait!"

Alex reached back for my hand as he hit the top stair. Helena crowded through the opening and–taking Alex's hand–scrambled down the stairs right behind Alex.

Trevor grabbed my elbow and steered me toward the door. Diego and Zena pushed passed us, and in their hurry to get away, knocked Trevor to his knees on the landing.

I turned to help Trevor up, and froze. The table—a regular, plain old card table—was suspended in mid-air, violently banging against the door frame, too wide to pass through.

"Trevor, come on!" I reached for his hand, but he was already up. Half carrying me, half dragging me, he took the stairs two at a time. As we hit the second stair from the bottom, I heard a crack as the ancient wood gave out under our weight. The broken stair caught our feet and we sprawled, face first, onto the living room floor. Looking back, I saw the heel of one of my boots stuck in the splintered stair. Helping me up, Trevor turned and slammed the stair door shut. The front door was wide open, and we headed for it.

Outside, standing in the blowing snow was Diego, trying to calm a hysterical Zena. And there were Helena and Alex by the Escalade. Her face was buried in Alex's chest, her arms wrapped tightly around him. Alex turned to us.

"Hey, Trevor, you got the keys! Let's get away from here, man."

***

I was in a total funk. Saturday night had just about finished me off. When I got home that night, I had thought about calling Sky and seeing if my best friend would sleep over with me. I was too petrified to sleep by myself. But then I realized I wasn't going to say anything to anyone—

not even Sky–for a long, long time. Maybe if I never acknowledged it, never gave the words utterance, it would be like it never happened. And then I wouldn't have to try to figure out how any of it was even possible. Instead, I slept with my bedroom light on, and I assigned Major and Minor to guard my bedroom door. I turned my cd player on loud. Way loud. Maybe ghosts didn't like loud noises.

Nor was I about to breathe a word to Mom about that terrible night, either; but she had sat there, expectantly, as I unwrapped my boots on January first. One boot missing its heel required an explanation. I hated it when Mom was right.

And now it was Monday morning. Ugh. The reality of school starting again took me even lower as I struggled through heavy snow in pitch black to get to the main road. The blizzard had left our long lane completely drifted in. The snow was deeper than my ugly, old boots were high, and my Levi's and socks were already drenched. Making it to the road, I stood panting from the exertion. I pulled my hood tighter around my head and held my glove to my face to block some of the cold Montana wind. I could see the headlines now:

"Local girl freezes to death waiting for ride to 6 a.m. dance practice."

Turning my back to the wind, I squinted through the swirling snow, catching glimpses of the old clapboard house that stood in the midst of the barren trees of our orchard. There it was, almost mirage-like, as it appeared and then disappeared in the gusts of snow and wind.

Dad had let his older brother, Joe, live in that run-down house, rent-free. Joe had never married. Mom mentioned once that Joe was a hard worker, doing handy-man work, but anything he earned, he hoarded. When Mom found out he was eating oats meant for our cattle's feed, she started taking him left-overs from our dinners. I had only a few memories of Uncle Joe. He wore thick glasses, the lenses making his eyes look huge, like a bug's. His hands, big and rough, were always grimy with grease, and there was enough dirt embedded under his fingernails to grow corn. He died in an accident when I was nine. I remember standing by his casket, eye level to him. He was the first dead person I had ever seen. His hands, scrubbed almost clean, were folded across his chest. Joe was buried; the house was boarded up. Joe left no legacy, his life made no impact at all, and our lives went on. I shook my head now, perplexed. It is so strange to have an uncle die, and to really not feel anything at all at his death; to have, really, no memories of him at all.

"Crap! And now I am going to die out here! Where are they?"

Bracing against the wind, I rooted for my English assignment in the bottom of my back-pack to verify it was there. I had written a Haiku in the wee hours of the morning for class today, but somehow I knew Mrs. Spencer wouldn't be too impressed:

Mean girl, Helena.

Intent to pour misery

In an empty urn.

I stuffed my paper back into my bag as around the corner slid a red Mini-Cooper, coming to a stop mere feet from where I stood.

"Holy crap! Now she's trying to kill me!"

Having to endure Helena first thing in the morning topped off my hating-life mood. Skylar, our buffer, was in the front seat, so I assumed my 'relegated to the back seat' status and immediately buckled up. The common joke around school was 'She drives like a bat out of Helena.'

"You're late, Helena," I snapped. I thought I could gain the upper hand if I put her on the defensive immediately. Helena turned up her stereo and took off, fish-tailing on the ice. I grabbed my seat belt, cinching it tighter around me and looked out the window, trying to take my mind off her crazy driving on such terrible roads. The road plows had been out already, but the freezing temperatures left a thin layer of black ice. Looking down at my hands, I noticed I was gripping the edge of the seat. I better understood now what 'white-knuckling' meant. Finally reaching the freeway, which was thankfully salted and free of ice, Helena merged into the traffic and sped up.

I looked at the backs of Sky's and Helena's heads. Had Helena said anything to Sky about what had happened the night before last? If so, Sky wasn't letting on.

"Hey, Lilly, can I borrow your phone?" Helena reached towards the back with an open palm, obviously expecting me to just hand it over.

Already suspicious, I asked, "Why, where's yours?"

"I think I left it at home; I want to call my mom and have her look for it."

"God must love stupid people; he made so many," I muttered under my breath. But, knowing it's not wise to argue with a crazy person, particularly when she is behind the wheel, I reluctantly relinquished it.

"Be fast, Helena. Alex is supposed to text me." I bit my lip for disclosing that, but too late!

"Lilly, I can check for you." Helena flipped open my phone, and, looking over at Sky, started laughing. "Hey Sky, maybe he's sexting her."

"Helena," I said with contempt, "have you noticed that you always laugh AT me? Always at MY expense? Give me back my phone, Helena."

Helena, completing ignoring me, read aloud the most recent text from Alex:

" 'Mornin, Hot Chick; skip Calc with me and let's hit

Starbucks.' "

Skylar turned to give me one of her black looks.

"I didn't know Starbucks carried pot," Helena interjected dryly.

Sky, looking forward, threw in her two cents. "Why do you persist with this jerk, Lil? I heard how he left you in his dust at the party Saturday night. Sounds like it should be Trevor you would want to hang out with, not Alex-the-Lion-Heart."

So, Helena had told Sky. It was bad enough being chased down a rotting stairway by a devil summoned from the deep, an experience that would give me nightmares for months! But even worse was Sky knowing that Alex had left me behind. The fact that he hadn't even looked back hurt me–totally–but that was a one-time thing. He wasn't thinking. Hell, we were all terrified! But with Helena blabbing all of it to Sky, Helena had finally crossed over The Line. I could no longer handle another tidal wave of gossip directed at me and Alex, which Helena—no doubt—had unleashed.

"Well," Helena responded sarcastically, "we have to give Alex some slack; he was drunk." Then, looking back over her shoulder, she added, "I would think you would have had your fill with drunks, Lil."

Unsnapping my seat belt, I lunged over the seat, not sure whether to go for my phone or her throat.

"You are a total bitch, Helena! Give me back my damn phone!"

***

If this were a dream, it was a really bad one. In this dream, there was no sound. The world went silent as the car did its 180 degree dizzying spin. Definitely, the feeling of slow motion added to the surreal effect. From the back seat, I could see Helena, her eyes wide with terror, grip the wheel, turn to Skylar and mouth,

"H A N G O N!"

And even though her mouth was wide open, her lips moving, there was no sound. The car slid sideways, the front and back tires catching in the frozen sod of the median. The Mini catapulted over and over again until it stopped, rocking crazily on its side. The glass shattered around us, but there was no sound of breaking glass. Sod and dirty snow filled the car and my lungs, leaving me gulping for air, but I could not hear my gasps. The roof crumbled above us, sandwiching me between it and the floor. But there was no sound of grinding metal. Nothing. When I had relived the dream for at least the 100th time, I saw–at last–Skylar. She was tumbling head-first through the windshield; I could not reach her, and then, she was gone.

Life's a Voyage

That's Homeward Bound.

– Herman Melville

CHAPTER FIVE

My mind moved back and forth between my silent dream and a dream that had stalked me since childhood. It was one of those infamous "reoccurring" dreams discussed in my junior year psych class. Reoccurring dreams could be significant, Mr. Cordon had said. It was the mind's way of trying to retrieve from the catacombs of the subconscious some memory stuffed deep down from long ago. This dream would come unbidden, its sporadic timing unnerving. It would lie low, not returning for months, and in the light of day I was hopeful that perhaps it was gone forever.

And then a random night would come, when I was just this side of sleep, barely aware of my body and my mind shutting down. The same intense foreboding would descend and suddenly I could no longer cry out, I could no longer move. Compelled to live it, unable to wake myself, I would lie frozen, almost whimpering. Always I could slightly turn my head; always from the right the figure would merge into my field of vision. The oppressive weight would settle over me, trapping me to the mattress. It was a dense, musty form, whose approach and presence would leave me in such terror as to absolutely convince me I could not survive. Then it was gone. I would be left curled in a fetal position, fighting sleep for hours.

And now a third dream was crowding in, vying for center stage. With all my heart I hoped that a dream was all it was, for—if not—a living nightmare awaited me just on the other side of my eyelids. I knew if I allowed my eyes to open, I would see myself immobilized in a hospital bed, my throat raw, my mouth like cotton, my head pounding. I knew I would not be able to keep out the swish, swish, swish of the respirator, the beep of the heart monitor, the smells of gauze and antiseptic, the stiff sterility of the ICU.

"No, it is only a dream," I determined. And I allowed myself to sink into that soundless world with my best friend, Skylar, and my nemesis, Helena, once again.

***

"Give, said the little stream; give, oh give; give, oh give.

Give, said the little stream, as it hurried down the hill.

I'm small, I know, but wherever I go, the grass grows greener still."

This was my mother's voice, echoing down the tunnel to me, reaching clear to the bottom where I chose to stay. Sometimes I could be coaxed midway up the tunnel from my hiding place when she would sing my favorite childhood song, or talk about a family trip we would go on just as soon as I was better. Occasionally, I would allow a smile, but couldn't understand why doing so brought such tangible joy into her voice.

Some times, I heard Luke's voice. "There were two muffins in the oven," he said. "One said to the other, 'Is it hot in here or is it just me?' 'Holy cow', said the other muffin, 'a talking muffin."

Other times I would hear Luke playing my favorite music on his guitar, or Luke naming off all my favorite foods I could be eating, if 'I would quit being lazy and get out of that bed.'

I would try to respond. I would try to come farther up the tunnel, but then his voice would fade, and I would know that I was slipping, sliding back down to the bottom, too weak to hold on, too tired to make sense of any of it.

I would dread the times I heard the doctor's voice. He would talk with my mother in subdued whispers, making it impossible to hear him. I didn't like him, for always my mother cried and every time, after he left, someone would invade my space and cause more pain. I would feel pricks in my hands and arms; I would gag and retch when a tube was forced down my throat. Hands would touch me, make me turn over, hurting me even more, so I would retreat, again, to the bottom of the tunnel.

"Lilly, Lilly," my mother's voice would call. "Can you hear me, Lilly? Can you wake up now, Lilly? Try to open your eyes, sweetheart, won't you?"

No one could reach me here. Here, at the bottom, I could leave my three nightmares behind and visit happier memories.

Today I chose to go to a magical time when I was nine. I was in the hospital to have my tonsils removed, and awoke to find my parents at my bedside.

Dad asked, "So Lilly, what would you like for a get-well present?"

I told him I wanted my own horse and tack.

Mom had answered in a ludicrous tone, "Oh, Lilly, you might as well ask for the moon!"

Dad had put his arm around her waist, and winked.

Money was scarce even then, I knew that. But just a week later I had walked to the corral to see my beautiful horse, Raven, tied to a post! Dad had beamed at my high-pitched squeal.

"Lesson One," he had said, "is to learn to put his halter and saddle on."

I struggled with the gazillion straps and buckles.

"Hey, Lilly," Dad had said, grinning, "You can do this. Be patient with yourself. It's a good start!"

Back then, I idolized my father. At the age of three, I was taking giant steps behind his boots as he strode to the barn in the brisk spring air. When five years old, I would ride behind Dad, clinging tightly to his Levi jacket as he spurred Duke into a gallop. At seven, I would tinker in his tool shop as he worked, making believe that I–too–was fixing a machine. Dad could fix anything. I corrected myself: He could fix machines. The time came when Dad became an unreliable and angry drunk, lost in booze; I quit riding Raven and lost myself in dance. By then, he could no longer fix himself. He couldn't fix me.

***

My mind turned reluctantly to my next hospital stay, when I had my appendix out. I was fourteen. The pain had started one morning when I was helping Dad in the hayfield. I had chalked it up to running in the heat, my head and side pounding with each step. Of course, crying hysterically could have contributed, as well. Dad had asked me to drive the truck earlier that morning while he bucked the last of the hay bales onto the truck bed.

Montana is hot in July and the scorching sun beat down on Dad as he walked along the side of the truck. I could smell cigarettes and alcohol in the sweat dripping off of him, stale odors left over from the night before. I had awakened at 2 a.m. when Dad bumped into the dining table while making his way to the bedroom. Mom had long ago vacated their bed, choosing to sleep upstairs. I hadn't wanted to be left alone on the main floor with my father. In the light of day I knew that my fear of his some day losing it and doing me serious harm was irrational. But in the dark of night, it seemed perfectly possible.

Watching him struggle alone that day, with 40 bales in the field, I had to give it to Dad; at least his work ethic wasn't broken. The Bubble Family had a machine that would stack the bales manually, but Dad said it wasn't worth it to borrow the equipment for so few bales. With most things, we were too poor to buy farm equipment –we had to lease–and Dad was too proud to borrow.

Every twenty feet I would stop the truck while Dad swung onto the bed and stacked the bales up against the back of the cab.

Finally, he yelled through the open cab window. "Lilly, we're full! Head for the haystack."

Reaching the haystack was not an easy task. There were several dikes to cross over, and one had to do it slowly, always on an angle, or the whole load could topple. I had never dumped a load. Not even when I was eight and could barely see over the dash. So, it was bound to happen on the hottest day of the summer when Dad was hung-over and I was behind the wheel. My stomach lurched. In the rearview mirror, I saw the load sway. It was Dad's string of cursing that made me shove the gear into park and jump from the cab. Two-thirds of the load lay on the ground.

In all my years I had never seen such a look of hate on Dad's face as that moment in the field. Where I got the courage to turn from him and run, I did not know, but his fury followed, nipping at my heels.

"Get the hell out of here, and don't ever come back! Ever!"

If only I could have gotten the hell out of there! But the pain in my side kept getting worse and did not let up even when I reached my bedroom to lie down. Mom was gone so no one would hear me, but I still put a pillow over my head. I would not cry. The person who cares the least controls the relationship.

By morning, the pain in my side had become so excruciating that Mom was finally convinced it was appendicitis. She put me gingerly in the car and drove to the hospital.

"Please Lord, just let me die," I had whispered from the

backseat. But I didn't. Skylar, Jason, and Luke had paraded in and out of my room over the next three days, with Luke bringing me a bouquet of 24 blue balloons, news, and my favorite— peanut M&M's. There had been only one person I was surprised to see: Dad. He came alone.

When he stopped at the door, he cleared his throat. "Um, Lilly, can I come in?"

I had just shrugged and turned to look out the window. We hadn't had a conversation for the longest time. What could there possibly be to talk about?

How long it had taken him to pick up the spilled load?

How many bales had busted open on the ground?

How much my medical bill was going to be?

He had stood awkwardly by my bed and asked, "Lilly, what would you like for a get-well present?"

I had almost laughed; almost, but then I noticed his hands were shaking, his voice quavering, and tears were filling his light blue eyes.

"Absolutely nothing, Dad. I'm fine. Really." I just wanted him gone. But he didn't leave. He just stood and looked at me. I tried to hold my expression steady. Aloof was best. Aloof was safe. Then, finding bravery that I seldom seemed to have, I went for it.

"What I want, Dad, you can't seem to do."

"I know what you would ask of me, Lilly. You would ask the same thing that your mother has asked. We all want me to stop drinking. You wouldn't understand why I drink, Lil, but I know I need help. No matter how impossible or difficult it seems to me. . ." his voice trailed off as he fought to maintain control. So unskilled in expressing feelings, he struggled on. ". . . I should be able to do it."

When he left, it was late and I was drained. How would Mom describe it? Oh yes, 'wrung out like a wet washrag.' My legs jerked from the tension in them. I sank deep into my pillow, my eyes hot and itchy from crying. Fortunately, Jason had called my room then and told me a bunch of one-liners to help me lighten up.

"A man walked into a bar and said ouch."

"I took an IQ test and the results were negative."

"Learn from your parents' mistakes; use birth control."

Jason had an uncanny knack for knowing when I needed him badly. Now Luke seemed to know, too.

***

So much had happened between my tonsillectomy and my appendectomy, between my appendectomy and now; now, where I chose to remain cocooned in my self-imposed prison.

What was happening to me now? There were nurses at my bedside again. I felt a swab freshening my mouth, salve rubbed on my lips. I heard one nurse recruiting another to help lift and turn me.

"One-two-three, turn!" I winced in pain. I would think about Jason.

What fun memories do I have of three-doors? I asked myself. Because he was four years older than I, I couldn't remember life without Jason. Knowing he would be home on leave from the Marines, Jason had invited me to go to my sophomore dance. I was excited because I got a new formal. Then Mom showed me an old favorite movie of hers, "An Officer and a Gentleman." An actor had strutted into a factory in his dress uniform, swooped a girl off her feet and carried her out, to live happily ever after. Mom suggested I ask Jason to wear his dress uniform to the dance, and he said he would. How cool was that? Then Jason found out that Zena had not been asked to the dance, so he took both of us. Zena did not want to go. She said she was tired of being my "duff" (designated, ugly, fat friend). Jason and I dragged her there. I fast-forwarded my mind to a frame where Jason, in all his glory, was doing his typical Jasonesque thing on the dance floor—the crab walk. He danced with me and Zena simultaneously. The three of us had a great time; we talked about it for months.

My mind locked onto Jason hip-hopping on the dance floor, and I put him in a freeze frame. Mom always told Jason he was an "Old Soul." He would look at her funny when she told him that, but there was no disputing it. Jason had depth. He had wisdom beyond his years. That quality didn't make him popular, but he didn't care. He wasn't the best-looking guy, but he didn't care. He seemed to have mastered this life by the time he hit junior high, and he was just putting in his time, helping us shallow ones who would only wear brand names, who weighed in five times a day, and checked every mirror when we walked by.

As Jason and I grew older, and times got tougher at home, I leaned on Jason more. He was there when Dad came home drunk one night and broke the kitchen window; Jason helped get Dad into bed, swept up the broken glass, and put plastic over the window to keep the cold out. Jason was there to hear Dad's last drunken tirade.

Hanging onto a kitchen chair for support, Dad was screaming at Mom. "You couldn't live with what I've had to live with. You'd have caved by now. You have no idea what I've done for you, for Lilly!"

He collapsed into a chair. With his face in his hands, Dad started sobbing.

"I've lost my soul, Jen; I've lost my soul!"

I don't know about his soul, but he'd certainly lost his mind, not to mention every last ounce of our respect. Mom simply couldn't take it anymore; she issued an ultimatum: Either get help or lose his family. Dad accepted her ultimatum. He chose drinking over us, and took off in his truck. I never saw Dad again. A year later Jason took the call from a hospital in South Dakota, telling us that Dad's drinking had finally killed him.

After Jason won the state championship in wrestling for our school and graduated, he joined the Marines. Jason was doing his second tour in Iraq when he was killed. Mom and I were knocked to our knees. But now Jason was captured in my freeze frame, and if I left my memory on pause and didn't push the play, he would still be in my life, forever. Jason. Dad. Maybe all those vivid memories weren't so great, after-all. The pain of missing Jason was almost as intense as the pain of once again thinking about Dad.

Don't come talking to me about

The consolations of religion,

Or I shall suspect you don't understand.

–"A Grief Observed" – C.S. Lewis

CHAPTER SIX

I don't know what finally lured me from my hiding place. I had realized a few days ago that the tube was gone from my throat. My throat was raw and it hurt incredibly to swallow, but it was glorious to calmly expand my lungs and take in air. I'd recently been moved to a different room, there were now fewer machines surrounding my bed, fewer bandages swaddling my head, fewer people coming in and out. It just felt safer, and I felt stronger; perhaps strong enough to face what I could no longer deny.

This was no dream; this was my new reality. But at least I felt myself strong enough to face what I knew Mom would be there to tell me when my eyes finally opened.

My eyes had been closed for so long that they moved like the stiff, old window shades covering my bedroom windows when I tried to open them. On the third attempt to raise my eyelids at least half-mast, the winter sun–blazing through my hospital window–blinded me. I carefully turned my head from the window and tried again. Slowly the room came into focus. There was a cot, pushed up against one wall, my mom's Bible, purse, and some magazines at the foot of it. Around the room were drawings, cards and posters taped to the walls. A bouquet of sickly green balloons–half-deflated–were anchored to the arm of a recliner. A vase, full of yellow, stagnant water, held pale, brittle red roses. I'd been here a while.

Trying to lift my head, I was met with such an intense, pounding headache that I gently placed my head back on the pillow. Refocusing my eyes, I started reading the posters on the wall opposite from me.

"Get better fast, Lilly." It was signed, 'Your Cronies.' It held 18-20 signatures.

"We love you, Lilly," signed, Zena, Heather, and Brooklyn.

I looked around the room for Sky's artwork. She was always recruited to do the posters for dance team events. I didn't see any greeting from her, but I recognized Luke's familiar scrawl.

"Get out of that bed, Lovie, and let's go dancing." Signed, Luke

I smiled at that. Luke hadn't called me "Lovie" for a long time. Of course, I knew why he had stopped. He simply didn't approve of Alex, and he let it be known far and wide. And, of course, Skylar sided right along with him. She called Alex Boozer/Loser to my face and who knows what behind my back. The more they razzed me about Alex, the more time I wanted to spend with him. They didn't know Alex like I did. Few of us were lucky enough to come from a "Bubble family" like Luke's. When nothing else had worked, Skylar hit directly below the belt and pulled out the 'Jason Card.'

" 'Jason would so not approve of you hanging out with Alex and his pothead friends.' "

I couldn't argue there because I knew it was true. Jason never drank. Never used drugs. Got straight A's. His influence had spread to Luke, Skylar, me and anyone else whose lives his life had touched. Contrary to their opinions, it wasn't because of Alex my grades had plummeted. It wasn't because of Alex I had started skipping my classes. I wasn't going to allow Alex to be tried and hung by my friends for what my father's choices had done to me, for what the Iraq war had taken from me.

Looking back at the vase of flowers, I searched for a card. Certainly they were from Alex. I would ask Mom when.....

My thoughts were interrupted by a shriek. Mom stood in the doorway, her hands to her mouth, her eyes riveted on mine.

"Lilly, you're awake. Thank God you're awake." She rushed to my bedside and grabbed my hand, crying harder still. "I knew you'd wake up, Lilly. I would pray, and a perfect calm would come over me. Against all odds, I knew you'd come back."

The phrase, 'against all odds' leapt out at me. I started taking an inventory of my limbs. If I had them, could I still move them? Two arms, two hands, check. Looking at the bottom of my bed, I noticed two mounds where my feet should be. I was relieved to see a twitch of my right foot. Pushing at the covers, I noted for the first time the cast from the bottom of my left foot up past my knee. When I felt my left big toe, not entombed in the cast, move upon command, I breathed a sigh of relief.

"Mom, how long have I been here?" Was the question I attempted to ask, but instead, slurred words in a mere whisper were what came out. I tried again, "How long?"

"Sssssh, don't try to talk right now, Lilly." Trying to regain her composure, and taking a deep breath, Mom began: "Lilly, you've been in a coma for three weeks."

"Three weeks!" My shriek was reduced to a raspy croak.

"You were in a very serious car accident, Lilly, but you're going to be fine, sweetheart. It will take a while, but you'll be as good as new."

Once again I attempted conversation. "Have Alex and Skylar. . . "

"Ssssssh, Lilly; don't talk. I'll call your nurse. Everyone will be ecstatic."

***

By the next day, my bed was raised a notch. It was so heavenly not to be lying flat on my back. I had vertigo, and my head pounded, but it was worth it to have a better perspective of my world. More heavenly, still, was to be actually drinking liquids, to feel the cool fluid go down my throat. I hoped I would soon feel stronger. I tired so easily. Two minutes of Mom's rattling on wore me out. A few friends were allowed to see me, but only for five minutes at a time. Luke was the first to come. He walked in, hidden behind a fresh bouquet of balloons.

"Hey, Lovie, don't worry about getting up!" he joked. "Do you know how hard it is to find periwinkle blue balloons, not to mention driving with a gazillion of them thumping around in the car? You need to pick a different favorite color!"

I had always been exacting about colors; I guess it came from memorizing all the colors in my deluxe box of crayons when I was little. "You're getting closer, two-doors," I whispered hoarsely. "Last bunch was a putrid olive-green color. At least these are blue!"

He tied the strings to the recliner and came to my bedside. "You look like hell wearing a halo." He smiled and kissed my cheek.

I gave him a half smile back. "You ought to see me after my respiratory therapy, Luke. Then I look and feel like road kill."

Luke, giving Mom a strange look, hastily continued. "Hey, I'll take you anyway I can get you, Lil. Black eyes or no black eyes, just as long as they're open."

Holding my arms against my ribs, I suppressed a laugh.

"Luke," Mom warned, "broken ribs don't like being jarred."

Mom and Dr. Kimball had finally shared with me the extent of my injuries. Three broken ribs on my left side, an open fracture of the tibia and fibula above my left ankle, serious brain trauma–hence my three-week coma–numerous cuts, scrapes, and abrasions. The ribs, cuts, even my brain were healing. It was the multiple fractures of my left ankle bone that devastated me. The very best scenario was that I would dance again. How well? Well now, that begs the question of how well one can dance with a weakened ankle! And the worst case scenario? Walking through life with my left leg significantly shorter than my right, which—in turn—would draw stares, completely turn guys off, and basically ruin my life. But, hey, I would be the proud owner of a handicap parking sticker. My contempt for Helena, my anger towards her, quickly turned into a hatred as hot as a blast furnace.

"Lilly, the Bubb. . . I mean the Hartmans have been such a help while I've been here with you. Luke and his father have taken Major and Minor for their daily runs. They're boarding Raven and Duke with their horses so they're getting fed. I've gone home to a plowed lane and his mom's food in our fridge, ready to heat and eat. They're literally angels at our door."

"Yes," Luke responded, with a grin. "Pardon me while I polish my halo."

The winter sun was shining through my window, trapping Luke in its rays. His honey blonde hair looked lighter, his dimples deeper, his smile brighter. Luke had been blessed with one of those dispositions that was always—obnoxiously—cheerful. He could turn a bad case of the flu into a positive experience. 'Look at how much needed rest I am getting,' he would say.

"I'm a realist," I would declare.

"No-o-o, you're a pessimist," Luke would counter. "And

I'm here to show you the error of your ways. It's much more fun to be an optimist."

I was brought back to the present when I heard someone coming down the hall. Maybe it was Skylar. I was so looking forward to launching into a rant about Helena and her driving with someone who had actually been there! This was all Helena's fault, driving so irresponsibly on icy roads. She could have killed us all.

As the footsteps got closer, I looked up to see not Skylar, but Alex. I was mortified. I didn't care if I looked like hell for Luke. He had seen me with peanut butter and jelly stuck in my hair and boogers hanging out my nose. Alex saw my look of horror and backed away. Or, was it how I looked that made him back away?

Mom tried to play peace-maker as Luke visibly bristled at Alex's presence.

"Alex, it's so nice of you to come. Lilly can only have visitors for a few minutes, as they're coming to do physical therapy, but. . ."

Alex, not even looking at Mom, talked right over her.

"Lilly, I'm so glad you made it. I brought you some magazines." He slipped a Vogue and Seventeen onto the foot of my bed and stepped back. No hug. No touch. No nothing.

"I've got to go; gotta go to work, but you keep getting better. I'll come again soon. As bad as you look, you're the lucky one!"

He stared Luke down briefly, and then turned and was gone; just like that. I barely noticed his exit. If my breathing wasn't already shallow from guarding my broken ribs, his blatant, left-handed compliment would have knocked the air right out of me. I tried to justify his comment to a stunned mother and seething friend.

"He was just feeling awkward. Who wouldn't with my body guard," I glared at Luke, "staring him down."

I then turned on Mom. "And he didn't need my mother reminding him he would be kicked out any minute!"

I felt my greasy, stringy hair, and ran my hand over my bruised face. It hadn't occurred to me til now that I could really look that bad, but I must, judging by Alex's reaction. But even worse was the last thing he said.

"Mom, what did Alex mean by 'I'm the lucky one?'"

Luke looked at Mom, gave her a warning glance, and shook his head.

"Don't do that, Luke," I said with panic rising in my chest. "Damn it! Tell me!"

Skylar hadn't been to visit me yet. She must be in the hospital too.

"Mom, where's Skylar?"

Their silence, the tears that sprang up unbidden, their own visible pain as they moved to my side spoke volumes. I stuffed my bed sheet into my mouth to muffle my sobs.

Through ragged gasps, I whispered, "Mom, did Skylar die?"

Luke reached for me, and I knocked his hand away.

Screaming now, I turned my wrath towards Luke. "Don't you dare! Don't you dare try to tell me I'm the lucky one!"

***

I quit speaking. I quit eating. Sleep was once again my drug of choice, my escape route. When awake, I feigned sleep, keeping my eyes closed when anyone came into my room. Mom wasn't fooled, however, and she, Luke, and other friends kept up a running monologue when they thought I might listen.

My mother was a walking Bible. She thought in Bible verses. Her faith was a constant, and I didn't usually mind, as that was the only thing that got us through two deaths in two years. But now, I had pretty much had it with her mini-sermons. Today was not a good day for another one. Having learned about Sky less than 48 hours ago, my life, as I knew it, was over. Like me, Skylar had not been wearing her seatbelt. Unlike me, she had been thrown from the car, and then it rolled over her, crushing her. She died there, right there in the median. There was not even an open casket at her funeral. Helena had not made it either. Her neck broken, she died on the way to the hospital. How predictable of Helena to take my best friend with her! I, alone, had survived the crash. Damn Helena, damn her reckless driving. Texting. . . while speeding. . . on slick roads. . .

And now here I lie, questioning why I was left to live. "Oh, yeah; that's right; I'm the 'lucky one.'"

"Lilly, we all loved Skylar. The Lord will comfort us, he'll heal us, Lilly." Mom had so often referenced her unequivocal faith, and this time her words had such emotion and truth behind them that–for a brief moment–I almost let myself believe. Almost. Unfortunately, my loss dwarfed her faith. Putting my fists up to my ears, I squeezed my eyes tightly shut, trying to close her out.

"Mom! Luke! Just leave! I don't want to. . ."

"We have to learn to live by faith, Lilly. You. . ."

Luke put his hand on Mom's shoulder, obviously trying to get her to back off, but undeterred, Mom pressed on. "Faith is what carried me through your father's leaving, and. . . and his dying. It is what got you and Luke and me through losing Jason. Faith is what will get us through this."

I rolled onto my back and turned my head to face my mother.

"Faith in what?" I was almost screaming. "Let me tell you what I have faith in, Mom! I have faith that if I love someone else–anyone else–they'll be taken from me too! I have faith that if I'm counting on something, oh, like maybe a career in dance, it will be pulled out from under me. In fact, I'm quite sure, Mom, my faith has graduated to a higher level. I now have sure knowledge that anything I treasure or cherish, or love, or. . ."

My voice cracked, as a new resolve settled in. I started again. "I have sure knowledge that. . ." I stopped. I wasn't going to show my hand to them.

I turned my back to her and Luke and faced the barren wall of my room. They finally gave up trying to penetrate my barricade and retreated to the hall. The low drone of Luke's deep voice, interspersed with Mom's crying, seeped back into the room. Another voice was added to the mix, the head nurse reassuring them that the hospital staff would guard the prisoner. For the most part, they did. Except for the five minutes it took me to struggle out of bed and pull the bottle of pills out of Mom's over-night bag.

Make yourself familiar with the angels

And behold them frequently in Spirit;

For without being seen,

They are present with you.

— St. Francis de Sales

CHAPTER SEVEN

Night came; they went home. I didn't care if I hurt Mom when I flung her beliefs back in her face. I didn't care if Luke looked like a whipped pup when I turned on him. And I tried to tell myself I most certainly didn't care that I so thoroughly repulsed Alex!

I lay in the quiet of my hospital room trying to figure out how to die. How does one quit breathing without it being considered suicide? I had always been taught that suicide was the ultimate selfish act. At one time I would have agreed. I had witnessed how heartbreaking it was for family members left behind when a classmate, Quigg, had taken his life just last year. Quigg's girlfriend, Danni, had broken up with him and that was all it took for him to waste himself. Danni's life took a nose-dive. She would never be the same. But I was dealing with far more than some stupid guy breaking up with me. So this I knew, of this I was certain: I would not stay in a world without Jason or Sky one minute longer than I had to.

Leaning up on one elbow, I reached for the call button. The nurse hurried right in, Johnny on the spot.

"I'm sorry, but I can't turn off my mind. Would you please bring me something to help me sleep?"

Back she came, giving me two pills – certainly a safe dosage of whatever it was. But the pills–combined with the several taken from Mom's purse and now secreted under my pillow– would hopefully not be so safe. I downed them in one gulp.

Sinking back into the pillow, I folded my hands over my belly. I wanted to be found looking peaceful. Maybe that would help Mom. My face twinged with guilt. Getting tough with myself, I whispered under my breath. "No weakening, Lilly. Start counting: One hundred, Ninety-nine, Ninety-eight, Ninety-sev. . ."

***

'Riding atop boxes and bags, piled high in the back of a wagon, I look around me. Duke and Raven are pulling the heavy load, gingerly stepping around rocks and weeds on the rutted trail. Foothills, rising to steep, snow-covered mountain tops, surround this high plain. The humidity and heat bear down on me, soaking my long cotton dress with perspiration. Dust swirls around my face, making it difficult to breath. My lips are cracked; my tongue is swelling, filling my mouth. My stomach cramps leave me unable to walk beside the wagons like all the others. I'm trying to remain quiet, trying not to complain, but I am hurting bad. Can't let the nurses know; ssshhhh, be quiet.

Clutching my stomach, I pull my knees up to try to find relief. I study my feet. My brand new winter boots are mud-caked and pretty much shot.

'Here's some herbs and roots. They are like medicine; they'll calm your stomach.'

I reach for them. My best friend, Anna, has a wooden bowl full of berries, and a piece of dried meat wrapped up in old cloth.

'This is for you when you're feeling better; maybe tomorrow. There's some for your children, as well.' Anna looks to her left and laughs. I look too. There is Sophie, dressed for tea, sitting at my little play table, atop some boxes. The jostling of the wagon tips her over. We laugh again.

I look at Anna. She's just as dirty; looks just as hot. She's straddling the boxes, trying to keep her balance, giving me some diet Coke. She's an angel. I must be dying.

With a cast on my leg, I'm walking along side Anna. My stomach is better now. Major and Minor run past us, playing in the sage brush. Anna and I sing and laugh as we walk and walk and walk and walk. Hanging out together makes the dust, rain and mud more tolerable. We approach a swift moving river. It's made of chocolate. Clinging tightly to one another, we cross to the other side, but Anna loses her ipod in the stream. I step from the river with my long turquoise dress wet and covered in chocolate. I lick my sleeve. Looking at Anna sideways, I laugh. None of it seems so difficult when I walk with Anna.

Our wagon train stops for the evening. Anna helps me take our dirty clothes down to the creek to wash them. I hand her a baby to hold while I scrub on the clothes. Wringing them out, I put them in the dryer and slam the door shut. Anna perches on a rock by the creek, bouncing little Lisbeth on her lap.

Now Major and Minor are barking and growling. Out of nowhere descends a band of mounted Indians. Before I can scream, before I can call for help, one Indian bends low over his Pinto and grabs Anna by her hair. Little Lisbeth tumbles to the ground. I stand, wild with fright as he throws Anna over his horse.

'Sarah, help me! Sarah, oh my god, save me. . .' Screams fill the canyon as he rides off with Anna.

I'm down on my knees, the dust from the retreating horses filling my lungs.

Our captain shakes his head. 'Sarah, the Indians are too numerous for our small band of travelers. It would be senseless to try and rescue her; we'd all be killed. We must go on.'

The wagon train pulls out. I collapse in the track of a retreating wheel, wailing. I am shaking from the horror of it, from the pain of losing her. Major licks my face and whines. My screams and cries are silent. I will never see Anna again. NEVER. I'm crying, I'm crying and holding my stomach. I am going to be sick. I am going to throw up.

***

Leaning over the side of the bed I heave, splattering stomach bile all over the tile floor. Again and again, I retch, gagging on the acid forced up through my throat. I gasp for breath, snot and bile streaming from my nostrils. Reaching for my sheet, I wipe away the strands of liquid stringing from my mouth, but then feel it coming again. My stomach cramps and heaves, trying to free itself of all the poison it has taken in. I reach for the call button.

***

The nursing staff was amazed at how violently my system acted to such a small amount of sleep medication.

"If you take these on a full stomach, you simply shouldn't have the reaction you did, sweetheart. I am so sorry the medication made you so sick."

Morning finally came. Was I happy to see the light of another day streaming through the window? Not so much.

Why was it so easy for other people to escape this world, and I couldn't seem to pull it off.

Burdened with two heavy canvas bags, Mom struggled into my room and dropped them on her cot. Three old, leather-bound journals tumbled out.

"Oh good, Lilly, you're eating some breakfast! They're putting you back on a bland diet to give that touchy stomach of yours a break." Without inhaling, she continued, "Today is your lucky day. Today you get to meet your family."

Could Mom get any weirder? I wondered. "Lucky me," I said flatly and forced another bite of rubbery egg into my mouth.

I eyed the journals warily. In a corner of our barn loft sat an old metal trunk. It had occupied that corner for as long as I could remember. When I was younger, at home alone and bored, I would climb the ladder to the loft, raise the heavy rounded lid of the trunk and rummage through its contents. I found magazines dating from the 1930's, old-fashioned hats, vintage quilting fabric and yellowed baby dresses. And among all that stuff were numerous old, leather-bound journals. They smelled musty and some of their pages were stuck together from moisture seeping in. There were several authors, as the handwriting and the time periods varied from journal to journal. Mom finally brought them into the house and made a special place for them in our bookcase. She became engrossed and read every page.

'Lilly, these journals are fascinating; it's like Mae and Thomas and Sarah have come back to life! These people are so real to me now,' Mom had exclaimed.

With her endorsement, I had thumbed through a few journals, but nothing more. Whoever these people were, I didn't know them. They were dead and long gone. Why would I care to read about people who were older than dirt?

"Listen to this, Lilly," Mom commanded, as though I had any choice. I was, after-all, trapped in a bed, with her between me and the door. Seeing my look, Mom compromised.

"Okay, I won't read all of it; I'll just pick out a few entries." She settled back into the recliner.

"This is a story about your great, great grandfather, Nephi Hunt. Now remember, Lilly, how it goes on your dad's side of the family: Sarah, Thomas, Nephi, Teancum, your Grandpa Benjamin, your dad, and then you. Nephi's soon-to-be daughter-in-law wrote this. Guess what her name was, Lilly?"

When I did not respond, Mom answered in exasperation, "Think! You were named after her!"

"My great grandmother, Lillie, wrote this?" Hearing something that my namesake wrote could be worth listening to.

"Lillie was smitten with Nephi's son, Teancum. I'll read

it verbatim from her journal, Lilly."

'One Sunday in July, 1919, Teancum invited me to go with him to the shearing corrals to watch him and his father, Nephi, shear sheep. I, being in love with Teancum, of course was delighted to go.

Granddad Nephi welcomed me with open arms. It was on this Sunday afternoon that I became acquainted with the man who would later become my father-in-law. I sat on a pole fence next to Granddad Nephi with my very best dress on. He told me of his courting days and the girls he used to take out to dances, transporting his dates in wagons, sleighs, and on horse-back. They used to take some kind of farm produce to pay their tickets: Perhaps a melon, pumpkin, chicken or potatoes.

I listened to his stories until the shearers quit for the day, and we all went back to the old Hunt home together, had a nice supper of fresh vegetables and homemade cookies. Soon after, Teancum and I left for entertainment more suited to our own likes.

I noticed when I got home that I had lost a button from my best Sunday dress. But the next time I was at the Hunt home, I noticed Granddad kept trying to get my attention. He was fumbling with his thumb in his front pants pocket. When he was sure I was looking, he pulled his watch fob out. . ."

"What's a watch fob, Mom?"

"You've seen old movies, haven't you, Lilly, where the men reach into their vest pocket and pull out a watch with a 'lid' on it that snaps open, revealing the face of the watch?

Well, the watch is attached to a chain and at the end of the chain is a small clasp that attaches to a button or a loop inside the vest pocket. Either the lid, or the chain, or the clasp could be considered a fob."

I nodded, remembering those kinds of watches, but still not understanding why it was called a fob.

Mom continued. ". . . *Nephi pulled his watch fob out and what do you suppose it was made of? Well, nothing less than the button from my favorite dress. I decided to act dumb, and said to him, 'What a pretty watch fob you have, Nephi. It kind of resembles the button from one of my dresses.' And he answered, with the same devilish twinkle in his eyes, 'Well, it might have been a button once, but it isn't any more.'* "

Mom looked up from the journal, laughing.

"Gee, Mom, that's really funny," I responded in a monotone. I reached for the remote. Mom got to it first and threw it onto the cot, definitely out of a cripple's reach.

"Your dad inherited that watch, Lilly. I think it's still with Garrison's things at home. Have you wondered much about the woman you were named after?"

I had to admit that I hadn't. I had never cared to know anything really personal about my great grandfather Teancum, whose land I had grown up on. I had never thought about the love of his life, who spelled her name Lillie. I closed my eyes and sunk deeper into the pillow. My immediate family was dysfunctional for sure, but all these people seemed pretty functional. I liked Lillie. I liked her a lot.

***

The ache in my left leg, which wasn't there when I went to sleep for the night, became increasingly more painful as each sleepless hour ticked on. By 4 a.m. I rang for the nurse and pleaded with her to give me something for the pain. This time she gave me a shot, 'to bypass my sensitive stomach,' she said. She took my temperature, smelled my cast and left to call the doctor. Dr. Kimball could not get there til he made his rounds at 6 a.m., but even with the pain killers I had been given, the intense pain from muscle spasms in my leg left me crying.

Upon his arrival, Dr. Kimball asked an attendant to quickly split the cast. Immediately I saw the foul-smelling drainage at the incision site by my ankle. I thought I was going to throw up. The smell drove Mom from the room. Mega doses of antibiotics were injected into an IV.

"Lilly, you have developed osteomyelitis, an infection at the site of the breakage."

Dr. Kimball stood there, looking more than a little discouraged.

"Splitting the cast will reduce the pressure of the swelling, and that will eliminate some of the pain, but I've got to be honest with you, Lilly. This is serious. You'll need surgery immediately to get the wound cleaned out. The surgery will take one to two hours dependent upon what we find, and then you'll be in recovery for two hours after that. You should be back to your room and feeling much better by early afternoon. "

I started crying. I had just about reached my proverbial limit!

A nurse stuck her head in the room. "Doctor Kimball," she announced, "an operating room will be available in less than an hour."

There are more things in Heaven and Earth, Horatio,

Than are Dreamt of in your Philosophy. . .

Hamlet – Act I Scene V – William Shakespeare

CHAPTER EIGHT

Everyone vacated my room and Mom and I were left staring at each other, both trying to absorb this latest news.

"Do you want to watch some TV, Lilly?"

Shaking my head, I lowered my bed and lay flat, staring at the ceiling. It would take more than an inane TV show to take my mind off this monumental setback.

"Is there anything remotely interesting in one of those journals, Mom?"

"Well. . ." Mom reached for a small brown book underneath the other journals and thumbed through pages filled with small, scratchy handwriting. "I read this the other day when you'd gone for physical therapy. Wait til you hear what your Grandmother Hunt has to say."

"Your grandmother, four generations back, was Sarah Hunt. She was born in 1824 in Derbyshire, England. You won't believe this, Lilly. She had nine children, but five children died when small of contagious diseases."

Mom quit speaking, the realization of the loss Sarah experienced sinking in to the both of us. FIVE children, dead.

"After her husband died, Sarah, her son–Thomas–his wife, Hannah and their baby left England in May, 1864 to come to America. Sarah was forty years old. There were 800 on board ship."

Mom was quoting directly from the journal now:

" '*May 3, 1864: It was raining dreadfully as we set sail. I could not see where the sea and the sky met. My dear son, Nathan, who will not leave our native land, stood on the dock, soaked to the bone, waving furiously. He disappeared into the mist as our vessel, the McClellan, slipped into the channel and on toward the open sea. In this mother's heart of mine, I know I shall never see my Nathan again.*' "

Mom stopped reading to launch into an editorial, "Can you imagine the feelings of her and her family as they sailed farther and farther out from the shores of their beloved homeland? That would take guts, wouldn't it?" Mom queried. With no response from me, she summarized several journal entries:

" 'Their voyage was long and wearisome, six long weeks on the water. As they neared Newfoundland, the ship hit an iceberg, causing a hole large enough for a man to crawl through. Children were crying, 'Will the ship sink?' and the reply was, 'Ay, Ay, never, never.' And so with skillful manpower, the ship was fixed and they arrived in New York in June, 1864. They slowly made their way by covered wagon to Omaha, Nebraska, July 19, 1864 for the last lap of their journey.' "

Even though I didn't want to admit it to Mom, I had to inwardly concede that some of this stuff was actually interesting.

" 'Sarah and her family lifted their faces toward the West and braced themselves for the 1200 miles of rivers, mountains and desert that had to be conquered before they could reach their destination. There were 329 in the company.' "

Mom read quietly, leafing through several pages. "Wow, they suffered. It says here that in Omaha, the wagon train captain bought a load of green corn for all the oxen pulling the wagons. They were told it was good to eat, so they ate it heartily, not knowing it should be cooked first. Sarah was the most seriously affected. She had to ride atop the wagons for many days."

Mom's voice faded into the background. I knew all this stuff. It was in my dream. I saw it. I was there! I looked over at Mom, trying to get something out. How was this possible? How did my long dead relative get in my dream?

"It took them five months from when they left England to reach the Great Basin, Lilly. Just think of her losses: Five children dead, husband dead, one son left behind in England. And, if that wasn't enough, Lilly, she even had her best friend kidnapped by Indians in the middle of the western plains! Can you believe it?" She sighed and slowly closed the journal.

"I think I'll go downstairs to the gift shop for a soda. Is that okay with you, Lil, if I'm gone for a minute?"

I nodded yes, too stunned to respond more. I didn't have an explanation. Anna! Anna was the best friend who had been kidnapped. She'd called me Sarah. My dream was right there in her journal. All of it. There was a connection here and it nagged at my brain, trying to form itself into words. Running my hands through my hair, I resorted to biting my lip, focusing hard, trying to pull it out.

***

Mom returned with a magazine for me, and a 7-Up for her. Plopping down on her cot, Mom let out a heavy sigh. I couldn't get into the magazine. I was way too preoccupied with how I was going to word my question to her.

"Mom, do you ever dream about dead people? I mean, do you think they can visit us in dreams?"

Mom sat up and studied me for several seconds. Standing, she scooted a chair up to my bedside and reached for my hand.

"What I am about to tell you is very special, very sacred to me. I know you have been through a great deal, but so have I, and many others because of this accident. But right now, I need you to really listen to me, and spare me your sarcasm and anger."

I could hear Mom's tone, and I knew she was in her going-over-the-edge mode. I kept my mouth clamped tightly shut.

"As a matter of fact, Lilly, I did see your father; but it wasn't a dream. Not at all. Garrison came to me a few days after he died. I didn't tell you, Lilly, because you have been dissing anything spiritual for a long time now. I thought I would wait until you had worked on forgiving him, and was a little more receptive. But it's been three years now, and you still aren't any closer to forgiving him."

Forgive Dad? Forgive him for negating Mom as a human being, for making me feel like a Big Fat Zero! Who walks away from people they love? Who does that? He had left us shattered! Forgive Dad? Never!

I guess Mom took my lack of response as an invitation

to continue.

"I was lying in bed one morning wondering how I was ever going to get through the day, get through the next hour, even. One minute I was alone in our bedroom, and the next minute your dad was there, sitting at the foot of our bed. He told me not to touch him. I can't remember if he said why I shouldn't."

Mom stopped, choking back tears. "He, he asked me to take care of his little girl, of you, Lilly; to watch over you, to protect you. I promised him I would." Mom was struggling to speak. "And that is why I know we live on."

Mom's sharing with me did give me pause. Refusing to start crying, I clenched my hands into tight fists. I would go to surgery, close my eyes, and hope that maybe, just maybe, Sky would drop by. What I wouldn't give.

I took a quick intake of breath! The light came on, and there it was—the connection: Anna. . . Anna was to Sarah as Sky was to me.

***

"Here's just a little poke, Lilly," The anesthesiologist slid the needle into a vein under the skin of my hand and secured it with tape.

"Okay, Lilly, you ready?" Dr. Kimball patted my shoulder, smiling. "This won't take long. You just relax, and take a few deep breaths."

I flexed my shoulders and tried to get comfortable on the operating table. I no sooner closed my eyes than into my mind came a soft loving voice; strangely, a voice with an English accent, sharing a Haiku.

A huge avalanche

Stripped the mountain's grand soul bare.

Avalanche of loss.

Great, great, great, great Grandma Sarah Hunt knew, felt, just how I was feeling. I smiled. Dr. Kimball patted my shoulder and told the anesthesiologist he was ready to start.

***

Suddenly plunging into darkness, I feel myself falling down, down, under a heavy mantle of wet snow. The weight of mud and metal compresses my lungs. I gulp for air. Kicking my legs, try to kick free, reaching up, reaching for something, someone. A cell phone, a red cell phone, floats, like dandelion down in the breeze, over my head, drifting beyond my reach. Stretching, I strain to grasp it. 'Give it to me,' I yell. But Dad shakes his head and tells me to cross the dike on the diagonal, or I will tip the load. I grip the wheel, and strain to see over the dash, but Sophie, dressed in one of my dance leotards, licks my face, blocking my view of the orchard, and the apricot trees. Uncle Joe reaches for my hand and we look for the kitty, but the white cur-

tain, blowing in the breeze, covers my face.

***

I was back in my room by noon. They had given me something to stave off the nausea that usually follows anesthesia and pain medication, and I was actually quite surprised how good I felt.

Once she knew I was settled, Mom turned my safekeeping over to Luke for a few hours and left for a mandatory faculty meeting. Luke had not gone back to college to start winter semester. He said he was tired of studying and needed a break. Here he was now, flipping through the channels, trying to find something we would both be interested in, but there was nothing good on in the middle of the day.

"Please leave it off, Luke," I said. "I'm not in the mood for TV."

"Too bad you don't feel good enough to play Scrabble, Lil. I would clean your jets. . . . . AGAIN." Luke looked longingly at the Deluxe Scrabble game sitting on a nearby table. Mom and I had played twenty games, the score 11-9, my favor. But Luke was the all-time champion. Whenever he would play with Mom and me, he'd annihilate us.

"Luke, see those old books at the end of Mom's cot? Those are my ancestors' journals. How about you read to me? Maybe reading aloud will help me to fall asleep. I am so tired."

"Sure, Lil, but since when were you interested in dead people?"

I snapped back. "Since Jason and Sky fell into the category of DEAD PEOPLE, Luke!"

Luke stood there, staring at me, obviously shocked at my short fuse; but, always so quick to forgive, he took my hand and squeezed it.

***

I awoke sometime in the middle of the night. I was alone. With the surgery having gone without a hitch, Mom and Luke had gone home to their own beds. Outside, another winter storm beat against the walls of the hospital. It was an ink black night, and the light fixture above the bathroom sink gave off very little light. I couldn't make out the time, but I felt it must be after two a.m. The nurse had been in around nine p.m. to give me more pain medication and check my I.V. I just wanted her to be gone as I was so tired, so weak, I didn't feel like I had the strength to turn over. Sleep was all I wanted.

But just now, what had awakened me? It wasn't pain. It was my heart. My heart was pounding out of my chest; my breath was coming rapid. This was a sinking feeling, a foreboding. Instinctively, I knew something was very wrong. I was slipping fast. If I could have moved to look beneath my bed, I wouldn't have been surprised to see all my blood pooling on the floor.

Try as I might, I could not lift my arm enough to reach for and push the call button. It was all I could do to turn my head to look for it. Now my vision was blurring; my ears, starting to ring. And I continued to bottom out until my body felt empty of all life force. Then even the bathroom light burned out, plunging me into pitch darkness. Never had my hospital room been this dark. Not even light from the hallway spilled through from the door standing ajar. I was getting claustrophobic; this was unnerving. I had to open my door and get some light, some air. Surprisingly, I had the energy to sit up. I swung my legs over the side, and stood upright. I shouldn't be able to stand without crutches, but yet, here I was. Two strong legs carried me effortlessly forward.

With arms outstretched in front of me, I groped for the wall. I took another step and felt the cool metal of the door. I slipped through the narrow opening only to find more darkness.

"Hello? Hello? Where is everyone?"

Nothing. My words seemed to bounce off distant walls, as though I was in a very large, very empty auditorium. Panic was setting in as I turned and felt along the wall. Then, my cheek brushed against something soft. It felt like a smooth, cool, silk curtain and I grasped it, feeling for an opening. There it was! Parting it, I stepped through into a brilliant, warm light, the intensity of it only exceeded by its warmth. I gasped at what lay before me. Acres of green rolling hills stretched for miles in front of me. The grass rippled and waved in the cool breeze. The fragrance of lavender floated over me. I inhaled deeply. I was standing in a glorious summer day.

The incredible scene before me kept my mind from registering for a moment that I was completely naked. As alarming as that should have been, it did not concern me in the least. I was simply too confused by this drastic change in scenery to deal with my wardrobe malfunction, nor to immediately recognize who was standing right in the middle of this perfect summer day with me. How could I miss the lop-sided grin, the wrestler's physique, the Marine's dress uniform?

Jason said softly, "Lilly, it's so awesome to see you!"

I had a quick intake of breath. How many times had I longed for a moment like this, envisioned it, dreamed it, but the joy of seeing my best bud quickly turned to terror. Reason told me that Jason was dead. If he was dead, then I was either having another vivid dream, or. . . A scream rose in my throat.

This was not possible. The scene before me could not be real. Jason wasn't really there. What the body does when it is dying was carefully explained to me in my physiology class. Errant endorphins and misfiring electrical impulses send bizarre images to the brain. People who had near death experiences mistook the dying brain's distress signals as some spiritual vision that guaranteed them life after death.

Oh, I was dying, I knew that. And I knew, too, that what and who was before me was only a last second desperate attempt by my brain to keep it and me immortal. Jason was nothing more than a hallucination, now forming in my temporal lobe. Very soon now, I would plunge into darkness and simply cease to exist, as the last weak neurotransmitter failed. Would I die with my eyes open, staring at nothing?

The boundaries which

Divides life from death

Are, at best, shadowy and vague.

Who shall say where one ends,

And the other begins.

– Edgar Alan Poe

CHAPTER NINE

"No, I won't!" Feeling a mounting panic, I turned to retrace my steps. Behind me was the ivory curtain I had parted and walked through. It was suspended in mid-air, five to six inches off the ground, and reached at least 25 feet into the air. The ivory material was semi-sheer, but I could only see shadows behind the curtain. The bottom of the veil swayed in the gentle breeze. The curtain stretched to the horizon to my left and right. But I knew, as I stood there, that I could not reach the curtain, for when I took one step forward, it retreated the same distance. For some weird reason, it remained elusively just beyond my grasp.

"It's made of a very fine matter, Lil." There was Jason's voice again. "And, too, physical laws take on different perimeters here, so once you have passed through the veil, it prevents you from returning; at least without permission."

I whirled back around to face my hallucination, fighting the fear and dread that had seized me. My hallucination had already read my face. Jason always could, and he rapidly moved to my side. After wrapping me in a white silken gown and tying it on the side, he enfolded me in his arms and held me tight. I felt warmth penetrate through the raw fear to my very soul. A profound peace enveloped me, and I almost allowed myself to give into it. Almost.

"Jason, I don't understand. This feels real, but I know it's not real. . . it must be another dream! And even if it were real–and I AM happy to see you–I don't really want to be here. I thought I did; I know I said I did, but not really. I must be dreaming, and I have to wake up, NOW, cause I don't want to be, to be. . . ."

All the words tumbling out of me came to a screeching stop as I choked on the dreaded "D" word.

"Dead?" The apparition asked gently.

"Yes, dead! I am sorry I said I did; I'm sorry I wished to be, but I don't want to be dead already!" I was fighting back tears.

"Sssssh, Lil, just stop a minute." His voice had a soothing cadence to it that calmed me. He turned me to face him.

"Lilly, look at yourself. Are you safe? Are you well? Are you whole? Does this feel like a dream to you?"

I looked at my leg, my ankle. No cast there. No swollen, hot skin. No red, jagged scar. Just a healthy white leg, ending in a perfectly operating ankle. I had to admit that I really was okay. I had to admit that I was basking in the warmth of the sun in its heaven, but even more-so, in the deep, abiding love that permeated Jason' entire being. I had never felt better, I felt, in fact, glorious! Holding my arms out, I twirled faster and faster. Then, catching my balance, I ran, taking great leaps into the air. Landing solidly onto two strong legs, I executed three perfect cartwheels. I stood up to see Jason, shaking his head and laughing at my performance.

"Earth life is the dream, Lil. Reality is only found on this side of the veil."

Done with being serious, Jason broke into a wide smile. "I was asked to come meet you, Lilly. I've been assigned to be your Guide. I don't know that anyone else even knows yet that you are here." Jason paused, lost in thought.

And here came his lop sided smile again. "Probably because you're not scheduled to be here for years."

I was only partially listening. Any lingering anxiety

was being replaced with wonder at the reality of the panorama before me. To my left was a very large, shimmering lake. It was overwhelmingly beautiful. The surface looked like liquid silver. Trees lined the shores, and—like the lake—were much more impressive than anything I had ever before seen. Their leaves and sprigs carried a variety of colors—deep reds, golds, shades of purple, and blues even. One stem held its own small bouquet of different blossoms, in different colors. And these hues made the colors I was familiar with muted and dull. These were colors I had never seen before, and, therefore, there were no words for them.

Looking down, my bare feet were buried in blue-green grass that felt like lush velvet. Where the grass ended several yards away, a field with masses of ivory flowers swayed in the gentle breeze. I inhaled deeply. The air was crisp and pure. No pollution here. Looking up, I saw distant mountain peaks reaching high into a brilliant blue sky.

"Jason," I gasped. "It's beautiful!" Trying to contain myself, I pulled back to really study Jason. I gushed, "You! You look incredible."

Jason's face was smooth, his skin radiant. His hair was longer than his usual military style, his black locks tucked behind his ears. His body was toned and tan, his Marine uniform accentuating his muscles.

"Well, I dressed up for this occasion, Lil. I wanted you

to see me in something familiar; it lessens the. . . the. . .

"The shock," I said, half laughing, half crying. I was crying now for a completely different reason. Seeing Jason, touching Jason, taking in the beauty I was standing squarely in the middle of, left me in awe. The profound peace here–where-ever 'here' was–poured over me like rainfall, leaving me drenched in happiness.

"I've missed these rib-smashing hugs, Lilly," Jason laughed as he picked me up and squeezed me so hard that I pled for mercy. But there was no pain.

"Stop! Stop!" I gasped. Jason was always strong, but now he was, what WAS that adjective? Substantial? Solid? It was hard to put my finger on it, but Jason was more solidly Jason than my old Jason. Even though I knew, full well, that his actual body was buried back in Missoula, Montana, this body, or spirit, or whatever it was, was intact: Eyes, ears, knees and toes. He was all there.

Jason had been in his dress uniform when he took me to the dance, but this uniform was awesome! It shimmered and radiated light. On closer inspection, it wasn't the material that was reflecting light; Jason was glowing! Somewhere within him, radiating out, was a beautiful light that enveloped even me as I stood close to him. I stepped back and looked down at my own ho-hum attire for the first time. It wasn't like I could ever afford to buy brand name clothes when I was alive, but I wouldn't have been caught dead wearing this. But here I was now, dead, and I was wearing it.

"That," Jason explained, "is an orientation robe. Once you've been here a while, you can choose to wear clothes familiar to you or robes. But, by wearing that, other people here won't expect you to know anything. So, it shouldn't be much different than when you were on earth." I looked at Jason. He grinned.

I slugged him in the shoulder, knocking him off balance. "Well some things never change, Jase; always the tease. But wow, then I really am dead-dead, aren't I?" A large lump formed in my throat. Was I ready to be dead? How does one get ready for this?

"Well, I'm not sure." For the first time Jason sounded uncertain.

"Not sure? What do you mean? I'm either dead or I'm not, right?" My hands went to my face. I felt my eyes, nose, mouth. I pinched my arm; I bent down and rubbed my hands over my legs. How was dead supposed to feel?

"Lilly, I just don't know. According to the schedule. . ." Jason stopped, looking confused. "Timing is everything. You could call it sacred, even. We shouldn't mess with timing on earth, and we certainly don't try to bargain with it here."

"Where's 'here', Jason? Is all this Heaven? "I twirled and made a big, sweeping gesture with my arms as I took in how far the magnificence stretched before me. No travel brochure from any country back home could even begin to compete with what was before me.

"No, Lilly. . .," Jason paused, then pulled me to a nearby bench and sat me down next to him.

"This is the Spirit World, kind of a weigh station before the real Heaven. But I can tell you it certainly felt like Heaven compared to where I'd been. One second I was sitting behind the wheel of a Humvee, and the next second, I swear, I was traveling at the speed of sound, being hurled towards an incredible light."

"Jason," I said, in almost a whisper, "you have no idea how big of a hole your death, your absence, has left in our lives. Why you?"

"It's that 'timing' thing again, Lil. Simply, my time was up. I'm sorry you've been hurt. I saw how upset everyone was at my funeral and. . . "

"You were there? I mean, I know your body was there, but this you. . . " I interrupted Jason as I gestured towards his form in front of me, ". . .You were at your own funeral?"

"Yes, Lilly. We hang around for our own funerals because we are responsible for our bodies until they are taken care of. You have a stewardship over your own body; afterall, without that body you could never have gone to earth. But I don't want to get into that right now, okay? Let me finish my point." I could tell Jason didn't leave his tendency for impatience back on earth.

"You have no idea how much I wanted to say, 'Hey, Mom, hey, Dad, it's cool here! I'm busy here. Don't mourn me!' Lilly, I did everything I was sent to do; and when I came to the end of it, Voila, I came home! I'm so happy here."

When Jason said 'happy', I felt his feelings, his satisfaction, his peace-of-mind. All those wonderful emotions had been absent in my life for so long.

"Well, you're wrong, Jason. Of course, I'm dead. For what reason would I come all this way—and quit smirking at me—just to turn around and go back? That's not possible, and besides, what purpose would there be in that!" I slumped down on the bench, stretched my legs out, folded my arms, and adopted my resolute position.

"Why, Lilly? Would turning around and going back be a waste of gas?"

"Funny, Jason, you're really funny."

"You know, that's not your call, Lil! You've always been headstrong, willful, and done your own thing come hell or high water! Well, you're not in Hell—yet—and we're not anticipating rain, so get over it."

This was Jason, alright! He always could put me in my place and make me like being there.

"Let's walk, Lilly."

Pulling me up, Jason steered me onto a marble walkway, stretching into infinity in front of me. Each side of the walkway was lined with lilacs, roses, day lilies, gardenias, orchids, leaving the air heavy with their fragrance. Beyond the beds of flowers were green, rolling hills extending as far as I could see. I turned back to the flowers, trying to name each flower I recognized from among the thousands I had never seen before.

"Jason, my Mom would go ga-ga here. You know how much she loves flow. . ." I stopped, mid-sentence.

Suddenly, from behind, I felt a crowd gaining on us. I turned to see several men and women, most appearing to be in their late twenties, intently closing in on Jason and me. Staring into the light radiating from them, I could see they all were wearing light blue robes that reached to their ankles, with a slit almost to their knees. The men wore a sash around their waists, with an outer vest-like white coat that reached to the ground. The women wore beautiful, ornamental belts, some studded with gorgeous gems. Their clothes seemed to shimmer like satin. And they were all most definitely wearing large smiles. One of the men, with a powerful demeanor, caught up to me. Wrapping me in his arms, he gave me a warm embrace.

"Little Lilly," he exclaimed, "it's so wonderful to see you again."

His words got lost in the flurry of images passing through my mind. I saw him as a little boy, as a teenager breaking a horse. Next came his wife, his baby. Vivid images came to me of him struggling to till the ground behind a single horse and a plow. The Bitterroot Mountains were in the background. I knew that view, that field! He was working our ranch! Last of all, I saw him felling timber in the Bitterroot. An instant communication had taken place. I realized that this man knew all about me, as well; my interests, my hopes and dreams, all of them now gone. However this 'instant messaging' worked, I realized it was effortless for me to know—and understand—this man. And with understanding came genuine caring. Wrapping my arms around his shoulders, and kissing him on his cheek, I gave my grandpa a long, tight hug.

I had not seen pictures of most of these people, but yet, I knew their faces. I had been with these people before, and wondered, in awe almost, how could that possibly be?

Jason stepped forward with introductions. "Lilly, this is your great grandfather, Teancum." Turning behind him, Jason motioned for a beautiful, petite blonde to come forward. She stepped up, and putting one arm around Teancum's waist, she offered her hand to me.

"And this, Lilly, is Lillie, your great grandmother." As everyone surrounded me, Jason stepped back to give us room.

I gasped. None of these people looked old enough to be anywhere close to a great grandparent, or even grandparent. Lillie, my great grandmother, looked younger than Mom.

"We want to have a reunion so we can get reacquainted," Lillie said excitedly, slipping her arm around my waist.

Here I was, this woman's namesake, born a hundred plus years after her, but she was acting like she had known me forever.

One by one, they stepped forward, introduced themselves and hugged me:

Sarah Hunt, her son, Thomas, and his wife, Hannah, who had traveled on foot with Sarah the 1200 miles to the American West.

There were Sarah's sons, Nathan–who had stayed behind in England–and Nephi, with his wife, Thomina.

Many more stepped up to meet me, and then, last of all, Grandpa Benjamin and my Grandma Rachel. With just a hug, an instant bond was formed with each of them.

I looked around to see who I might have missed, and noticed a lone figure, radiating no more light than I, split from the group and move quickly away from us. She was skimming above the grass, moving faster and faster away, her red hair flowing behind her. Finally, she slowed and stopped, perhaps sensing that my eyes were following her. She deliberately turned, and making eye contact with me, gave me a look that could have killed, if I weren't already dead! I gasped.

"Helena! Jason, that look's like Helena!"

"Are you sure? Jason quickly took a protective stance in front of me, breaking our stare-down.

Helena turned her back to us and was soon out of sight. I didn't know contempt could exist here–I must have brought it with me–because there was no denying that I felt it towards Helena every bit as much as I had back on earth. Obviously, the feeling was mutual.

"It's so great of all of you to come see Lilly!" Jason turned me back towards my family.

"Oh, it's so good to see all of you," I exclaimed. Their love enveloped me and I couldn't contain my relief to be among people I felt safe with.

Hannah took my hand. "You are beautiful! I see your dad in you."

At the mention of my father, I looked around nervously. That was the other person in this new world that I definitely did not want to run into.

A blur of white made me look down. A small white terrier, with her tail furiously wagging, had trotted up to me. It couldn't be, but it was! I would recognize that lolling tongue anywhere.

"Sophie!" I shrieked. Falling to my knees, I reached for her.

Sophie pounced on me and started madly licking my

face. I tipped backwards into the grass and everyone laughed at Sophie mauling me. Jason gestured for everyone to form a circle and they all sunk into the lush grass around me.

Teancum knelt directly beside me. "We have loved helping you and your parents all these years."

I didn't understand what Grandpa meant. I shook my head, thrown at how I had found myself in the middle of this strange continuum.

As though he was reading my mind, he continued, "Lilly, all your family here has been involved in your life there. When your mother has prayed, when you have struggled, it has been one, or many of us, who have been sent to assist you. Who would love you and want to help you more than your family and friends. . . and, Sophie, your dog?"

Kneeling in the grass, with Sophie pressed against me, I knew the answer to that. No one. Absolutely no one.

Time never changes the memories;

The faces of loved ones, who bring to me all that I am,

All that I come from, and all that I live for,

And all that I'm going to be.

My precious family is more than an heirloom to me.

– Author unknown

CHAPTER TEN

I was pretty much speechless by now. Nobody would believe this.

"You're right, Lil; they wouldn't," Jason agreed.

I looked at Jason. His lips had not moved; his words had not been audible. His voice was inside my head; he had spoken to my mind. This was eerie.

"Lilly," Sarah explained, "We do not need to talk with our mouths. We have with you so as not to alarm you. It is much more exacting and accurate when we talk spirit to spirit. So much is lost in any language; but when it is spirit to spirit, you receive what I am saying with all of your senses."

It was true. I not only heard Sarah's words inside my head, but I felt her love, and her greater insights, penetrate to my bones.

Grandpa Benjamin jumped in. "When we were born, Lil, a veil was drawn over our memories. We forgot everything about this world. But don't worry. Now that you're back, everything will come back to you, over time, with practice. You won't be learning so much as you will be remembering. Til then, we'll make sure you hear both ways for a while."

"This certainly beats texting," I exclaimed.

I looked down at Sophie, curled up now in my lap.

Sarah stooped down and petted Sophie's head. "You know, Lilly, on Earth our pets can understand us when we talk to them. It is our ability to understand our pets that is taken away from us when we take a turn there. Their personalities are like that of a sweet little child, but often they are the teachers. They teach us how to love when we struggle to love people."

Sophie looked up at me, and she then proceeded to vent years of frustration inside my head.

"You have to know, Lilly, I hated that blue striped doggie sweater you made me wear in the winter."

I gasped!

"Think about it, Lilly. I always came when called, and I kept your feet warm at night. And what did I get in return? Cheap, bargain dog food! What I wanted was popcorn! Lastly, my definition of a 'walk' is not out the front door, around the house, and back in the front door."

Staring at Sophie, I was left astonished.

Jason laughed. "Wow, Sophie, do you feel better getting those things off your furry chest?"

"Did you ALL hear Sophie's rant?" I looked around at them, not knowing if I liked all my thoughts just being out there for everyone to hear.

"Yes, Lil, we all heard her," Sarah explained. "But not everything is 'out there' for everyone to hear.

"Well, that was, Sarah! You were just inside my head hearing that I don't like my thoughts read," I replied in exasperation.

Sarah tried again. "If Sophie had wanted to communicate with just you, Lilly, she would have projected out to just you. But probably wanting to get group sympathy," Sarah looked down at Sophie and winked, "she projected her thoughts out to all of us. When you want your thoughts to be private, they will be. You just have to be patient with yourself. You just crossed over, you know."

This was absolutely mind-boggling to me. The spirits of people and animals could communicate with each other the same way humans did.

Standing up, Teancum pulled me up beside him. Reading my thoughts, he continued with them. "All animals have their own unique personality; things they like–like popcorn–things they don't, just like us. Here, in the spirit world, our pets decide if they even want to be with us. Just desserts, I think. Sophie is here because you and your mother were so wonderful to her, contrary to her litany of complaints."

I remembered holding Sophie in a vice-like grip when I was four. I was trying to get her to drink imaginary tea from a little plastic cup in my tea set. I am sure there were many injustices that perhaps I should admit to. Then I thought of Tweetie. Ah-hah! I did have something over on her!

"You're forgiven, Sophie-girl." I smiled and Sophie–looking very relieved–wiggled out of my grasp and trotted off to join a cute little wiener dog taking a walk with his owners.

Sitting there within my circle of family, I realized that absolutely no one was in a hurry. We were all relaxed, basking in the peace of knowing that all was right with this beautiful, new world.

"Is it time for breakfast. . . . or lunch?" I blurted out. I wasn't hungry really, but didn't family get-togethers call for food?

"Aaah, yes," Grandpa Benjamin nodded, smiling. "We forgot the time."

Everyone started laughing at what was obviously an inside joke. There was something about time that was different here. I had no sense of how long I'd been here. Was it hours? Days? Did the sun ever go down here?

Then, into my mind came Grandpa's voice. "It is with relish that I share with you one of the biggest reasons the Spirit World is so Heaven-like! Here, Lilly, there are no hours, minutes or seconds to tick by. Time does not fly. Time does not stop. We don't run out of time. We don't have too much time on our hands. We can't be late. We don't show up early. We don't measure or mark time."

Practicing my telepathy, I responded. "You mean, Grandpa, that my Calculus homework would never be late?"

Benjamin explained. "When we pass through the veil, Lilly, we enter a timeless dimension. On Earth time is passing, but to us, everything happens in the moment. Past and future do not even exist here in the Spirit World. All 'time' is now. So, no, your homework would never be late here."

Okay. That did it. I felt my eyes glaze over. Whatever Grandpa had just said was the very reason why I did not take Physics. Science was never my strong suit and I saw no reason to pursue it here.

Obviously, Grandma Lillie knew that, too, and took pity on me. "Jason, why don't you take Lilly and get her something to eat." She grinned as though her suggestion held other surprises for me.

Jason took my elbow. "Excellent idea! Lilly, let's glide."

"Come see us at our home, Lilly," Grandma Lillie said," and we'll visit some more."

***

Waving goodbye, Jason took my hand in his, and I felt myself rising into the air. Putting his other arm around my waist, Jason gently guided me towards a distant skyline of buildings. For the first time in my life, I was floating. And maybe falling. I clung to his hand tightly, looking at him in panic.

"Don't worry, Lil, I've got ya! This is something that you're going to. . ."

Clinging to Jason's arm with my other hand, I interrupted him. "I know, I know. . . I have to relearn this, too, if I can just survive the fall. I have to remind myself that I can't die twice, huh, Jas?" I looked down and around me nervously.

"Lil, get a grip! We are only ten feet off the ground! This is an awesome way to travel. It's just like when I taught you to rollerblade, remember? After a while, you let go of my hand and did it on your own."

All around me people were gliding peacefully by. Biting my lip, I realized how ridiculous I must look clinging to Jason. I felt like a cirrus cloud on a summer breeze. With my new body being weightless and so mobile, reason told me this floating thing shouldn't be so hard to master.

Trying to take my mind off the fact that my feet were not touching the ground, I asked Jason a pressing question. "Why do 'my older than dirt' ancestors look so young?"

Jason smiled. "When we die, we return back here looking as we will always look from this point on – in our prime. Some people might like to hang onto their grey hair, but underneath the grey is a young face between twenty-seven and thirty-three years of age."

"Well," I replied, "that is still OLD."

We were quickly approaching a downtown area much like the ones on Earth. But the outline of buildings looming above the horizon was the only similarities to Earth's cities. There were no cars; everyone walked or 'flew'. I didn't know what else to call it, this floating thing we were doing. The streets, the sidewalks, all paved with what looked like alabaster, were spotless. There was no dirt, no cigarette butts, no litter anywhere. Reading my thoughts again, Jason interrupted them.

"Hmmmmm. What would graffiti in Heaven say?"

"I've died and gone to Heaven?" I responded. "Or, a different four-letter word, like 'LOVE' YOU!"

"The Angel Gabriel was here?" Jason contributed.

I poked Jason in the ribs. "Stay out of my head! That was mine."

Lowering us to the ground, Jason shook his head. "I must say, Lil, 'thought spillage' appears to be your biggest challenge!"

Looking over Jason's shoulder, I noticed a small form standing at the top of a nearby hill, silhouetted against the sun. I squinted, trying to make out who was watching us so intently. Then I saw the spiky hair and it finally registered to me. Breaking into a run, I moved faster than I thought myself capable of.

Arms outstretched, I ran into the open arms of my best friend, Skylar, knocking her over. We fell to the grass, screaming and laughing and crying all at once. People passing by stopped momentarily and laughed with us. We pulled each other to our feet.

"Skylar, I can't believe it! It's you. It's really you." I stood back, holding her at arm's length to get a better look. "Sky, you look fabulous." Then I lost it. I wrapped my arms around Skylar's neck and sobbed. She didn't say anything; she just hugged me and let me cry.

"Lil, it has seemed like forever, hasn't it?"

I nodded. Trying to get a grip on my tears, I blurted out, "Why did the accident have to happen? Why did our lives have to end so soon, Skylar? It's wonderful here, but I want to take you and go back to our dance club, and to boring world history class, with boring Coach Kress, and even to the crappy school lunches! Our turn on earth wasn't long enough. We didn't get to LIVE, Sky!"

Skylar stood there, her hand in mine, letting me go on and get it all out of my system.

"Lil, I felt the same way when I first came; honest, I did. But you'll find that the longer you are in the Spirit World, the more you'll remember your life here before you went to earth. It will all make more sense, and you'll get understanding. Once you see the bigger picture, all the homesickness leaves."

Jason stepped up and hung his arm around Skylar's neck. "Sky, Lilly showed up here a tad early. Maybe she'll be going back for more of that delicious cafeteria food."

"Yeah, right, Jase." Sky begged to differ. "People don't just drop by here for a visit."

I looked first at Jason, then at Sky, my face screwed up in confusion. I, too, wasn't convinced that my life was ended for good. A nagging feeling told me my turn on earth was not over, though it certainly appeared so standing here with my two very best, very dead friends.

Growing up doesn't

Change anything.

It's the changing that

Makes you grow up.

— Author Unknown

CHAPTER ELEVEN

We were among the buildings now and Jason was on a serious hunt for our favorite ice cream. Skylar had gone on and on about the ice cream here being better than Italian ice-cream, gelato, but I was highly skeptical. The buildings were not tall, maybe five stories max, but they were elaborate in their architecture. Their facades were a variety of different periods and styles. I recognized Victorian, Egyptian, Greek, Russian, gothic, and colonial designs; yet, their outer walls were of the same alabaster material.

Perfectly placed between the buildings were all kinds of trees, flowering bushes, large vases of flowers filling the air with their perfume. People were everywhere, but the corridors were so spacious that we didn't feel crowded.

"I suppose it is obvious to you, Lil, that we don't have to eat! We eat because we want to; AND, Lilly, we can eat all that we want," Skylar glowed smugly. "Can you imagine unlimited chocolate, and no worries about weight gain?"

Jason, speaking into an imaginary megaphone, commanded: "Okay, Ladies! Put the chocolate cake down and step away from the platter!"

"Wait!" I groped my gown, feeling for pockets. I realized I hadn't been issued a purse to match my ensemble, and definitely not a wallet with any money in it. "What are we going to do for money?"

Sky looked at me like I had three heads.

"Why would you think that we would need money here? This is Heaven!"

"Guys, HELLO! Remember back on Earth when we couldn't do ANYTHING without money?" I remembered that grim fact vividly, because Mom and I never, never had enough of it.

"Well, Lil, you won't need money on this world," Jason responded. "The absence of money here is the great equalizer. Back on Earth, the amount of money a person has defines him or her to a great degree."

"But here," Sky said, pointing to a girl passing by us," no one knows what car she drove back on Earth, and no one cares!"

"We have abundance here, Lil: Sufficient for our needs, and some to spare. No need for designer shoes here," Jason said.

"I have died and gone to Heaven," I declared. There was a pause, and then all three of us started laughing. "Literally," I added.

***

We reached an area Jason called the Plaza where there were rows and rows of counters, all with different foods I had never seen before, being artfully prepared by people I could tell loved doing it. We filled our trays from the huge selection and found a table with three chairs under a Weeping Willow tree. But the leaves on this tree were not green like the leaves on our tree back home; they were light blue. And they twinkled.

A scent wrapped itself around me and stopped me in my tracks. Closing my eyes, I inhaled deeply; again. . .and again. Opening my eyes, I turned to Jason and Sky.

"What IS that?"

"What is what?"

"That smell; that incredible smell?"

"You mean the fragrance all these trees give off?"

I knew I could never find the words to describe the scent: Fresh peaches? Mixed in with delicate wafts of vanilla? Whatever, I wanted to live among those trees forever! And I experienced the same ecstasy when I slid Heaven's ice cream across my tongue. It was better than anything back on earth, as was the cake, and the cookies, and the candies, and the drinks.

***

Between bites I asked Jason, "Why did I come through a veil and you were just hurled here?"

Jason always talked with food in his mouth, and he did so again. "Our world here is every bit as big as the earth. People enter the Spirit World at different locations, in different surroundings. Depending upon where someone is when they cross over, they could pass through a veil like you did, Lilly, or. . ."

I laid my fork down. "Jason, what happened the day you died?"

Jason took a deep breath and the mood suddenly became very somber.

"Where do I even begin?" he said, shaking his head at Sky and me. For the first time ever, Jason's eyes looked very sad. He slumped down in his chair and stared straight ahead, beyond the horizon, back to Earth, back to Iraq.

"You might think that I would have passed on a return trip to the fiery furnaces of war, but, oh no, not me. Some patriotic zeal catapulted me there for a second time.

"You know, guys, everything about that place stank. The war had taken a toll on the people, their homes and businesses, the soil and the air. Raw sewage, burned out vehicles, wild dogs, very few buildings left undamaged, and only putrid, thick air to breathe. I could return home to clean air, sheets, streets and water, but those poor people would continue to wake up in the same despicable conditions. Yes, we were liberators, but I lost sleep wondering what more we could do to help rebuild.

"On my second tour, I was Platoon leader of the First Platoon, Bravo Company. Two teams had been deployed to stop all traffic from crossing the main bridge just north of where the Euphrates and Tigris River converged. Any vehicle entering the bridge would be given a volley of warning shots and allowed to turn around. If the vehicle continued, we would presume it to be hostile and would stop it advancing by the use of deadly force. My Humvee was equipped with, among the usual deadly killing weapons, a .50 caliber machine gun. It was certainly capable of taking the head off any driver attempting to cross the bridge, and depositing muscle tissue and bones fragments on the upper side of the First National Bank of Baghdad, three blocks past the river. "

Sky's eyes widened. "P L E A S E, Jason! I think I'm going to be sick."

"Sorry. I forgot I was talking to girls." Jason straightened in his chair and continued. "I sat in my Humvee, with my usual guests—a swarm of flies that covered the complete interior."

Jason's whole face wrinkled up, and he gave us a disgusted look. "Don't ya just HATE FLIES! With packs of wild dogs feeding on the dead nearby, you might think the nasty, black winged maggots would have stayed a little closer to death."

I looked at my precious, brave Jason and couldn't help but think that perhaps the flies knew they were staying close to death; death just hadn't arrived yet. I shivered, and hoped Jason had not noticed my reaction.

"Dusk turned to dark, and through my night goggles I saw an old blue sedan barrel onto the bridge with the pedal to the metal. It was gaining speed when permission to fire was requested.

"Do it!" I said. "Light 'em up."

"My gunner stood in the back seat behind the machine gun, and with the precision of a surgeon, took out the driver and the passenger. The car slammed into the side rail and exploded in a giant fireball, its reverberations shaking our Humvee.

"Enemy! Enemy! The radio crackled as Team Two spotted movement to our right. Enemy AK-47s started popping around us: 'POP! POP! POP!' It sounded like a fireworks factory had been set ablaze."

Jason was sitting on the edge of his chair, totally reliving the whole thing. Sky and I were riveted.

"Talk to me, Team Two' I shouted, but there was no response. Then, down the road I saw a light come on in Team Two's Humvee as it moved away from my position. The Iraqis had our vehicle, you see, including two .50 caliber machine guns. I knew our only chance was to overtake the Humvee before it could be hidden off road or lost in some building."

Jason looked at us, shaking his head.

"Heaven forbid our weapons be used against us or our friendly forces. Ready to give chase, I turned the ignition and, as I did, the corner of my eye caught the red streak coming from a grove of palm trees. Then, everything happened in slow motion. An RPG round came through the open passenger side door. It slammed into my door and exploded in the cab of my Humvee. There was a brilliant flash of light and–as I looked down through my night goggles–I could see both my hands had been blown off at the wrists. Cauterized in the blast, I was amazed to look at the stumps where my hands had been and see no blood! My legs were not within my field of vision, and my own intestines were sloughing over the edge of the seat."

Jason ran his hands through his hair. Sky paled and covered her mouth. I just sat there, stunned, fighting back tears.

"But, man, I didn't feel any fear, ya know? I guess the endorphins kicked in, protecting me from the shock of it all. Then, while in the midst of assessing my personal damages, another brilliant light filled the interior of the Humvee, only this time it was even brighter and more glorious.

"Glowing, as he sat next to me, was my grandfather.

" 'Let's go home, son; drive on,' Grandpa said.

"And I turned the key and we rounded a bend to here, where we are today, Lilly."

"Jason," Sky said, finally remembering to breathe. "It must have been horrible."

"It was hell, Sky," Jason said matter-of-factly.

Jason paused to look at us. The agitation he had been feeling was replaced by peace and calm. I could tell Jason was done. There would be no more talking about this.

"Sky, tell Lilly about the circuitous route you took to get here."

Looking over at me, Jason shook his head and said, grinning, "I wouldn't want to take the detour Sky did!"

"Oh, I don't know," Sky countered. "It kind of reminds me of beginning at a water park, then entering the Haunted House at the County Fair and then ending on a Tilt-A-Whirl ride where you feel weightless and euphoric."

Sky looked at me like I should understand what she was describing. I didn't. I picked up my fork and reached for another piece of chocolate cake.

"Well, okay, let me start from the beginning. After the car stopped rolling I stood up and brushed myself off. Then I realized that I felt flimsy, almost transparent. I had lost my. . . my hardness. It was a very strange sensation! I looked down at a girl lying in the snow beside me and had absolutely no idea who I was looking at."

Skylar started laughing, thinking that was funny. I was horrified.

"I bent over to get a closer look and realized I was seeing a three-dimensional me! I had never seen myself before, guys! It was just weird! Think about it; we've only seen ourselves two-dimensionally, in a mirror. The solid, space-filling me I didn't recognize at all." Skylar paused, looking disappointed and then–feeling her nose–she said, "My nose is bigger than I thought."

I urged her on. "Skylar, hurry up! This is fascinating."

"I suddenly felt an enormous amount of energy around me. I felt the power behind it, and a rushing sound swirled above me, lifting me carefully up into a whirling, huge, black mass."

"Like when I used to suck my dirty socks up into our vacuum at home," Jason interjected, impressed with his own analogy.

"Hardly," Skylar replied dryly. "I wasn't scared; it was a wonderful sensation. I had never felt so calm, or had such a sense of peace. You know how you swoosh down the slides at the water park, Lilly? In a reclining position, feet first, head raised? Well, that's what this was like, but the speed was incredible. I looked around and realized that there were a lot of other people–and animals too–traveling with me. We didn't talk. We were all just content to be on the ride. I then drew closer to what looked like a dense fog–this is the haunted house part, Lil! I entered the fog and felt masses of people floating by me. They seemed to be in agony; they were actually moaning."

Jason elbowed me. "See what I mean, Lilly?" He faked a shiver.

Skylar rolled her eyes. "I could feel their remorse, their torment. They were in the depths of despair, and I somehow felt all of it. I was choking on their anguish. I thought, 'Oh my gosh! Am I in Hell?'" Skylar stood up and started to pace.

"I pleaded to be taken away from them, and I was. I was pulled forward through that moving mass, towards a brilliant light. Peace and warmth enveloped me again, and then I stopped. Here." Sky held her arms out wide and spun around, as though drawing all the beauty of her newly found home to her.

Sheesh! In comparison to Jason's and Sky's stories, my exit from Earth was downright boring! What was there to say about it? I felt yucky, and then the lights went out. Whoo-hoo!

Picking up my fork, I pointed my next bite of magnificent chocolate cake at Skylar and declared, "You win! Your entrance tops mine."

***

Jason, Sky, and I were lying back in long grasses, making angels' wings with our arms while savoring all the tastes from our eating binge. If I had eaten this much back home, I'd be feeling like a beached whale. Nearby us fruits and vegetables were growing on many of the bushes and trees, there for the picking when we were ready to look at food again.

All I felt was contentment. Well, almost contentment. While devouring our ice-cream, I had sat across the table from Jason and Skylar, noticing their individual glows. They 'glowed' differently from one another, giving their robes different colors and hues. And I? I didn't glow at all, or at least not much. I felt like a Plain Jane compared to Skylar. But I didn't know how to ask, and I wasn't sure I even wanted to know why.

"Don't feel bad about that, Lil," Jason said.

"Didn't I tell you to stay out of my head, Jason!" I retorted. "Sheeesh! There is peer pressure here, too! I didn't think I'd have to worry about what I wore once I was dead!"

"Lilly, Lilly," Jason said in a placating tone, "don't take it personally. Just because you look like your own little nightlight. . . ." He didn't get any further because I rolled over, straddled him, and started stuffing handfuls of grass into his mouth.

"Stop it! Stop it you two," Sky said, laughing at the both of us. "Lilly, you have to remember that you are in an orientation robe, and that does make a difference. Jason and I have been here longer, so we've got our permanent robes. These robes are a visual measure of the progress we made while on earth."

"Progress? Progress!" I tried hard to not take her comment personally, but it wasn't working. "Well, apparently I didn't make any progress, Sky, by the looks of me! But it's not just this ho-hum robe that's bugging me, Sky! Why are you two glowing differently? There are all different degrees of glowing walking by," I said with annoyance, pointing to the people passing by us on the sidewalks.

Jason explained. "Lil, the brightness does vary from person to person, and the hues, as well. It all has to do with how each of us lived our life while on earth, the choices we made, the service we gave, the love we shared, how easily we. . ." Jason paused here. ". . .forgave."

I got it. I stood up and brushed the grass off me while I tried to get control of my anger. It didn't work for I was now seething.

"Oh, yes, that 'forgiveness' thing. Well, I'm surprised I am here at all, then, even for a short visit. I may not ever be more than a dim flashlight."

Before either of my sparkly friends could object, I continued. "So tell me, Jason, should I just magically forget now about Dad walking out on Mom and me? Is it suddenly okay that Mom was devastated, my self-worth wiped out?"

I whirled around to face Sky. "And tell me, Skylar, are you and Helena just as tight as ever? Is it no big deal that we're all dead waaaay before our time? Don't you care that you won't be graduating, or going to college? Is it no big deal that your father won't walk you down the aisle to be married to the love of your life? Do you not want to know what it feels like to make love, to have your very own baby?" I was screaming now, and screaming probably wasn't allowed in Heaven, either. I looked around and didn't see any Noise Patrol approaching, so I continued. "Crap, Skylar, she KILLED us!" I sank to my knees and started crying. I would never glow. I was unfit to be with my friends in Heaven. So just where did that leave me?

Jason pulled me down beside him and put his arms tightly around me. "Lilly, you have a right to feel those feelings. Maybe that is one reason why time is not kept track of here in this world; we each are allotted all the time we need to work things through, to understand, and to move on."

Sky knelt beside us. "Do you remember reading Emily Dickinson in our literature class last year, Lil? Remember how much we liked her? There was this quote: 'We never know how good we are until we are called upon to rise.' Emotional betrayal, abandonment calls upon all that is good within you to rise, Lilly. We must all rise!"

"I know what you're trying to say, guys, really I do. But there is a big difference between Helena hurting us, Skylar, and actually killing us!" I could tell Jason did not like the direction this conversation was going. He gave Sky one of his 'don't go there' looks, but she ignored him.

"Lilly," Skylar was talking slowly, weighing her words. "I don't remember it that way. Helena didn't cause the accident. Accidents are. . . .are accidents; it was no one's fault. You were just reaching for. . ."

"SKY!"

Sky and I jumped!

Realizing he had yelled, Jason lowered his voice. "I mean, uh, Sky, it's time for Lilly's Orientation classes. Why don't you go with her? It pays to sit through some of these courses more than once."

"Yeah, right, Jason. I'm onto you," Sky said. "You just

want to go hang out with Analeise."

"Who's. . .?"

Too late. That's all I got out. Jason was there one second. Gone the next.

I am still learning.

– Michelangelo

CHAPTER TWELVE

I felt like I was at an airport back on earth. Sky and I were scrunched in the middle of a huge crowd, under the dome of a large pavilion, looking at multiple screens above our heads. Information on each screen scrolled quickly past us.

"How do I know which ones I'm to go to?"

"Look for the green screens, Lil," Sky answered. "Those are all the classes for new arrivals."

That didn't help much. There were several green screens overhead, with lines and lines of courses. To the right of the courses, words flashed on and off: FULL or ROOM FOR FIVE. I started reading down the same screen as Sky:

- Natural Laws Explained
- Understanding Pure Energy
- Vibrations and Frequencies
- Adjusting to Mental Telepathy
- Levitation 101
- Thought Travel
- Service Assignments
- Intergalactic Travel

All those sounded too cerebral for my current state of mind. Where was the creative stuff? I looked through other screens and stopped on the third one from the end.

- Robe Design and Creation
- Creating Heavenly Music

Oh, that sounded interesting. I made a mental note to go to that one as soon as I could. But where were the dance classes? I was good enough to teach dance. I knew I was. I could begin with ballet, go onto contemporary, even teach some tap, ballroom, or jazz.

- Cooking Schools
- Chocolate Dipping

Pointing to a screen, Sky grabbed my hand. "That's a good one. Let's go."

"Are we going to the chocolate dipping class, Sky?" I asked hopefully.

"You wish," was her only retort.

***

We were sitting on the aisle, three quarters of the way down, in the middle section of a large ampetheater. I looked around me. There must be 1,000 seats, I thought. And they were all occupied.

A petite woman floated in through a side door and stood behind a podium. Looking at all the faces staring down at her, she smiled a broad smile.

"Good day. I am Miriam. Welcome back to the Spirit World. We are happy for your return."

Everyone smiled back and nodded. I wasn't feeling it. Somehow, some feeling I couldn't explain, made me think that I was the only one who didn't belong here.

"The official title of this course is: Spirit Guides: Helping Your Earth-bound Associates."

Miriam glanced at her notes. "However, there are several units we will study under this general topic, some of those being:

The Ministry of Angels;

Different Types of Spirit Guides. . ."

My mind raced back to what seemed a hundred years ago. I was in Diego's upstairs bedroom, with Alex and other friends. Zena had said maybe we were talking to a spirit guide. R I G H T. Vlad was certainly a different type of spirit guide, alright. If I was going to be a spirit guide, I was going to be a nice one, not one that made teenage girls pee their pants.

Miriam was skipping through random topics:

- Knowing When and Who to Help
- Making Contact through Dreams
- Physical Appearances and Visitations
- Respecting Privacy
- Miscellaneous Do's and Don'ts.

"We have much to cover, but. . ." our instructor looked around the room, "we do have all the time in the world."

Everyone laughed. Everyone but me. I squirmed in my chair. Did I? I wasn't sure.

Miriam smiled up at us. "Let us begin. Perhaps some of you, while on earth, were aware of the presence of spirits around you. Perhaps others of you, for many reasons, were closed off to that possibility. Whatever your mindset back on earth, you are now vividly aware that was, indeed, the case. None of us were ever alone there. How many times we were pulled, or diverted, from harm's way, we cannot count. How many times you and I were prompted to do something, or NOT to do something, we cannot count."

Miriam looked around the room. "How many of you have had your life's review?"

Every hand went up. Every hand but mine. My stomach clenched.

"What the freak, Sky! What's a life re. . ."

"Ssssssh, Lil, listen."

I turned back to the instructor.

"You have all been shown, then, all the times you were helped, protected, taught, directed, comforted, and yes, even chastised. Who were some of your guardians?"

A deep voice from way in the back shouted out, "My Uncle Stan was my guide. He was my favorite uncle back on earth. He died in Viet Nam."

Another female voice from down in front, "My childhood friend, Debra, was my guardian angel. She died of cancer when we were seventeen."

The class volunteered more and more names and the circumstances under which they had been helped. My Great grandpa Teancum had said members of my family had helped me, but when, and how? I had no idea. This was starting to feel like high school. I hated it when everyone knew there was to be a test and was prepared and I was clueless.

"I see many of you refer to your helpers as your guides; others, as your guardian angels. These are not interchangeable positions, people. There are numerous levels of energies here in our Spirit World, and whether you are a guardian angel, a spirit guide, an archangel, etc., depends entirely upon the frequency with which you vibrate."

Oh, no. Inwardly, I groaned. This was sounding like physics again. Time for my eyes to roll back in my head. I slouched down in my seat and stared upwards at the ceiling high above me. If I were organizing classes up here, what would they be?

- Ground Rules:
  - Accepting that you are really dead
  - There are no do-overs; please do not ask
- Areas off Limits:
  - The Importance of avoiding down elevators

I laughed out loud. Sky looked over at me.

"Aren't you paying attention?" she hissed. "This stuff is important."

Whispering, I lied. "I am, Sky; really."

I stared straight forward again but turned my mind inward. This was fun:

- Harps and Crafts
- Using Bleach for those Lasting Stains
- Lunesta: For those Days without End

"Psssst. Psssst."

I looked around. There was Jason, crouched down in the aisle, trying to get our attention. I nudged Sky and–looking back at Jason–he signaled for us to follow him up the stairs and out a door at the back.

Out in the hall, Sky turned, exasperated. "What are you doing?" First you send us to class and then you drag us out and right when it was getting interesting."

"Sky, how would you like to take Lilly back home for a quick visit?"

Skylar and I–staring at him blankly–both shouted "W H A T?" simultaneously.

"What ARE you talking about, Jason! What a random question," I exclaimed. "I just got here!" Actually, I didn't know how long I had been in the Spirit World. It was impossible to tell. By earth's measure, it would take a long time to see everything I had seen, talk to all the people I had met, and eat all the food we had devoured. Maybe I had only been gone for a few days; maybe I had been dead and buried for three weeks.

"Lilly! Skylar!" Jason was trying to be patient while inserting some mock self-importance into his explanation. In a deep, authoritative voice, he continued.

"As your Official Guide, it is my duty to re-instruct, retrain, inform and direct. So, I'm informing you. Members of both of your families could use a little help right now, and it would be better if you left sooner than later."

We looked at him blankly.

"Well, that is what we DO, right? We help! You two can't just sit around, eat, and have a giggle fest," Jason said.

"And besides, you, Lilly, will get to experience instantaneous travel."

"Count me in." Sky was oozing her usual confidence. "Lil, this will be a great gig! We'll be real angels!"

"But," I argued, "I don't know HOW to be a real angel. Didn't she say we had to be vibrating at a certain frequency?" I looked down at my torso. "Am I even vibrating?"

"Let's go," Sky begged, pulling at the sleeve of my robe. "We certainly don't have anything else on our social calendar."

Butterflies took flight in my stomach. I had to admit that I was excited about going home but panicked at what I would find there. Just maybe we could take a quick detour and go see Alex. In spite of his 'no show' after his first visit to the hospital, I missed him! Oh how I missed him! But wouldn't that be like rubbing salt in a wound? I couldn't talk to him; I couldn't kiss him.

"Okay, guys," I conceded. "Let's get this party started!" Gathering my robe around me, I hung on tightly to Jason's arm. The three of us broke the gliding limit, I am sure, getting to the specific location of my entrance through the veil.

Coming to a stop, Jason turned to us. "Lil, your Mom doesn't need any more hurt in her life. Her boyfriend is bad news. Simply, she needs to be warned. And Skylar, your sister, Ali, will soon be putting herself in a very dangerous situation. No one knows or loves them more than you. You'll know what to do." Jason then slipped a blue elasticized band off of his arm and handed it to Sky. "Here; take this. Remember, back on earth you're dealing with time."

As I grow to understand life less and less,

I learn to love it more and more.

– Jules Renard

CHAPTER THIRTEEN

Reassuring me that he would be at the same place when we returned, Jason parted the veil. Sky and I effortlessly stepped through. What had been impossible for me to do when I first arrived here was so easy this time.

We left Jason in our dust as Sky and I moved forward, traveling faster through space than any plane could ever fly. We sped above the surface of deserts, oceans and mountain ranges. The terrain appeared more forested now, with deep snow drifts piled upon the ground. We passed over roads and rivers. Freeway lights lit up the night. In no time I looked down, astonished to see the tops of trees under me. Soon we started to slow, and below me I saw the south forty acres of our ranch. Sky and I came to a stop, suspended 60 feet above my house, our feet touching the bare, upper branches of our cottonwood tree. We were not cold; we were not hot; we were not tired. I could not comprehend what had just happened, but yet, it had happened. We were back on earth.

I looked longingly at our house, at the barn and corrals, Dad's tractor, buried in the snow, had sat in that same spot aside the barn for three long years, as though waiting for Dad to come back, start it up and do some spring planting. When was the last time I rode with Dad on the tractor through the orchard, past Uncle Joe's old house, to reach the south forty? That life seemed like a millennium ago.

Below me Major and Minor were whining nervously and lunging at the fence of their dog run, trying to get out. I knew that my sweet dogs saw us. They kept looking up to where we were standing. But–to be exact–we weren't really standing. The only word I could think of to describe this suspension in mid-air was levitating. I could sense Major and Minor were not scared of Sky and me, but they were upset about something.

"Mom must not have gone to bed yet, Sky. The lights are still on in her office."

Whoosh! Thinking of Mom's home office immediately put us there. There we were, standing in front of her bookcase in the warmth of our home. I was so busy trying to process how the "thinking there/being there" thing worked, that it took a minute for me to realize that our house was being invaded. Papers were scattered on the floor; Mom's desk drawers were gaping open. I heard file drawers opening and slamming shut. Turning, I realized that Sky and I stood only four feet away from Carl. That A-hole was rummaging through Mom's files. Mom's obsessive compulsive need to be totally organized was coming back to bite her. She had made it very easy for Carl to find her 401K file, her savings account file, her life insurance file.

Carl spent a few frantic minutes flipping through each file, obviously taking mental notes before he hastily shut the drawer and headed towards Mom's bedroom. We followed. Mom's bed was empty. Now Carl started pawing through Mom's personal things. I felt my face turn red; my hands rolled into fists; my temples started throbbing as my anger built. I was going to explode any second. If only I wasn't such a lightweight. If only I still had substance! What I wouldn't give to knee him in the groin and drop him to the ground!

Our resident creep, glancing up, walked over to the window and checked the latch. He then zipped up his leather jacket and went back to his plundering.

"He feels us," Sky said. "We make the air feel colder when we are around the living. It has something to do with our vibrating at a higher frequency than they."

I was in no mood to be tutored when Carl was stealing from Mom. "So, you're saying we create a breeze?"

"Heh, I know what I'm talking about here," Sky said indignantly. "Unlike someone else, I listen in class. Energy moves at different speeds in different dimensions. Jerk Face here, and everyone else on the Earth, is in the third dimension. We vibrate faster because we are in a fourth dimension, hence why we are invisible to people here. So, I'm just sayin temperatures DO change when spirits are around."

I moved up right behind Carl and blew on the back of his head. He just pulled his collar up around his neck.

Sky turned to me and winked. Standing almost IN Carl now, Sky let out an eerie, blood-curdling howl, and yelled, "BOO!"

Nothing.

"Give it up, Sky. The brain dead can't see or hear us." I stepped to the bedroom door and looked into the living room. Mom was nowhere.

"Where is Mom?" Tearing up, I thought my worst fear. "Do you think he did something to her?"

"I think he would have left the state by now if he'd hurt

her," Sky replied "Could she be at school still? Maybe at Parent Teacher Conferences?"

Looking at Mom's alarm clock on her night-stand, I shook my head. "Not at 10 p.m."

Sky tried again to reassure me. "Maybe she's gone to stay with relatives; you know, just to get away for a while after your funeral?"

That seemed logical to me. Mom could have taken a leave of absence from school and gone to Arizona to stay with Aunt Robyn.

Carl moved to another dresser tucked behind Mom's closet door. Mom and I had pushed and pulled that dresser to that spot six months after Dad's death. The dresser held all the nonessentials Dad had not taken when he left us. Shoving the top drawer closed, and jerking open the second, Carl rummaged through old ties, spent batteries, an empty money clip. He held up an old watch with a chain dangling from it. He turned it over in his hands, obviously studying it to determine if it had any value.

"Lilly, don't let him take that!"

I looked at Sky. She was standing there, calmly observing Carl. She hadn't heard the voice that had come, unbidden, into my head.

"Do something," the voice commanded me.

Looking around, I saw Mom's CD player sitting on her nightstand. I was there in an instant. I switched up the volume and hit the ON button. A country western song filled the room:

'I'm so blue, without you-u-u-u-u-
My heart has gone and broken in t-w-o-o-o-o-
And I'm drowning my heartache
In this bottle of booze
Cause I can't face the truth
Of losing you.'

Dropping the watch, Carl jumped. Letting go a string of expletives, Carl abandoned his mission and was out the door before I could yell 'Get lost, dirtbag!'

"Way to go, Lilly, I knew you could do it! I knew you could."

A long time ago I had heard that same voice tell me I could do hard things. I hadn't heard that voice for over three years! Somehow Dad had been here with us, and just as quickly as he had come, he had left. The myriad of emotions I was feeling–fear, loneliness, and hope–left me confused and shaken.

Sky had flopped to the floor and was making a wide sweep with her arm under the dresser. She produced a bauble of some kind. Turning it over in her hand, she said, "This broke off the watch. It looks like an old button."

A smile spread across my face as I remembered whose

button this once was. "Well, it might have been a button once."

Skylar held the button out for me to take. Upon arriving in Heaven, Jason had mentioned that my ability to touch or move objects with my mind–innate abilities I had possessed before coming to earth–would return to me slowly over time. Until then, my efforts would be hit and miss. As with everything else, Sky was already a pro. Putting all my effort into it, I focused on taking the button out of Sky's palm. For the life of me I couldn't grasp it.

"Focus, Lil," Sky coached. "Don't let anything else enter your mind but picking up the button!"

Inwardly I was envisioning a live person coming into Mom's bedroom and seeing a button suspended in mid-air. How weird would that be? Feeling like my eyes were going to pop out of my head, I stared at the button with all the effort I could muster. Placing my thumb and index finger on each side of it, I slowly moved it from Sky's hand and held it up in the air.

"You go, girl!" Sky laughed.

Feeling like I had just performed an amazing feat, I studied the button closely. Why had my grandpa Nephi liked it so much? There was nothing really special about it. It was metal, gold, with some antiquing, and it had been shaped to look like a flower. I looked closer. The button was a lily!

"Lil, put it back and let's go. We've got light years to travel before we eat, and light years to travel before we eat." Sky had put a new spin on one of her favorite Robert Frost poems, but in our situation, it fit.

Sky left the bedroom, walking slowly through the living room into the kitchen. Looking around Mom's bedroom, I saw her favorite coat draped over a chair. I tucked the button deep into the pocket of her coat.

"Maybe, Mom, just maybe, when you find this button, you will somehow know that I was here. I promise I will never be far from you."

Tears filled my eyes. How I missed her. I stepped out of her bedroom and, focusing intently on her bedroom door, it slowly swung shut. I was getting this down!

Sky stood in the middle of the living room, scoping out the room.

"What are you doing, Sky?"

"I'm looking for your funeral flowers. Think about it, Lilly! Even if you'd been gone a few weeks, there would still be plants, baskets with wilted flowers, programs, something left over from your funeral, don't you think?" Skylar was quiet now, studying me.

"You're still in your orientation robe."

I looked down at my gown, almost devoid of any light. "Why are we caring what I'm wearing, Sky?" I said impatiently.

"I think your Mom is at the hospital!"

"Why? So you DO think she's hurt," I said in alarm.

"No, Lilly, she's got to be at the hospital with you. Think about it. If your body was no longer able to sustain life, you really would be never-coming-back dead, and you'd be out of your orientation robe by now." Sky looked smug, like she had explained everything with perfect clarity.

Nothing was making sense. If my body was still able to sustain life, if the synapses in my brain were still firing, why had my spirit taken off? I was dead, and I had been dead for a long time; of that, I was certain, wasn't I? No matter how timeless Heaven was, my mind still told me that it had taken some time to do and see and experience all that I had there.

So very confused and frustrated now, I found myself almost shouting. "If I'm not dead, but yet I'm not alive, than what AM I, Sky? You have all the explanations. Is it not my time to die?"

Sky wilted before me. I sunk into Mom's old couch, and regrouped. "Sky, I'm sorry. It's not your fault. This is just so, so baffling to me."

Sky nodded her head, trying to empathize. "It would be hard not to know if you were coming or going. 'I'm in. 'I'm out. 'I'm in. I'm out.'" Sky hopped back and forth over an imaginary line.

"So what do we do now?" I felt too defeated to do my

own thinking.

"Well, first to the hospital to check out your room because only then will you know for sure, Lilly, if you're dead. And then to see what trouble Alli has stepped in."

I reached for the front door, opened it almost effortlessly, and stepped back to let Skylar pass. She looked at me, shook her head, and laughed.

"Lilly, remember that we don't need to open and close doors. We can just pass through, you know."

"I know. Humor me here," I said, "I just wanted to feel normal, to be in my old life again, if only for a second. Strange how we human beings don't appreciate what we have until we lose it. In spite of school and always worrying about how we looked, life WAS wonderful, wasn't it Sky?"

Closing the old, weathered door gently behind me, I turned and studied Sky. She didn't seem to miss her life on earth at all. She seemed completely comfortable passing through doors, at peace with being dead. But, then, maybe it was because she knew she was really dead.

Lifting off into the cold night sky, I whispered a silent prayer: "Please, please may Mom be there. Please, may I be there."

Realizing what I had just said, I had to smile at my condition. Being dead did have its laughable moments. Was this what it meant to have a 'split' personality? Did this give new meaning to being bi-polar? I thought back to a scribbled note my absent-minded English teacher, Mrs. Spencer, had left on her office door one afternoon after school:

"I am not here. I have gone to find myself. Should I return before I get back, keep me here."

Sky and I had laughed over that for days. And now, ironically, here I was, leaving to go find myself.

***

We stood outside Room 430, on the fourth floor of the South wing of the hospital. I had spent so much time in that room there should be a plaque with my name on the door.

"I don't dare go in, Sky. You go. Go in and come back out and tell me."

Sky passed through the closed door. A minute later, I saw her arm penetrating the thick metal door, waving me in. Telepathically I heard Sky singing in my head, "You put your left arm in, you put your left arm out. . . ."

"Stop it, Sky," I said between gritted teeth. "This is serious stuff here."

Passing into the room, I saw that a light shone from a lamp by the recliner, casting shadows in the room. Mom–looking exhausted–was safely asleep on her cot. My eyes immediately went to the hospital bed. A three-dimensional, horizontal me was lying there, on my back, my hands to my sides. I wasn't moving. The horizontal me was taking shallow breaths, looking no more than one inch away from death's door.

The translucent, vertical me started to cry.

"What do you think is happening, Sky?" I was totally confused. Here I was, in Spirit, and there I was in the bed. W E I R D.

"I don't know." Sky was staring down at me in the bed, looking a tad horrified herself.

This was so very troubling. My coloring was a ghastly grey; my hair was greasy and matted around my face; a bag was suspended on a pole above my bed, slowly dripping plasma into a vein in my right arm. The room smelled stale and sickly. My left leg was elevated on some pillows tucked under my leg. The freshly opened incision was dark red, my entire leg swollen. Under my gown, I could see that a dressing covered my lower abdomen.

Skylar didn't need to whisper, but she did anyway." You are definitely having a bad hair day." Then, her head turned to an angle to get a closer look at my face, she pressed on. "Do you think your nose looks bigger than you thought it was?"

"How big my nose is or was isn't my biggest worry right now, Sky!" I replied tersely.

"Just trying to lighten things a bit," Sky whispered softy. "So, what now?"

Looking around the room, I saw my Deluxe Scrabble game sitting on a nearby table. Picking up some tiles, I quickly re-arranged them on the board. Sky looked around me at the board.

I spelled out horizontally the words D O S O M E T H I N G. Using the S , I spelled out vertically, the word S T E A L I N G. Breaking all the Scrabble rules now, using the A in 'stealing', I spelled out horizontally, C A R L.

Skylar nodded approvingly. "Novel idea! You're the Bomb!"

We both quickly looked up. Someone was struggling to push the door open with their backside, trying to not spill two fountain drinks and a late-night snack from McDonald's. The familiar smell of my favorite fast food–bacon cheese burgers–drifted over to where Sky and I stood by my bed.

"Did you know that Spirits salivate?" I asked Sky telepathically. "Because I certainly am."

Luke dropped the sacks into the recliner and set the drinks on the table next to the Scrabble game. Looking around, he looked relieved that Mom had slept through his entrance. He walked softly to my bedside. Sky and I hovered inches from him.

"Well, good evening, Lilly," he whispered, bending down by my ear. "You look your usual gorgeous self."

Skylar and I exchanged looks. "W H A T E V E R," I

mouthed.

"Any more scares like that and Jen will ground you for life." Luke stopped, cleared his throat, and struggled for a moment to get anything out. I could tell he was trying very hard to not cry. Having his little brother, Landry, die just last year would make another death all the harder for Luke.

"I do promise you this, Lilly. You will live. I'm not going to let anything take you away. Keep hanging on, Lilly. Just hang on."

I couldn't stand it any more. Now I knew: I wasn't dead. I also knew that discovery opened up a ton of questions. What did it all mean? Why had my spirit abandoned my body? I shook my head at the difficulty of this impossible puzzle that somehow I had to piece together.

And I also knew I had to get out of there. I headed toward the door, Skylar close behind me. Then, pausing, I turned back to the game board. Finding the tile I was looking for, I focused on it with everything I had. It slowly slid to the edge of the table and then dropped to the hard tile floor. Luke turned sharply to see it bounce and slide to a stop. Bending over to pick it up, he tried to make out the letter in the darkened room. He glanced up quickly towards the door, his eyes looking right through me, and then looked back to the bed, where I slept. He shivered.

"Luke, that cool breeze . . .that's us," I whispered. "Keep

your promise, Luke, please keep your promise."

We floated up, up through all the floors above us, through the roof and out into the night, leaving the hospital far behind.

"What tile was that, Gorgeous? I mean, Lil?" Sky asked.

"Very funny, Sky. It was the letter 'L,'" I replied, "for me, for Lilly."

"Or," Sky said, looking at me sideways, "the L could stand for 'Luke,' or 'Love.' It looks to me that those two words are pretty much synonymous, don't you think?"

Darkness cannot drive out darkness;

Only light can do that.

Hate cannot drive out hate;

Only love can do that.

— Martin Luther King

CHAPTER FOURTEEN

We were traveling in a straight line–'as the crows fly' Dad would say–through the pre-dawn light above the streets of Missoula. I followed at a distance behind Sky. Would I ever get used to being a Spirit and having travel take no time at all? Taking the few nano-seconds I did have, I tried to process why I had left so much of my heart back in that hospital room.

There had been a time that whenever Mom talked to me

my eyes glazed over and my brain made a 'click' sound as it turned off. She seemed to always invade my space. Now she would wake up and not even know that I had been in her space. I would give anything to talk to her, to have her tell me that everything would turn out okay. What I needed was some of Mom's faith, because I had so very little of my own. One of Mom's favorite Bible quotes came to mind: 'Lord, I believe; help my unbelief.'

But what would 'turning out okay' even mean for me? What did I want? What did I know for sure? I was so happy in Heaven with Jason, Sky, Sophie, Sarah, Teancum, Lillie–all my family. There were peace and safety there, and a love so penetrating. Those feelings were in short supply in this world. But then, didn't Jason tell me that I had a responsibility to that broken body in the bed? It was pitiful looking. I shouldn't care, really, about it. Couldn't I view it as just an outer shell that I had shed? For even though I had lost my hardness, it was great to feel no pain, to move freely, to be no longer subject to accidents. Afterall, you can only get dead once, and I'd taken my turn.

All that being the case, I just couldn't shake the feeling that I had unfinished business here. I felt almost a compulsion to climb back into that body and fix it. But was it fixable, and did I really want my body back if I couldn't dance?

Also left behind in that hospital room was Luke. By

some off chance I ended up back here for another go at life, I had to look at this. I had to face it. The only other time I had been the object of such love was back in the Spirit World. The love I felt from Luke was the same kind of unconditional love I had felt there. My leg could reek; my hair could stink; my breath could knock over a line-backer, but Luke loved me, really loved me. That, I knew to my core. What I didn't know was what I was going to DO with it. Where had Luke learned to love like that? I thought of Luke's little brother, Landry. Did Luke's vast ability to love grow inch by inch, while changing a four-year-old's diaper, while spoon-feeding a nine-year-old who couldn't speak, while lifting a twelve-year old in and out of a wheelchair? Was I even capable of loving like that? For a long time now, love–for me–was synonymous with hurt. If I could stay in Heaven, I wouldn't have to risk again; I wouldn't have to deal with any of it.

And lastly was the Alex factor. Unfortunately Alex and Luke occupied the same town in the same world. Had Luke forgotten how hung up I'd been on Alex? And, in spite of Alex's glaring absence at the hospital, I was still crazy about him. I felt like a jerk even admitting that to myself. Luke was such a sweetheart; well, unless Alex was within 100 yards of him and then not-so-much.

Had Alex come to see me after my most recent setback? I had to wonder how Luke and Mom would have treated him. Of course Alex would be a total basket case over possibly losing me. Although some girls might envy me, juggling two guys wasn't what it was cracked up to be. If ever given the chance, I would have to tell Zena that.

And there it was. The peace Sky and everyone else seemed to be immersed in was not available to me, plain and simple. I was torn between two worlds and the vacillation–do I stay or do I go; am I alive or am I dead–was exhausting. But, after-all, what did I expect? It was my life I was describing. I couldn't even die right.

***

Sky was descending now and we were slowing. We were in a richer area of Missoula, entering through the walls of what–to me–looked like a mansion; a trashed mansion. Even though it was almost dawn, the party we had joined didn't look like it was going to end any time soon. It was the mother of all raves. In every room, on all three floors, there were kids. Lots of them I knew from my high school, more I didn't know. With no place left to sit, kids had taken to the floor, many downing pizza and beer. Others were sharing kisses and joints. Strewn everywhere were empty bottles; mashed into the carpets were pizza crusts and chips.

Sky and I had been at only one other party like this. The pressure from friends—Jason called them frenemies—

to drink, to use drugs, was intense. If word had gotten back to any high school administrator, we would have been kicked out of Dance Club without discussion. It wasn't worth the risk and we had split. Well, we certainly didn't need to worry about a Skylar/Lilly sighting now!

Sky and I backed up against a wall and stood there, pretty much astounded. Name your drug of choice, your favorite drink, and they were there for the asking. Sky and I were peering at each other through a dense cloud of smoke. Was it drugs, drinking, or boys that had brought Sky's fourteen-year-old sister here? Alli was somewhere among these two hundred stoned partiers.

Seeing how concerned Sky looked, I tried to lighten the mood. "One tequila, two tequila, three tequila, floor."

She didn't laugh. "See her anywhere, Lilly?"

"No. Let's split up. I'll go downstairs, you go upstairs," I replied. We struck out through the crowd.

"Excuse me, excuse me," I said as I tried to get through the mass of dense bodies. Seeing that a head on collision with a guy and his girlfriend was imminent, I yelled, "Watch out," and reached to push him away from me. And then it happened. My arm penetrated his chest and they walked right through me.

"Ugh! Oh, yuck."

I turned and headed back to the safety of the wall, feeling nothing as I walked through several dancing bodies.

Somehow, I felt violated and I had the sudden urge to take a long shower. To have strangers, well anyone for that matter, just walk right on through me was disgusting. It's one thing to go to a party and get lost in the crowd. It's another thing, altogether, to have someone not know you're even there!

Standing a foot from me was a tall guy, with blonde dreadlocks, unwittingly blowing smoke from his joint directly in my face. I couldn't resist the impulse to reach up and flick it right out of his fingers just to see his reaction. I tried, and I tried again. Unlike the button, I couldn't make contact. All my efforts to knock his joint to the floor did nothing.

An utter helplessness swept over me. In this world I had been reduced to nothing. I didn't exist. In the Spirit World I was solid. I could touch others; they could touch me. I could love; I could feel the love of others. I was somebody there. I made a difference there.

A profound loneliness settled over me like nothing I had ever experienced. Somehow, I had to get back to that. . . .that hardness that other kids could see and could touch. But if that wasn't to be, I didn't want to spend another minute on this earth. We were going to find Alli, do what we needed to do, and go home!

I glided down the stairs to where it was even more crowded. The draw down here was the surround sound–

currently shaking the whole house–and the theatre-size screen on the wall. A horror movie was playing. Too bad Alli was a five-foot, 80 lb.blonde. She wouldn't be easy to spot.

Looking for the nearest wall, I moved toward it. It felt like I was slogging through tar, the atmosphere in the room heavy and dank. Kids were flopped on the furniture and the floor three-deep. Or were they? I looked again. Mingled there together were live people and dead people–spirits. Why were other spirits here besides Sky and me? I estimated there had to be 80-100 of them mixed in with the invited guests. A thick, dirty energy surrounded the spirits. In stark comparison, silhouetting the living was a yellowish-gold aura outlining their bodies. It looked very much like an electric field was surrounding them, and it was vibrating ever so slightly.

Sky came up and stood next to me, watching, too, the scene before us.

"Why are you holding your nose?" she asked.

Only then did I realize I was. The dirty spirits smelled like wet dogs who'd been eating their own dung. My gag reflex kicked in.

"I've seen this before," Sky said.

"Say WHAT?" I asked incredulously. I was totally unnerved by the sensation that I had made a wrong turn and found myself in Hell.

"Remember my telling you about the dense fog I traveled through on my way to the Spirit World? Well, that fog is the very first dimension beyond the earth and the higher spheres. It vibrates very close to the earth's realm, and that fog was filled with spirits much like these."

"What is keeping them from going towards the light?"

"These spirits are earth-bound, trapped here by their addictions," Sky answered.

I stared at the countless spirits who were obviously going through heavy duty withdrawals. They were crawling over the party-goer's and–just like me–they were reaching for cigarettes or grabbing for cans of beer, held in the hands of the living. But–also like me–the dead could not grasp anything. Some spirits moved from target to target, frantically reaching for their drug of choice, and coming up–every time–empty handed. They were in agony!

"So-o-o." I tried to put it together in my head. "So, it isn't just our bodies that get addicted, is it? Our spirits must, too. That means we take our cravings with us!"

Skylar, with her signature sarcasm, replied dryly, "Hence, you over-dosing on chocolate and ice-cream ever so recently; or don't you remember YOUR addictions?"

Refusing to acknowledge the truth to that, I turned to the near-by wet bar and studied the faces there, looking for Alli. I gasped! Sitting there was a pretty, dark-haired girl; it was Danni, Quigg's old girlfriend.

"Do you see Danni there?" I asked Sky, pointing towards our friend.

"Do YOU see who is standing by her?" Sky replied. "It's Quigg."

I looked closer and saw a tall, skinny guy. One year dead, from suicide, Quigg stood shoulder to shoulder by Danni. Sky and I were next to them in a nano-second. Not having had any classes with Danni this school year, I hadn't seen her for months. She looked like she had aged ten years since Quigg's death. He didn't look much better, still tall and thin, and every bit as transparent as us. And now, Danni was Very Drunk. I couldn't figure out what was keeping her upright on the stool.

Quigg was cradling Danni's head against his shoulder. Tears were streaming down his face.

"Danni, go home! You don't belong here. I'm so sorry, Sweetie! I'm so sorry."

Danni was oblivious to Quigg, to the tragedy being played out around her, but I could hardly bare to look at his anguish. Tears sprang to my own eyes

Quigg's begging continued. "Go home, Danni; please go home. I love you. I'm sorry. I'm so very sorry."

"Is Quigg trapped here, too?" I asked Sky inside her head. My heart ached for him.

"I'm not sure," Sky replied, shaking her head sadly. "You've got to remember that I haven't been in the Spirit

World much longer than you, Lil. But I do remember hearing that those who commit suicide are never free from the consequences of their choices."

"Are any of us?" I asked flatly.

Danni swayed to her right, barely being caught by a guy next to her. He eased her to the floor, then—with twenty spirits hot on his heels—pulled her to an over-stuffed chair, lifted her up, and plopped her in it. Danni's head fell forward onto her chest; she was completely wasted. What I saw happen next was horrifying.

Starting from the top of Danni's head, the thin barrier of light aligning her body split and the light peeled away and down, leaving her head, torso, then all of her exposed to spirits waiting to enter her body; and enter they did. As fast as her aura began to split, the spirits who had followed her to the chair clawed, pushed, and scrambled to get to the opening at the top of Danni's head. One dove in, completely disappearing, to be followed in by six or seven other spirits.

Quigg was instantly at Danni's side. He stood in front of her, swinging his fists for all he was worth–to no avail–to keep the others off of her.

"Get off of her! Get away! You Bastards! Leave her alone!" Knowing how futile his attempts were to protect her from these parasites, Quigg collapsed on the floor beside the chair. Putting his head in his hands, he started to sob. I couldn't even imagine his anger of not being able to protect Danni, his frustration of not even being heard.

Sky–watching all of this unfold with me–grabbed my arm.

"Oh, this makes so much sense now!" Being too shocked to even respond to her, Sky continued. "Doesn't this make total sense, Lilly? When we are conscious, we are in control of our bodies; but once we're wasted we become vulnerable to all the spirits loitering here on earth. Being as spirits need to be IN a body to feel anything, the only relief they're going to get from their cravings is the amount of time they can be in the bodies of the unconscious!"

So, that was it! Sky's take on what we were watching made perfect sense to me. The compassion I might have felt for those trapped by their cravings was overshadowed by the revulsion of having a crowd inside of Danni as we stood there discussing the whys. Danni was totally unaware of who she was playing host to.

"Just as there are degrees of light in Heaven, there must be degrees of darkness among the spirits trapped here," Sky said, shaking her head.

"Well, duh," I thought. Sky didn't usually miss the obvious. Some of the spirits who had curled up inside Danni looked as though they had crawled up through the floor from some dank, dark abyss.

There was nothing we could do for her. Danni was

out cold.

Watching the invasion of disgusting characters into Danni's body convinced me. In our search for Alli, we had indeed stumbled into Hell.

One makes mistakes;

That is Life;

But, it is Never a Mistake

To have Loved.

– Romain Rolland

CHAPTER FIFTEEN

This 'errand of angels' wasn't all that it was cracked up to be.

"Lilly, I don't think Ali's here; I've looked everywhere," Sky said in exasperation.

"Well, we can't go back without finding her. Where else do we look?" I asked, getting frustrated myself.

"Come on, Lilly! We haven't been gone that long. Where did we hang out after parties or movies?" Sky asked.

"Well, I don't know where your favorite parking spot was, Sky, but Alex and I always park–I mean parked–above the ravine." I stood there, thinking back to how delicious Alex's kisses were, and how much I longed to have him hold me. Realizing that I might never again feel his lips on mine, or even smell his cologne, left me feeling sick and empty. How was he coping? How many months would it take him to find someone to take my place?

Sky pulled me from my reverie.

"Okay, then, let's go to the ravine." Skylar headed for the nearest exterior wall. We passed through the plaster, wallboard and brick, quickly rose above the trees, and headed toward Hellgate Canyon.

"So, I guess we just assume that when Danni comes to those disgusting creatures will crawl back out and slither away?" I asked.

Sky wasn't answering me. She was already five miles up ahead.

***

We were heading west in a moonless night, our feet skimming the tops of the quaking aspens and pine trees being tossed about in the winter wind. We arrived at my favorite parking spot, an overlook above a deep ravine. We descended and landed softly on frozen ground. It was pitch black but for the gazillion stars in the sky above us.

To think that I had been on the other side of those stars only a short while before. I shook my head at the irony: Life was strange, and death was stranger.

Now we stood behind a line of eight-ten parked cars and trucks. I surveyed the cars to see if I recognized any of them. Of course I did. There was Val's Mustang. Next to his was Jimmy's Silverado. The red Camaro belonged to Gibb. I looked farther to my right, to a spot away from the traditional line of cars. My heart started racing. Parked there, close to the edge, in Alex's and my favorite spot was. . .was Alex's Toyota. Why would he be up here alone? Unless it was to meditate, to think about things. That was probably it. He was probably mourning the loss of us.

Skylar, following my gaze, recognized the truck and looked sideways at me. Seeing my bewilderment, she looked at the ground and cleared her throat.

"What?" I almost yelled. "He's not up here with anyone, Sky! You've always thought the very worst of him! Come on! Let's go over there and you can see for yourself!"

I was at the back of Alex's truck, and up on the bed in a split second. I stuck my head through his back window, hearing Screaming Infidelities playing in his CD player. Two bodies were slumped on the seat, some chick buried in the bulk of his arms. It was readily apparent that Alex was quickly making his way to third base with her. Pushing the chick's sweater above her breasts, one hand was fumbling behind her, trying to unhook her bra, while his other hand unzipped her jeans and started working them down over her hips. Gasping, I pulled my head out and slowly moved to the back of the truck bed. I sank down on the tailgate.

"Oh, Lilly, I'm so sorry. This must make you feel terrible," Sky whispered softy, putting her arm around my shoulders and sinking down next to me. Grief washed over me in dark, heavy waves.

I didn't need to whisper, but I found myself doing so as tears rolled down my cheeks. "He has already moved on. I'm not even dead and buried yet."

Shaking my head in total shock, I looked at Sky for some kind of comfort or reassurance. But, for whatever reason, I could tell that none of this was really news to her. She didn't respond. Sky just studied her feet, dangling above the snow-covered ground.

Finally, Sky shrugged. "I don't know what to say, or rather, how to say it. But, if they weren't at the party, I knew they would be here."

Sky could have doubled up her fist and given me a direct hit to the face and I wouldn't have been more stunned.

"They? You knew he was with someone?" I felt my temples bulging at each side of my head. Through tight lips and clenched fists, I accused Sky. "We didn't really come back to look for Alli, did we?"

Sky was still refusing to look at me. "Yes and no. Lilly, I knew. . . ." She paused, choosing her words carefully. "I knew that if we found Alex, we would find Alli."

That chick was ALLI? There were no words. I was left speechless. Sky scrambled on, trying to salvage a now totally botched mission of mercy.

"I am so sorry, Lilly. Alli will need our help–soon."

Sky consulted the blue band Jason had slipped her at the veil and that was now wrapped around her fore-arm. It housed a miniature screen. Looking closely, I could see a small truck cab, containing two horny people.

"Why don't I have one of those?"

Sky grabbed my chin and pulled my attention back to her. "But, too, Jason felt that if you could see the real Alex that it would be easier for you to get back on your path, to move on."

"My path? I wasn't aware I had taken myself off my path, Sky," I replied testily. "Helena did a real good job of doing that for me." I turned away from the truck.

"Come on, Sky, let's go."

"We can't, Lil! Alli will need our help any second." Sky moved to the back window of the cab. Without any effort she penetrated the glass window. A few seconds later her upper half reappeared. The frightened look on Sky's face compelled me to spy on them once again. The music had been turned up. Alli was trying to say something, but

Alex's mouth was hard on hers. With her bra now off and tossed to the truck's floor, Alex started unzipping his own Levi's.

"Alex, get off me! Don't," Alli squeaked beneath the weight of his body. Alex's only reaction was to reach over and turn the music up even louder, drowning out her protests. Tears sprang to my eyes, but then sudden, explosive anger built inside me.

"An angel's errand, my ass," I said between gritted teeth. I was going to make certain Alex never made it to home plate with Alli! I was going to mess with his mind just like he had messed with mine. He'd never know what hit him.

This would be a real test of my ability to influence inanimate objects. I had been able to hold the button that broke off Dad's watch, and I had been able to slide the Scrabble tiles into place. But my effort to grab that guy's joint back at the party had been futile. Perhaps it was easier to move objects if my intent was to perform a service, or at least bordering on moral.

"Hmmmm, I wonder if harassing Alex would qualify as a service," I mused to myself.

I reached over the struggling couple for the knob on the CD player. I jabbed at the knob with my finger: On/Off; On/Off; On/Off. The music blared and then silenced. Alex jumped and sat up.

"What the Hell?" Alex yelled.

I reached for the lever controlling the windshield wipers. Swish/Swish; Swish/Swish.

"Holy Shit," Alex exclaimed, running his hands through his hair. Alli, struggling to get out from under him, sat up–wide-eyed and shaken.

Moving to Alli's side, I whispered in her ear, "Get out of here, Alli! Now!" Alli jumped, hitting her head on the ceiling of the truck. "Right now, Alli!" I stressed. "Go!"

Alli struggled to pull up her jeans while groping in the dark for her bra. Giving up on finding it, she pulled her shirt down, grabbed her purse, threw open the passenger door, and jumped out. Sky moved quickly to Alli's side. Leaning into her, Sky whispered something in her ear and Alli headed down the dark canyon road, reaching for her cell phone as she plunged through the drifted snow.

Alex stared through the windshield, watching the hood of his truck raise itself. Before Alex could exit the cab and scramble to the front of his truck, his tailgate slammed open and shut; open and shut. Spewing expletives, he hastily moved to the back of his truck where Sky and I now stood.

"I don't know who you are, you S.O.B., but I am going to kick your fat ass when I catch you," he yelled into the night air. Sky and I looked at each other, unruffled.

"Do I have a fat ass?" I asked with mock concern, turning to look at my backside.

Sky giggled. "Why, no, Lilly. Wasn't Alex always telling you how much he loved your butt?"

"As a matter of fact, he was," I replied. "Tsk, tsk. Guys can be so fickle."

As he reached to close his tailgate, poor Alex was oblivious to the fact that he was standing with one leg in me and one leg in Skylar. I bent down, placing my hands on the back bumper.

"You can't be serious!" Sky asked, wide-eyed.

"I'm as serious as a heart attack," I said between gritted teeth. "Are you in?"

"I'm in!"

Moving to the front of the truck, I reached into the cab and slipped the gear shift into neutral. Joining Sky at the tailgate, we pushed with all our might, focusing intently on the desired result. The rear wheels started to slowly creep forward through the frozen snow.

"Oh, Shit!"

Alex quickly moved to the driver's side door with the obvious intent to jump in and slam on the brakes. I grabbed his left foot and tripped him, face-planting him in the snow. Safely sprawled on the ground, Alex raised his head just in time to watch the front end of his beloved Toyota tip over the edge, the back end quickly following. His chick magnet disappeared into the dark hole below us, bouncing off boulders, rolling end-over-end, until it came to a crashing stop on the ravine floor. Kids were pouring out of the other cars, yelling and screaming as they ran to where Alex lay. He rose to his knees, wiping the snow and the disbelief from his eyes.

I didn't look back. Skylar would just have to use her highly developed powers to find me. One more visit to my hospital room to say a final goodbye and then I was going straight back to Heaven. Alex could go straight to Hell and proceed to burn there.

God offers to every mind its choice

Between truth and repose.

Take which you please–

You can never have both.

– Ralph Waldo Emerson

CHAPTER SIXTEEN

The force with which I made my head-on pass through the fat metal door into my hospital room sent me tumbling into the dimly lit room. Getting to my feet, I looked around and found me–of course–and Mom and Luke. Mom was sitting in the recliner; Luke was standing to her side, his elbows resting on the tray table holding our Scrabble game. Mom was crying. They were obviously lost in deep conversation.

"Are you in love with Carl?" Luke asked.

Mom shrugged her shoulders. "I don't know. I don't really trust love anymore, Luke."

"I can understand that," Luke responded. "Considering what you and Lilly have been through, I don't know why you would even want another relationship."

"Because I don't DO alone, Luke. When Lilly gets better, she'll go away to school, and I'll be really alone then."

Who was Mom kidding? I looked over at me in the bed. Sky and I had been to a rave party, witnessed an invasion of the dead into a friend's body, stopped a potential rape, and pushed a truck into a big hole, but my body hadn't moved an inch. I didn't think Mom would have to worry about me going to college anytime soon.

The good news was that, finally, I was feeling detached from my body. I didn't need it, obviously, to perform incredible feats. In fact, I had no clue why my heart was still beating in my chest. If I could have found a plug, I would have pulled it, just to end the monotony.

Even better news was that the light had come on for me. Sky had been right. I did have unfinished business. My feelings for Alex had kept me looking back, one foot in my old life, but now I felt only contempt for him. I had ties that bound me to Mom and Luke. Despite Luke's promise to keep me here, I had to undo those ties. It was way past time for me to move on. Maybe my body was just waiting for my permission to let go.

"My family was Garrison and Lilly," Mom continued. "Garrison is gone, and Lilly. . ."

Mom's voice cracked as she looked towards my bed, more tears rolling down her face. "I don't know where my faith has gone, Luke. I sit here, day in and day out, not knowing. Will she live or will she die this time? Is this how her life is supposed to end? I'm terrified of losing Lilly and I don't know if I can endure her loss alone."

"Being alone is better than being trapped in a marriage to a thief and a liar," I screamed!

My words–thin strands–floated up and away, getting lost in the long silence. I could tell Luke was struggling to know what to do with his new found knowledge, neatly laid out in tiles on the game board he was hovering over. I didn't envy him his task. How would he ever break it to Mom that her low-life boyfriend was ripping her off while she was here watching over me?

"Have you noticed anything about Carl that could be a red flag for you, Jen?" Luke, being so careful, so gentle, was now venturing into more shaky territory. "I mean, what if you find out that he isn't what he is portraying himself to be?"

Mom shook her head again. "Are any of us? Don't we all put our best foot forward initially, and then 'surprise'! Some time later we discover Jekyll turned into Hyde?"

"Amen," I agreed silently, as I thought about the 'Hyde' I had left cowering in the snow above the ravine.

"There are good people," Luke offered quietly. "There are people you can trust with your heart and with your life."

The word 'trust' jumped out at me. Our lives the last few years with Dad's addiction had been chaotic! Did chaos feel normal to me now? Was that why I chose bad boys who were exciting over kind guys I could trust? Unlike Alex, I knew my heart was safe with Luke. And maybe safe–at the end of the day–was always better than exciting. Now I was trusting Luke to safely lead Mom through the mine field she was unwittingly wandering in.

"Yes; Garrison was one of those good people," Mom responded in a whisper. "I absolutely adored him." Mom shook her head in resignation. "I always will."

I looked at Mom incredulously. She had officially gone around the bend. It was–without question–time to up her medication! Dad was good? The last seven years of his life he sure wasn't! And she still loved him? How had she gotten so emotionally unhealthy?

Luke cleared his throat. "I guess there is always a reason why people do what they do, Jen. Why do you think he let his drinking get out of hand?"

"I know exactly why," Mom replied with quiet conviction.

I moved closer to Mom. I wasn't going to miss a word.

Her justification of his behavior was bordering on insane. I shook my head in bewilderment.

Mom spoke softly, her eyes cast down at her hands resting there in her lap. She seemed to be almost void of energy or emotion. Her words came out flat.

"Do you remember Lilly's Uncle Joe?"

"Not really. Didn't he die when Lilly and I were about nine and ten? In some kind of farm accident?" Luke asked.

Mom, not answering his question, continued. "Joe was nice enough, but he was strange, too, Luke." Mom paused, struggling to state the facts. "Strange, and very sick." She now had Luke's and my full attention.

"When Lilly was little, I was just getting back into teaching. We couldn't afford a sitter, so Garrison took Lilly as much as he could during the fall harvest. It was good for them because Lilly loved her daddy, and Garrison's whole world was our little daughter. I was always telling Garrison not to ever leave Lilly with Joe–to wait til I got home from school to go run his errands or to do the work he couldn't do with a little girl at his side. He thought I was being paranoid for no reason. Garrison was very loyal and loved his brother very much. Plus, it was pretty much impossible to put his work on hold til I got home.

"Garrison never let on to what happened or when it happened, but–over a few month's time–I figured it out.

Sometimes Garrison would look at Joe with absolute disdain; sometimes with pity, but Joe knew to stay away. I guess Garrison felt too embarrassed to have ignored what I asked, too ashamed to have put his little girl in harm's way, and too full of hate towards Joe to ever vocalize the reality of it to me. Perhaps he thought that if he stuffed all the guilt, he could make it as though it never happened. We never went near Joe's house, and he was never welcome in ours. A few years later Joe was killed. . ." Mom shuddered. "It was so horrendous; ranching accidents with those big machines always are."

Luke and Mom couldn't have known that I had sunk down into Mom's cot, a few feet from where Mom sat. I put my head in my hands and tried to get my brain around what I was hearing.

"S H U T U P! J U S T S H U T U P!" I yelled.

I didn't want to hear any more, I didn't want to know any more. The image of Joe, with his buggy eyes behind those thick glasses weirded me out. How old would I have been? Four, five? Why didn't I remember?

Mom looked up at Luke, seeking understanding. "Joe was gone. I thought perhaps everything could get back to how it had been. Lilly had no physical signs but I watched to see if she remembered any of it; I waited for the emotional damage to surface. Lilly really seemed to be fine, but Garrison was a different man. It was then he lost all control."

"You mean. . ." Luke was struggling to keep his anger under control. His face was blotchy red, his eyes bulging, his hands balled into fists. "You mean you and Garrison NEVER TALKED about Lilly being abused? You never dealt with it? You never dragged Joe's sorry ass into jail?"

Mom was crying softly now. "To have acknowledged what happened to Lilly would have been to acknowledge the other."

"What other, Jen! I'm not following this!" Luke's voice was getting louder.

"Because of his drinking, Garrison wasn't thinking clearly. Maybe Joe's death was no accident, Luke. For five years, Garrison wrestled with exposing his brother and throwing him in prison; for five years, he drank to forget, but obviously, he couldn't forget." Mom's voice dropped. "I think, out of his love for Lilly, Garrison killed Joe."

I slowly raised my head to see Luke, looking aghast, trying to get some words out. He failed. Mom leaned back into the recliner and closed her eyes. She was spent.

***

It was a hot August day. The air was so still that I could hear the flies buzzing around the rotting fruit on the orchard floor. I was wearing my favorite sundress, the one with red bows on the shoulder straps and the pockets. My pockets were bulging with apricots. With my pockets and hands full of fruit, I stepped high through the long grass in the orchard, dodging cow pies, and walked under the shade of the big trees to Joe's front step, where the screen door was hanging open on one hinge. The bright sunlight outside made his small living room look dark. But it was cool inside. Joe was sitting in his old green recliner, smoking a cigar. I didn't like the smell of it; I wrinkled my nose.

"What ya got there, little girl?" he asked.

I tumbled the apricots into his lap and looked up at him for his approval. He laid his cigar in an astray on a small brown table by his chair.

"These look mighty good, don't they Lilly?" he said.

I sat crossed legged on the worn carpet and we ate our apricots in silence. When Uncle Joe was done with his, he stood and went into the kitchen. He came back with a damp cloth, wiping his fingers on it and then wiping off my hands. He took the pits from my lap and tossed them into the tall weeds of his front yard.

"Lilly, should we go find that ole cat, Whiskers?"

I nodded yes. He took me by the hand, his rough, thick hand enveloping mine tightly, and led me all the way up the brown wooden stairs, my little black shoes clattering on the bare wood.

The dream came again, unbidden. Once again, I could

not move; I could not cry out. I felt the weight; I smelled the mustiness of the room; the pungent smell of a cigar, the sweetness of apricots. The terror settled over me, always as before; but this time, when I turned my head a man was there. He knelt down beside me, where I lay, and he spoke to my mind.

"Lilly, my precious child; my precious, precious child."

He picked me up then. I wrapped my arms around his neck, squeezing him tightly, as he held me tenderly to his chest. I looked back at Uncle Joe as this man carried me away. He carried me away.

***

Finally, I understood. I had stuffed this long ago. The memory of it had tried to surface, tried and tried, but I wouldn't let it through. And this part of the dream, of the man carrying me away, I had never remembered until now. But wasn't it Dad who had come to my rescue? Dad must have loved me; at least for a time, he really did love me.

Looking up at Luke, I knew that he and Mom would work things out; they would have to. Luke would fall in love with some girl, and get married. Mom would dump Carl and choose better with the next guy. Over time, the changes in their lives would become the norm, and life would go on for them.

I was on my feet. I walked to the bed where the old

Lilly lay. Bending over, I whispered softly, "Hey, it's okay; you can let go now; I'm going home."

One Life–

A little gleam of time

Between two eternities

– Thomas Carlyle

CHAPTER SEVENTEEN

Just thinking about Heaven got me moving. With increasing speed, I shot through the darkness past specks of light that could have only been stars. In the briefest of moments a distant glow appeared in the blackness, drawing my spirit towards it like a magnet. The light took on the shape of my new world. I started to slow, and then Voila, I was back from where I had started: at the veil.

I turned and took a look back at the numerous planets, big and small, suspended in the universe spread out before me. I searched until I spotted the Earth among them. A dark shroud of clouds covered much of her surface. The only world I had ever known looked like a discarded, dirty rubber ball. I hated to think that Mom and Luke still hung out there. But I was here now, and once again a total peace would greet me on the other side of the curtain. My concern for those I had left back there was quickly replaced by the joy I felt to be so close to Heaven's entrance.

Parting the veil, I stepped once again into a beautiful summer day. Jason was good for his word, as he was there with Sky and another girl I'd never seen before. The threesome was basking in the radiant sunshine, waiting for me. It felt so great to feel the growing familiarity with this world, and to have closure with my life on earth. Slowly shaking his head, Jason was fighting a smile. Sky had obviously already informed him about Alex's misfortune.

"Hey, look at you! You found your way back all by yourself. We were just about to organize a search party." Jason was heckling me, as usual.

"Try not to look so surprised," I responded dryly, but I couldn't wipe the perma-grin from my face, either.

"Did Sky brief you on our Mission Impossible?" I asked.

"Oh, yeah, I did, Lil!" Sky exclaimed. I told them how Carl about messed himself when you turned the music on; I told them about your brilliant Scrabble idea; they heard all about us finding Alli with . . . .," Sky looked at me and abruptly stopped.

"It's okay, guys! Really! You were right; Alex was a lying dirt bag. All that matters," I concluded, "is that Alli is safe, Carl has hopefully slinked back to the infernal pit from where he came, and Mom and Luke can now let go. Because. . ." My mouth went suddenly dry as my words caught in my throat. I swallowed hard, and started again. "Because I have."

I projected to Jason's mind alone, "Thank you for sending us, Jason. No more loose ends." I didn't feel like sharing my newly-found knowledge about Dad just yet.

Because I can multi-task like no other, I could project to Jason while checking out the girl standing next to him. I quickly surveyed her from head to toe. She looked familiar to me, but then everyone up here was starting to look familiar. This spirit even outshone Jason and Sky. But it was more than her glowing robe that draped softly around her obnoxiously perfect proportions. She was elegant, disgustingly so. Her long chestnut hair fell below her shoulders, almost reaching the gold belt that wrapped itself twice around her 18" waist. If even she had ugly feet, or just one crooked big toe! But no where on her 5'7" frame did she have so much as one misplaced freckle. She was drop dead gorgeous and it was, to say the very least, intimidating. She stood there, straight and tall, her warm smile drawing me in. Could she really look like that and be humble, too?

"Hi. I'm Lilly."

Jason remembered his manners. "Lil, this is Analiese." There was an awkward silence. Stepping forward, I held out my hand. Analiese took it and smiled.

"So?" I thought to myself. I could tell Jason didn't want to do a lot of explaining right that minute.

"Analiese and I met each other soon after I got back here," Jason offered.

I looked at Sky. She just shrugged her shoulders with that 'I know more than you' grin. As usual, she was in the loop.

"Expound, Jason; don't just leave me hanging."

Jason and Analiese exchanged glances, obviously sharing memories that showed all over their faces. They had no intention of projecting their thoughts out to us, however. Giving me another warm smile, Analeise decided to disclose.

"Like Jason said, I went to earth before he did, and we didn't meet til he got back from his own life there."

'She didn't know him before she left,' I silently repeated to myself. What a novel concept. This had been alluded to before, this pre-earth thing, but with everything else going on in my head, there wasn't enough room in my brain to comprehend everything.

Interrupting Analeise, I projected to my friends, "I

don't remember anything before my birth. Shouldn't I by now?"

"It's complicated, Lilly," Jason replied impatiently.

Skylar jumped in. "Oh, you will, Lilly. Over time all of our memories start coming back to us."

"You see, Jason," I said dryly, "I can keep up with simple explanations. Sorry to interrupt, Analeise. Please go on."

Taking a deep breath, Analeise started again. "I was born in 1841 in Rhode Island, in America. My mother contracted typhoid fever while attending to the wounded at a field hospital during the Civil War. She passed away soon after. Then, my brother, Sam, and daddy went off to war. Daddy died fighting at Gettysburg, and I thought Samuel was lost, too. I didn't hear any word from him. I was sure I was an orphan and started supporting myself as a seamstress. I wanted to believe that I was strong and brave and that I could make a new life for myself. I saved every penny I made. There was a lot of migration to the West, and my aunt and uncle had migrated three years before. I wanted to join them and make a new life with family. Finally, when I was 23, I made my way to Nebraska, joining a wagon train starting its journey across the western plains." Analeise stopped talking and looked at Jason, hesitating to go on.

"You know, Analeise, we can get into all this later, don't you think?" Jason asked gently.

"Well, I'll just wrap it up by saying that the rest of my life didn't go quite as planned." Analeise looked at Sky and me and smiled that beaming smile of hers again.

Sky spoke up. "Remember that saying, guys: 'if you want to make God smile, just make plans!'"

We all laughed at that, but my mind quickly went to the major plans I had made for my own life.

"Yeah, like planning on becoming a great dancer, until some idiot wrecks it for you by. . .by. . . wrecking," I said ruefully. "So what happened, Analeise?"

"Our wagon train had stopped for the evening, and a friend and I took some children down to the river to play. I, I . . ."Analeise stopped talking. I could tell that she was remembering years and years ago in another world far away. Was Analeise still struggling with the reality of her waylaid plans?

She shrugged her shoulders, shook her head, and with a half smile continued. "Simply, I was kidnapped by some Indian braves. At twenty-three years of age. I finished out my life as an Indian squaw among the Cheyenne tribe. I died during a hard winter in the middle of a cholera epidemic, twenty years later. And here I am," she finished, smiling at Jason, Sky, and me.

Sky and I stood there, like two mutes. I was trying to go way back in the catacombs of my mind to retrieve some vague memory. This was sounding so familiar, but from where? I had heard a story like this before. Had I read it in a book when taking American history from Mr. Draper?

Sky projected to me alone: "Well, that certainly explains Analiese's radiance, doesn't it?"

I looked at Jason's gorgeous girlfriend in front of me and tried to get my mind around what I was hearing.

Analeise lived during the Civil war?

Analeise, an Indian squaw?

Analeise never drove a car! She never had a cell phone! No text messaging, no E-mailing, no Facebook! How did she ever survive? Why had it not occurred to me that all of these people around us, passing us by on the sidewalk and levitating above us in the air, could have lived, DID live, maybe 200 or even 500 years ago.

Analeise continued. "I met Jason right after he returned from taking his turn on earth. We haven't had much time to get to know each other."

Jason chimed in, getting lost in Analeise's eyes while he spoke. "Yeah, only a few years, so we've had to cram in as much time together as we can." Jason took her hand and squeezed it.

I looked at Sky. She, too, was caught up in their happiness. Even though we were just friends, Jason and I were the closest of friends. We had hung out together every spare minute back on Earth. I thought I knew everything about him; I thought I had seen all sides of him. But never had I seen this side of him. He was ga-ga over this girl.

Turning and looking at the new couple, Sky oozed, "Well, this is so cool."

Knowing I was acting like a self-centered brat, but not wanting to concede my place in Jason's life quite yet, I fired back a mental message to Sky.

"What could she and Jason possibly have in common? It must just be a mutual physical attraction. What is she going to talk to him about? How to rub sticks together to start a fire?"

I laughed. Sky didn't. And then I knew why! I was horrified. I had projected out to all three of them! Crap! I was simply going to have to quit thinking, period! Thankfully, before I had to get down on my knees and actually grovel, Analeise, obviously being the bigger person, excused herself.

"Jason, I'm going to go find Sam and enlist his help to get ready for the party. I'll see you all later, okay?"

Analeise stood up on tiptoe, kissed Jason on the cheek, and smiled at Sky and me like we were all the best of friends. Must she be so sweet? I had just royally put her down, and I had received nothing but a genuine smile in return. Rays of golden light streamed from Analeise's robe as she moved towards the alabaster city in the distance, once again reminding me of my own lackluster attire.

"Well, that went well, don't ya think?"

Bless Sky's pointed little head. Always the peace-maker. Jason continued to stare me down.

Trying to take the heat off me, Sky pressed Jason. "What party? When? Where? Why?"

"Well, whatever the 'what, when, where, and why's' are, I'm not going," I stated with all the determination I could dredge up. "I refuse to be seen in public in this orientation robe one more min. . ."

For the first time since coming back I looked down at my robe. There was no explaining what I was seeing because I knew for a fact that I had not changed clothes. My robe was no longer a drab off-white. Coming from beneath the robe, so obviously from me, was a gorgeous mother-of-pearl shimmering light that made my gown almost translucent. And even more, the light did not stop at my garment, but radiated outwards from me for several feet in all directions. It was beautiful!

"No," Jason corrected, once again taking the liberty of being inside my head unannounced. "You're beautiful."

"So, what happened?" I was astonished at how good I looked!

"Maybe you should tell us," Jason replied. "Remember our conversation, Lil, when you first arrived, about why different people radiate different amounts and colors of light?"

I nodded. "You said it was a measure of their decisions

and choices on earth, right?"

"Everything is recorded, in here." Jason pointed to his head. "Our minds are like indestructible hard drives. Our subconscious records everything–our thoughts, our motives, our actions."

Jason walked to a nearby oak tree and plopped down under its massive branches. Sky and I sprawled in the fragrant grass on each side of him. Lying on my back, I stared up through the millions of leaves. They filtered the golden rays of the warm sun above, casting dancing shadows on our faces and robes.

Jason laughed, almost ruefully. "What we plant there, ladies, we sow here. The law of the harvest is inescapable. You can't plant crab apple seeds and get Golden Delicious apples. We can't plant selfishness and harvest blessings. Our universe operates with natural laws, and not one of us can escape reaping what we sow."

There was a long silence while both Sky and I were lost in thought. I, personally, was remembering many petty, cruel words spoken; many actions and reactions that had hurt others. I had known better. Why hadn't I done better? And even worse, I was the exact same person here. All my insecurities, my sarcasm, my negative attitude, all of it had come with me! With my having just offended Jason and Analeise, it was quite apparent that death didn't change who I really was, at all! And even AFTER dying, I had crossed over to the dark side long enough to vent my anger at Alex! Nope, there was no automatic halo for me here! Precious time on earth had slipped through my fingers. It really was like sand through that stupid glass thingy. And now, there was no going back to fix things.

"So," Jason said, "what happened when you were home, Lil, that was significant enough to make you all glowy?" He gestured at the brightness surrounding me.

Being careful to keep my thoughts private THIS time, I thought of the revelation regarding Dad and his protecting me from Uncle Joe. Once I knew the entire story, once I understood why Dad drank, why he buckled under all the guilt, I could better understand his leaving us. It so wasn't right what he did, but I knew now he must have loved Mom and me.

Wow! Another epiphany! All this golden, pulsating, shimmering radiance surrounding me resulted from allowing myself to consider forgiveness.

"What is it about forgiveness, Jason?"

"Forgiveness reaps forgiveness, Lil. Unconditional love reaps unconditional love. That is the stuff Heaven is made of."

"Speaking of L O V E ," Sky asked, "Do you think Analeise is THE ONE for you?"

I rolled my eyes. Must we keep revisiting this oooey-goooey theme? I was so done with all the drama around romantic love I was ready to declare a life of eternal celibacy.

"Definitely," Jason replied, obviously eager to resume talk of him and Analeise.

I was compelled to mess with his pat answer. "Oh, really? What if you had met someone on earth instead and fell in love and married her before you died? Why wouldn't she have been THE ONE?"

Jason threw his hands up in the air and, shaking his head, gave me a look of extreme exasperation.

"Lil, I refuse to let your skepticism derail me from knowing what I know. Before I ever left for earth, I knew I wouldn't meet anyone there. I knew I would die young and single, and I knew I would meet the love of my life when I returned here. I just didn't know who or when! Of course, once on Earth, I didn't remember what I knew up here, but as you can see, it ALL played out."

"How could you have known that?" I countered.

"Must you be so difficult, Lil?" Jason suppressed a grin. "Let me try talking slower."

I swung for Jason's arm and he dodged the blow.

"Lil, listen! I knew because before we leave for earth we choose our lives, our families, our experiences."

"Let me get this straight! You're telling me I chose my family, even with all our issues? You are telling me I knew my dream to be a professional dancer would never come true, thanks to Helena, and I still chose my life?"

"Yup. That's what I'm saying." Jason smiled widely and poked me in the chest with his index finger.

Even Sky wasn't convinced. She pressed him, too.

"Jason, why would people who have really pitiful lives make that kind of choice? And what about Analeise? Why would she choose to be kidnapped and have to live the rest of her life captive in a totally foreign culture?"

"Because basically we knew we were being sent to earth to learn. So, we chose–at least in general–those experiences we could learn the most from. It's by DESIGN, Ladies."

After pausing a moment to let what he said sink in, Jason continued. "Some of the more advanced spirits here really didn't need to go to earth to prove anything. So, they went to test, and the rest of us went to be tested."

"As in who?" I prompted.

"Showing is better than telling," Jason replied. "The word on the street is that there's some action up ahead. Do you want to play some ball?"

"We must all suffer from one of two things:

The Pain of Discipline, or

The Pain of Regret."

— Jim Rohn

CHAPTER EIGHTEEN

Jason stopped us up-short at the side of a baseball diamond, surrounded by the din of enthusiastic fans whistling and cheering.

Looking around, I saw my grandpa Teancum in the crowded bleachers. I waved, and sent a 'hey, I'm here' message telepathically. Teancum glanced around, and then spotting me, waved back.

Jason nudged me, pointing to the player up to bat. What initially looked like a bright orb of light, brilliantly shining there to the side of home plate, became, upon closer inspection, one handsome guy. I could make out a fresh, gorgeous face staring intently at the pitcher, watching for the perfect pitch to come his way. Never, in any of the time that I had been back in the Spirit World, had I ever seen such a beautiful being. I highly doubted there was anyone to compare to him.

"Uh," Sky said, moving back behind Jason so that the comparison between her and the glowing star on base wasn't quite so drastic, "Do you have any idea who that is?"

"Of course I do," Jason replied. "And so do you."

Sky and I exchanged quick glances.

"It's Luke's little brother, Landry. He had mastered most things–specifically himself–before ever getting to earth. He had nothing to learn there. Landry went for others."

I shook my head; it made me sad thinking about the life Landry didn't get to have. He never got to stand on two strong legs; he never got to kiss a girl, he never got to just hang out with friends, other than Luke.

Jason gave me a long look. "And the way his older brother took care of him. . ." Jason paused. "I would say Luke is passing his own test with flying colors. Wouldn't you say so, Lil?"

Staring ahead at Landry, I could only whisper, "Yes, I would say so."

A loud crack as the bat met the ball got the crowd on its feet. The spectators roared as Landry's ball sailed through the air and splashed into a lake, 150 yards away. Then, our own personal 'sun', Landry, sped around first, second, and third base, barely sliding into home plate before his teammates swarmed him.

I thought back to my life on earth. I had spent so much time at Luke's house. Never had I seen Landry walk, or even talk, but now I watched his perfect form run bases. I grabbed Jason and Sky and gave them a hard group hug.

"It can't get any better than this!"

"Ah, but it can, Lil." Jason looked at Sky and winked.

***

After the game, Jason left to go help Analeise get ready for that Big Bash they had in the works. I was tugging at Grandpa's Teancum's arm to get him moving faster.

"Grandpa, thanks for inviting us to have some of Grandma's famous dessert; I love her bread pudding."

Every Christmas, Mom had referenced a yellowed recipe card with Grandma's neat handwriting on it. It was one of my favorite Christmas customs, and now I would get to have some from her very own kitchen.

I had yet to be in anyone's home. Since getting to Heaven, my spirit had experienced a whirlwind of activity: Levitating here; gliding there! I had heard that my friends and relatives had gone 'home' after our first meeting, but I had no concept of what that meant here. Why did we need homes when we were all wispy, and didn't need shelter, or even sleep?

Gliding along, arm-in-arm with Grandpa and Sky, I remembered the story Mom had shared with me. "Grandpa, Mom told me about your father using the button off of Lillie's best dress and decorating his watch with it."

Exchanging looks, we spoke simultaneously: "It might have been a button once." I dropped Grandpa's arm as we broke out laughing. Sky gave us a look like we'd both lost it.

"It's a long story, Sky," Grandpa said, patting her arm. "Yep, we Hunt men are big teasers, Lilly. We had a sweet courtship, your grandmother and I. That was all years and years ago, back on a ranch in Missoula, Montana on the planet Earth. We are so far removed now, in time and space, but yet, in my mind it happened just yesterday."

We came to an area that–from our vantage point high in the air–was like a well-designed residential community back on earth. Looking over the rooftops, the rows of homes–laid out in large grids–went on forever, millions of them. From the catacombs of my mind, I dredged up a memory from my Bible class.

"In my Father's kingdom, there are many mansions. I go to prepare a place for you."

Is this what was meant? Unlike any subdivisions I was used to, where the houses all had a similar, dated style to them, not one of these homes were alike. Some were small; others gigantic; one home looked like it was moved from a 1800's Southern Plantation and plopped down here. Another home resembled a large tepee; a third home could have been nestled in the Swiss Alps. There was no rhyme or reason to any of what I was seeing. Rising up to meet us were the sounds of water splashing in ornate fountains, tumbling down beautifully designed rock waterfalls, meandering down slow, sloping streams. Sage, pine, roses, thyme–a myriad of fragrances planted around each home–wafted up to where we were. I inhaled deeply. It was the variety of scents here in Heaven, floating in the crisp air, which always reminded me of just how very alive I was.

Grandpa pointed to a particular home below, and as soon as he did so, I found myself in front of what I assumed to be our destination. From the air, each home had appeared very close to one another, but now it seemed that this home was all by itself, sitting on a large, tree-covered acreage, with no neighbors for miles.

From the front yard, which was covered in mountain flowers, and scrub oak, I looked up to a beautiful mountain cabin with a large wrap-around porch. The logs on the exterior of the cabin were interrupted only by large windows on each side of a huge cobble stone chimney, hinting of a warm fireplace within. We glided up to the porch and planted our feet on the pine boards.

Grandma Lillie stepped out onto the porch to greet us. "Well, hello, Lilly; hello, Sky!"

I studied Grandma more closely. Something was different. Where was her gown? Grandma was decked out in an old-fashioned apron–complete with rick-rack–covering a simple cotton dress.

Standing on tip-toe to reach my cheek, Grandma gave me a kiss. Then, putting her arms around my waist, she escorted us through the screen door.

I found myself transported back to the 1930's on earth. It all smacked of my great grandmother's early life. A wood burning stove was to the left of the door. To the right was a dry sink and wash stand. A wall of cupboards with glass doors occupied the wall above. To the right of the cupboards were two sets of windows that looked out over a large, high mountain pasture and–closer in by the house–grandma's prized flower garden. A kitchen table sat under the windows.

The floor was cushy under my feet. Looking down, I saw that the floors were covered with large rag rugs, probably Grandma's creation. I peered around the corner into the adjoining living room. There was a large upholstered couch and a rocking chair. Above the couch, mounted on the wall, an old pendulum clock ticked loudly. Next to the rocker was an ancient treadle sewing machine, piled high with quilt blocks. It was a bright room; the sun's rays pouring in and spilling over all of my grandparents' treasures. Grandma answered my question before I could ask it.

"My happiest moments on earth were when I was a young mother, raising my children, working along side Teancum, Oh, it was hard work, all of it, but those memories are my best memories." Grandma looked around fondly at what she had designed." I wouldn't want my house to be any other way."

Sky and I looked at each other. Oh, the possibilities! I was already designing my space in my head. Ocean front, swaying palm trees, warm sand. Modern, lots of glass to let in the sky and the sea!

Sky and I sank into Grandma's overstuffed couch while Grandpa helped her dish up the bread pudding. Cinnamon, vanilla, caramel, all those scents co-mingled, filling the cabin.

"I'm salivating like Pavlov's dog. How about you?" Sky asked.

Before I could respond, here came our hostess with a tray filled with bowls of steaming pudding.

"I heard you and Sky went back to earth on an errand. How did that go, girls?"

Sky and I exchanged looks.

Handing me my bowl, Grandma asked, "You hit a

rough patch on your trip home, Lilly?"

"Well, Grandma, that's an understatement." I smiled weakly.

Grandma squeezed in next to me on the couch and studied me intently.

I slowly inhaled. "Sometimes I don't think life has been fair to me."

"As in?" Grandma sat there patiently waiting.

"Ah, you know, Grandma." I was sure she saw from her vantage point up here when my home life started sucking down there. And besides, I was in no mood to talk about any of that now.

"Whose fault is that?" Grandma looked at me as though she didn't have a clue.

Standing up, I turned and I stared at her incredulously.

"Who's fault is it?" I repeated. "Well, how about Helena's? Or even Alex's? Or, we could look at Uncle Joe?" I was now pacing the floor. "And then there's God, Grandma! I am supposed to trust God, but look at what He's let happen, and not just to me! To Jason, to Landry, to lots of people. How can I trust someone who takes people away? People that I love?"

Grandma just sat there, blinking. Hmmmmm, perhaps she was seeing the Other Side of her great granddaughter. No doubt I was now losing points with her.

Sky sank deeper into the couch, trying to blend in with

the big floral print, and busied herself inhaling the bread pudding.

Grandma stared me down. "You are right, Lilly. You could just go on being mad at everyone. You have a right, you know; after-all, you are the only one who has ever been hurt!"

Before I could point out that sarcasm may not be below me, but it was most certainly below her, Grandma barged on.

"What Joe did was so wrong. He should pay, shouldn't he. But then, so should the neighbor kid who sexually abused Joe when Joe was just a small child. After-all, Joe didn't get sick all on his own. So the neighbor's boy should pay, too.

"Shouldn't you blame our son, Benjamin? Benjamin was Joe and Garrison's father. Boy, he really screwed up his sons. What did Benjamin do to cause your father to become an alcoholic?"

Before I could defend my beloved grandpa, Benjamin, my great grandmother pushed on.

"So, perhaps your grandparents, AND your great-grandparents–Teancum and I–are ALL to blame, Lilly."

I stared at my grandmother. For a five-foot, one-hundred pounder, she sure could hold her own!

Sinking back into the couch, my grandmother quoted a scripture. "The sins of the fathers will be upon the heads of the children unto the third and fourth generation."

I remembered reading that scripture, as well. All the stuff that had made no sense back in Sunday school was now becoming a little clearer.

I sat down next to Grandma and put my hand in hers. Benjamin, Grandpa Teancum, Grandma Lillie. I loved them. So very much, I loved them. How could anybody be mad at them? My voice came out in a whisper. "It's not your fault, Grandma; and it's not Grandpa's. It's, it's. . ." I shrugged and started playing with the folds of my gown.

"So, Lilly, how far back should we go with the blame?"

I shook my head, understanding now. "We don't."

Grandma answered softly, "You're right, sweetheart, we don't. We don't waste a minute placing blame. We don't desecrate another precious second counting our hurts and offenses. We were all just mortals, stumbling around trying to find our way. Sometimes we didn't conduct our lives like the children of God that we are, but we were in a sphere where it was easy to forget who we really are, and from where we came."

Grandma stood up, and brushed the wrinkles from her apron. "But you are here, now, Lilly; and now, let it go."

***

I felt myself lapsing into a food coma from my triple helping of bread pudding. I was so tired. Not like on earth when my body was totally done in after dance practice. This wasn't bone-tired; this was soul-weary. Sky headed to the kitchen for her fourth helping, and I took the liberty to stretch my legs out, laying my head on the arm of Grandma's couch.

Taking a crocheted afghan, Grandma Lillie pulled it gently up under my chin. Patting my back, she stooped to kiss my cheek.

I projected–loudly–into the kitchen. "Just a quick nap, Sky, and then we'll go, okay?"

Somewhere behind me, a clock was ticking out a soothing cadence that filled the room. Tick-tock. Tick-tock. I couldn't wait for Sky's response. I closed my eyes, and sleep came.

***

"I don't know what is freaking me out more–the ugly orange jumpsuit I'm wearing, or the gun-toting heavy weight at my elbow. As if I dared bolt and run! Duh! Led to the front of the bench, the judge stares down her nose at me. Turning to the jury, she asks for the verdict:

"Involuntary manslaughter, your Honor."

Bang. Bang. Bang. The gavel slams down three times.

My heart is racing. My mouth is dry. I see my life, my dancing career, slip away. How many years locked up? How many?

Turning back to me the judge's eyes hold mine, her voice re-

verberating as though talking into a tunnel.

"The problem with lying to yourself, Lilly, is that you don't know you're lying because you're lying."

***

I awoke with a jerk. "What the . . . !" Looking quickly around I realized I was in the safety of my grandparents' living room, not in a courtroom at all. The soft, quiet drone coming from the kitchen told me Lillie and Teancum were close by. Slowly sitting up, I wiped away the sleep from my eyes. The nagging apprehension I couldn't seem to shed.

All things were made by Him;

And without Him was not any thing made

that was made.

– John 1:3

CHAPTER NINETEEN

For the first time since reaching Heaven, I was alone–without Jason, my Guide, or even Sky. I was hovering thirty feet above a glass-smooth ocean, only 100 yards offshore.

I had awakened from that hideous dream to have Grandma tell me that Sky had left 'for work.'

"For work? Sky has a J O B?"

"Apparently so," Grandpa answered. "She's on Selsia."

"Selsia! What's that?"

Grandpa had a bright twinkle in his eyes. "You'll see, Lilly! What do you kids say? It will 'blow you away'?"

Giving me a reminder on how to 'think myself' to Selsia, Grandpa kissed me on my cheek, and I lifted off the porch. "S E L S I A!" I commanded. Instantly, I was there.

'There' was a small parcel of barren land, flat, no trees or foliage of any kind for as far as I could see. The only thing that told me I was not off some miniscule mid-Pacific island back on earth was the color of the water. Looking at a violet ocean, pale yellow soil, and a spinach-colored sky, I realized a master artist was at work here. The colors harmonized beautifully, lending a sense of balance and tranquility to the entire landscape. The scent carried on the ocean breeze around me smelled like Mom's favorite flower, lilacs. I closed my eyes and took a deep breath.

"It kind of looks like an unfinished painting doesn't it, Lil." That was Sky's voice.

I spun around to see my best friend with a pen and sketch pad in hand.

"Well, it isn't done. This world is not ready for humans yet. It is only half created. But isn't it looking just cool!"

"This is a NEW world?"

"Yeah, one of oh, a gazillion other worlds." Taking on a classroom lecture tone, Sky gave me a brief synopsis:

"Galaxy type, spiral;

"System type, solar, multi-satellite, planetary;

"Plant Type, rocky core, ocean coverage;

"Life forms? Will be various–animals and plants;

"Intelligence? Yes, some day, human beings. Pretty much just like Earth."

Sky waved her sketch pad at me. "You didn't think Earth was the only planet with people on it did you?"

"You know, Sky, I haven't really had time to think about that possibility while sitting through tons of lectures, and flitting to earth and back! My mind is so packed full of sensations and revelations that I can't take much more in."

Trying to not rain on her parade, I tried again. "Yes, it IS awesome, Sky!"

"I was asked to come help some other spirits that are here working. This is my first assignment, but wouldn't it be so exciting to have some of my ideas actually used, Lil?" Sky pointed to her drawing, so carefully sketched out on the page. I tilted my head. Was it an amoeba? A plant? I wasn't about to ask. I moved on to a safer subject.

"How long will it take to finish?"

Sky looked around her, shaking her head slowly. "Not so sure. Maybe thousands of earth's years. Mountains have to be pushed up; lakes and streams need to be placed; plants need to be designed and planted; animals need to be sketched out and then created. There's tons of work left before people are placed here."

I shook my head at the long to-do list some creative spirits had before them.

"Wait a minute." Thinking back to my Bible classes, I finally had some knowledge to share. "I thought the earth was created in seven days, so why is this world taking so long?"

"Because a day here is the equivalent of a thousand years on Earth, Lil. You have to quit thinking in Earth's terms."

Here came another brain cramp. Squinting my eyes shut, my hands went to my temples, trying with everything I had to hang onto this complicated thought and make some sense out of it. My brain's processing speed ground to a stop. Why was it that my brain immediately went into freeze mode when presented with this kind of information?

"And speaking of incredible things, come here; I want to show you someone." Sky grabbed my hand and we moved quickly to the land mass, where three guys–two shorter and one taller–were intently studying large sheets of designs rolled out on the ground.

"Isn't he drop-dead gorgeous?" Sky pointed to the tallest of the three. They were so lost in their conversation they didn't even notice us.

Facing into one of three suns over my head, I squinted, trying to make out his face. "He's got a cute backside, Sky.

What's his name?"

"No clue, but I will most certainly be finding out. And some how, some way, I am staking my claim."

I looked at Sky. Her eyes were glassed over. I had never seen Sky be so love-struck with some guy she'd barely laid eyes on! I looked back at her guy. From where we stood, he didn't seem to be all that to me, but whatever floated her boat.

"Well, you go, girl."

Sky moved in closer to me. "Someone else stopped by here, too." Sky's voice had dropped to a whisper. It sounded ominous.

"Wh. . .?" But before I got it out, I knew.

"Helena?"

"Yup. I don't know how she knew where to find me, but she did."

My voice was actually shaking. "What did she say? What does she want?"

Sky shook her head. "She said that she wouldn't be staying. She said she was 'going back.' She said that there was a body waiting for her back on earth."

"SAY WHAT! How does THAT work?"

"I don't think that's possible," Sky replied. "I'm sure she had to sit through the Orientation when she got here, just like we did. Do you remember their saying anything about getting to go around twice?"

"Me? You are the authority on Heaven protocol, Sky. I have no clue; but what does it matter anyway? We're here."

We both stared over the sea of glass reaching to the horizon, each of us lost in our own thoughts, trying to figure out what Helena meant.

Finally, shaking my head, I sighed; there was no understanding it.

"But you know Helena," I said. "What she wants, she gets. If anyone can get around all the rules of Heaven, it's Helena."

I looked at Sky for some kind of approval of my assessment. I didn't get any. Sky was busily penciling in trees and bushes–or were they more amoeba–in her sketch pad. Biting my lip, I tried to introduce another subject as inconspicuously as possible.

"Sky, remember that unit Mr. Cordon did on our subconscious and dream states?"

"Oooh, yeah! I loved that part of his class, didn't you?"

"Me, too, but what all do you remember?"

"Just remember bits and pieces. He said that our frontal lobe, where our rational thoughts form, is turned off when we sleep. But he told us that a lot of electrical connections are still firing, and some neurons are more active during our dream state than when we are awake, even. Why?"

"Did he say why we dream?"

"Well. . ." Sky paused, thinking hard. "Didn't he say that there are some things in the living's conscious world, things that happen in the lives of the living, that can only get processed in their dreams?"

I felt a heaviness settle around my heart.

"Well, I don't think all dreams make sense, do you, Sky?" Inwardly I knew that in a courtroom back on earth this would be considered as 'leading the witness.' But desperate people do desperate things. "Very few dreams matter in the real world, right Sky?"

"Right; some dreams are just stupid," Sky agreed. "But, still, I remember Mr. Cordon saying that when we are asleep, our dream state creates a perfect environment to know."

"To know what?" I pressed.

"To know what we don't want to know when we're awake."

Or, I thought, to know what we don't want to know when we're dead.

Do not suppose, my dearest ones, that when I have left you,

I shall be nowhere and no one.

Even when I was with you, you did not see my soul,

But knew that it was this body of mine from what I did.

Believe then, that it is still the same,

Even though you see it not.

– Cicero

CHAPTER TWENTY

The three of us soared above the ground, moving closer to the music. Sky and I had no sooner got back to Heaven than Jason tracked us down.

"Time to dress for the ball, girls."

Looking at Sky, then Jason, and then back to me, I wondered if I would ever glow more than now.

"Only a little while ago I was finally feeling proud of how I looked in my new and improved robe."

Jason tried to encourage me. "When you have your

Life Review, Lil, you'll see how much you've grown and learned."

"My WHAT?"

Jason and Sky–startled by the alarm in my voice–stopped dead in their tracks.

"Your Life Review," Jason said again in a tone that should have elicited some reassurance in me. It didn't.

"Oh, this sounds bad; very, very bad." I dropped Jason's hand and hung back from them.

"Not at all! You'll see," Sky responded trying to reassure me. "It's like going back in time in a Time Machine. It's actually very. . . . ."

"How's that even possible?" I argued.

Jason tapped his head again. "Remember our hard drives? That's how it's possible."

"Everything's stored on my hard drive? Everything?" I was already racing down the corridors of my memories, trying to see what files I could somehow delete before they were out there for everyone to read.

"Absolutely everything," Jason replied, "everything except. . . . ."

"Except what," I asked, sensing a glimpse of hope.

"Except those things we repent of. Those things are all gone, wiped out as though they never happened." Jason stopped talking. All of a sudden he was choked up.

"Imagine going to war, guys. Imagine being in a battle and doing about anything to keep yourself and your buddies alive. Imagine that and then you'll know just how wonderful the option of repentance is."

Jason drew from some verse in the Bible: *"For I will forgive their iniquity, and I will remember their sin no more."*

Sky looked like she was going to respond, but her words were cut off in the racket of party-goers just ahead of us. We rounded an ivy-covered stone wall and saw before us a huge crowd of people, eating, talking, and dancing.

"How weird," I yelled to Sky above the music. "Everyone here looks so familiar, but why would they be?"

Looking around, I saw Lillie and Teancum dancing on the edge of the crowd. Thomas and Hannah were sitting under a tree, balancing a plate of food on their laps. Sarah was standing on the side-lines, laughing and talking with Analeise, like they went way back or something.

"Why does everyone look familiar?" Jason parroted back to me. "Probably because it's your family reunion, and you have a BIG family."

"A family reunion? I'm related to these hundreds of people, Jason?"

I was terrible with names but, looking more closely, I recognized most of the party-goers. No, not recognized; 'remembered' was more accurate! More memories of an earlier time were stirring in my head. Finally, I was losing the veil of forgetfulness that had accompanied me to earth and had clung to me still upon my return.

Looking over at the band, I realized nothing I had heard back on earth came even remotely close to what I was listening to now. The musicians had set up their instruments and speakers under a grove of magenta-colored trees.

Yelling above the music, I asked Sky and Jason. "How can five people be responsible for such incredible surround sound!"

I could hear and feel the rhythm, the different tones, the vibrations coming from all directions. It made all the music back on earth sound like a two-year old banging on a metal pot. This music, in contrast, I could not find the words to describe; and somehow, it left me feeling elated.

"I can't wait to dance, guys!"

I hadn't realized just how much I had missed my passion, but with Jason and Analeise being an item, who was I going to dance with?

Analeise broke away from Sarah and ran to Jason's side. Lifting her off her feet, Jason twirled her around. In a blink, Analeise dragged him off to dance.

Looking back at Thomas and Hannah sitting under a low-hanging bow of the tree, I noticed the cutest little girl sharing their shade. With honey blond hair framing her cherub face, she dipped and swayed to the music. Her feet were bare, her little blue robe billowing out around her as she twirled to the music. Perfect in her features, she was simply adorable.

I poked Sky. "Look at that little girl, Sky! I wonder who she belongs to."

"Oh, that's Ava. She's one of the little spirits waiting to go down."

"Ava," I said aloud. "Ava. What a cutie. "She's just like you and I, Sky. Dancing must be in her spiritual DNA, too."

A new song had begun. I looked back to the dance floor and spotted Jason and Analeise. Jason effortlessly picked Analeise up and flipped her over his arm. It was obvious Jason was crazy about her and so happy. How could I deny him that? As I watched I knew that Jason's and my relationship had changed forever. When I first got back and Jason had told me he was my assigned guide and mentor, I thought everything would be like old times. We would just hang out together in Heaven forever. Wrong. I shook my head and smiled at my naïveté. To my mind came another one of Mr. Cordon's Cordonisms: 'The only constant in our lives is change'. Analeise was becoming his whole world, right before my eyes. I studied Jason's face as they danced and swayed in each other's arms. From this point forward, if I loved Jason–and I so very much did–I would love Analeise just as much. Love is a decision, and my decision was to do all I could to add to their happiness. But for me? I, for one, would never give my heart to anyone again.

"Come on, Lil. Let's go dance. We don't have to wait for some dumb guy to ask us," Sky said impatiently, pulling my arm toward the dance floor.

"I would be honored if you would dance with me."

The invitation to dance came from somewhere immediately behind Sky and me. We both turned slowly, looking over our shoulders. Sky spotted him first.

"It's that guy from Selsia!" Sky shrieked inside my head.

Looking up, I saw her guy gazing down at us, smiling a delicious, crooked smile. His green eyes locked with mine, and try as I might, I could not look away. He was smoking hot! Somehow, from somewhere, I knew this guy! Was he a distant uncle or something?

Falling all over herself, Sky was beaming from ear to ear. "Hi," she said, offering her hand. "I'm Sky. And this," turning reluctantly to me, "is Lilly."

I nodded my head. Forget trying to get a sound out. I was acting like a deaf mute. Jason and Analeise walked up to my side.

"Sky, Lil, please meet my brother, Samuel Coltron," Analeise said proudly.

This Adonis was Analeise's brother? This was the Civil War Samuel? Trying to get my brain back in gear, I offered my hand. "Hi, Samuel, it's great to meet you. I just love your sister, Analeise."

Sky looked at me. "Yeah, right, Lil. Get real!"

Okay. Admittedly I wasn't too proud of my disingenuous comment, but what I wouldn't give to dance with this guy. Whatever I said must have worked because Samuel smiled directly into my eyes, bowed, and once again offered an irresistible invitation.

"I would be honored to have the next dance, Lilly."

Dang it! Loyalty and love overruled. I couldn't do this to my best friend. I shook my head. "Oh, Samuel, I'm a lousy dancer. You should see Sky dance! She's incredible." I turned to Sky and pushed her forward.

Not even acknowledging my pretext, Samuel reached around Sky, took my hand firmly in his and guided me into the crowd of dancers.

I glanced back at Sky and mouthed, "Sorry. I tried, really I did."

Sky telepathically sent a pseudo threat right back: "Be afraid; be very afraid. I have W-A-Y-S of getting even."

Samuel turned to face me. In a split second I had taken him all in. His hair was a golden chestnut brown, curling at the nape of his neck. His high cheek bones accentuated the angular features of his gorgeous face and his full, luscious lips. He was the ideal height for me; our bodies just fit!

The band started playing an old-fashioned waltz. Samuel held me tighter as we moved with the other couples on the floor. 1-2-3; 1-2-3. Was there anything more glorious than dancing with a hunk who could dance maybe even better than I? Feelings stirred deep within me that I thought I had left far behind on earth.

Sam was holding me so closely I could smell his skin. His cheek brushed mine. How I wished I dare kiss his cheek, his neck, his mouth. Suddenly, I had the overwhelming sense of knowing that I had been here before. Not here on this specific dance floor, but here, in Samuel's arms, many, many times.

The beat of the music changed and, as I watched Samuel dance, having his moves down perfectly, another memory sprang up: Samuel and I were walking down a secluded path, our arms around each other's waist. I was laughing at something he was telling me.

Wide-eyed, I looked at him now!

Samuel moved closer. "It's coming back to you, isn't it, Lil?" Samuel whispered softly, his lips pressed against my ear.

I stopped dancing, dropped his hand, and stepped back in shock. I remembered it all now. Another time at another dance, before either of us had taken our turn on earth. We had been doing the swing that time; Sam had twirled me too hard and I went flying.

I then saw us sitting in a park. I was pulling up tufts of grass and throwing them at Sam. We were talking about what our lives on earth would hold for us. I was feeling really bummed, because Samuel would go to earth, and be back, long before I could even take my turn.

Another, more sobering, memory played out before me now. I was there, in spirit, on a battle field. Samuel had been made a major in the Second Rhode Island Volunteers. He was so ready to see action because he felt so strongly that the North's cause was right. The war had barely started and he and his men were not trained; they were hopelessly outnumbered. In that very first battle of Bull Run, the Union soldiers launched several assaults but the Confederates had stood their ground. Many of Samuel's men started panicking and wouldn't hold the line. They ran, leaving only Sam and a few of his men left to fight. I knew all these details because I had watched it all, standing on the edge of the battle field, in a grove of trees, patiently waiting. Samuel was killed that day, July 21, 1861. And I was there; there to comfort him, to be his Guide, and to bring Sam home.

Now, on the dance floor, I grabbed Samuel's hand, pulling him out of the crowd into a dense grove of Austrian pines. The only other life around us was a Whippoorwill high in the trees, lending its serenade to the ambiance of this perfect summer evening. Standing on tip-toe, I wrapped my arms tightly around Sam's neck and planted my longest and best kiss on him.

Sam stepped back, holding me at arm's length, and

laughing softly, exclaimed, "You're here! Oh, Lilly-Bug, you're really here!"

"I am," I said, half crying, half laughing. "Can we ever make up for lost time, Sam?"

"We'll use every minute we have, sweetheart." Sam pulled me to him for another kiss.

And then it dawned on me. "Where in Heaven's name have you BEEN? Why weren't you there, at the veil, to greet me, Sam? I've been back for the longest time!" Hurt and indignant, I punched him in the arm to punctuate my frustration.

"Oh, babe, you have no idea how hard it's been to stay away from you since you got here. But Jason and I had talked, and he was right! We knew you had to go back to earth and deal with some stuff, Lil. It was important, and I didn't want our reunion to get in the way of the loose ends you had to wrap up there. Timing is everything, Lil!"

"Strange, that's exactly what Jason said. I don't know what is so special about 'timing.'"

"Be honest, Lil! You went back, in part, to see Alex. With your stubbornness, could anyone have made you go if you had remembered me, or us? And then, who could have helped your mother or Alli?"

A big smile spread over Sam's face. "Only you would shove a truck over a cliff!"

My mind went back to that tiny blip on my memory's

radar screen. Alex? Alex? What on earth did I ever SEE in that jerk? It seemed eons ago that I was on earth, that I was THAT girl; that girl who saw no farther than a self-centered player with a cool truck. All the energy and angst I put into that relationship with Alex, when all along, the love of my life, a Real Man, my best friend, waited for me here. But Sam was right. I might not have gone back to help had I remembered Samuel Coltron in the least degree.

"Thank heaven for memory loss. I couldn't have stood it, Sam, being away from you these past eighteen years."

Sam pulled me down to the grass beside him. We lay there, our arms and legs entwined, and he kissed me as only Sam could.

"Read my lips, Sam. I am never, not ever leaving you again. YOU, mister, are stuck with me, FOREVER."

Sam gave me a long, serious look, not responding. Finally, he lightened up and with a mock sigh, said, "Well, you're a lot of work, but I'll give it a go."

Before I could respond, Sam covered my mouth with his and I melted against his body.

For a damned soul is nearly nothing. It is shrunk, shut up on itself.

They will not, in the end, they cannot

Open their hands for gifts, or their mouths for food;

Or their eyes to see.

– The Great Divorce; C.S. Lewis

CHAPTER TWENTY-ONE

Much later Sam led me back to the dance. For the duration of the party, Sam and I would dance fast dances, we would dance slow dances, and with every turn I would remember more incredible times spent in his company. Sam and I had danced and laughed and loved for a long, long time; long before the earth was even formed. Funny how our perspectives so quickly change. When I had first arrived back to the Spirit World, I really thought I'd landed square in Heaven. Perhaps, for some, this place was Heaven. But for me, now, being with Samuel was the only heaven I would ever need.

Finally, as family and friends started leaving, Sam and I pointed ourselves in the direction of where Analeise, Jason, and Sky were standing. They appeared to be engaged in a fascinating conversation.

"I learned to love him; I really did."

Analeise was trying to reassure Sky, who was looking a bit dubious. It was obvious that Analeise was sharing details of her kidnapping with Sky.

"Blue Horse became Chief of our Cheyenne tribe soon after I was brought into camp. I was treated as a slave for the longest time. I was forced to sleep out, with no shelter. But then Blue Horse made those who were mistreating me stop. He brought me into one of his wives' teepee and he commanded her to treat me well. Then he named me White Fawn. I realized at that point that he had plans to make me his wife." Analeise stopped talking for a moment, perhaps wondering how much she wanted even Jason to know.

"We broke camp and moved often, following the buffalo over miles and miles of plains. Sometimes I would see covered wagons snaking through the brush, as close as a half mile away. I knew they were my people–white people. Like me, they wanted to start a new life out West. Blue Horse would always make me ride behind him when we were close to the wagon trains. I think he was afraid

I would try to run. When they would go to war with the whites, I was always kept out-of-sight, hidden behind buffalo robes in his teepee. I knew it was futile to try to escape; I would have been killed. Our band was one of the smaller ones in that region, but it was known for being quite savage. I'm sure Sarah saw them as savages when they rode through the camp and grabbed me by my hair," Analeise said sheepishly.

"That was YOU!"

My mind was racing: Back to my other life; back to the hospital room; back to Mom reading from one of the old family journals. "You were Anna," I shrieked? "You were Sarah's best friend? The one who helped her when she got sick in the middle of nowhere?"

"I was," Analeise answered sweetly. "I thought Sarah had told you. I thought you knew."

"I didn't know. No one told me." It was Analeise! SHE was the Anna in my dream. Quietly I mouthed under my breath, 'Analeise is to Sarah as Sky is to me.' It was bizarre enough that Analeise was Sam's earthly sister, but more-so, Jason's girlfriend had actually walked the plains with my grandmother, had nursed my grandmother back to health. If Sarah had died, I wouldn't have been born, or at least not to the family I was born into. I looked at Analeise through different eyes. I had felt such love for her in my dream; and I was feeling that love again now.

Analeise was wrapping up her story. "I lost Blue Horse to cholera. He was one of 2,000 souls, two-thirds of our tribe, to die of the epidemic. Very weak myself, I watched a few braves, his friends, lift him into a tree, his burial place. With his death, there was nothing left for me to cling to. I died a few months later."

We all stood very quiet and solemn, feeling intensely Analeise's loss.

"The Cheyenne were a brave and proud people. They became violent in their desperation to survive. If my life on earth taught me nothing else, it taught me that there is a reason why people do what they do. I had been transported into a foreign world, not understanding the strange language spoken by browned-skinned people. I saw them as my mortal enemy at first, as monsters almost. But I adapted. Over time, I learned to love them. They learned to love me."

I looked at Jason. He had tears in his eyes as he wrapped his arms around Analeise. I wasn't about to ask where Blue Horse was now. Perhaps he was with one of his other wives, walking along their own secluded path here in Heaven, hand-in-hand. I was quickly learning that–once here–people quit sweating the small stuff like culture, or color of skin.

With Sam by my side, I was letting go of some of my anger towards Helena. But hearing Analeise's life story, I could not wrap my head around how she had forgiven the Cheyenne and moved on while back on earth. But the fact that she HAD certainly explained why she outshown all of us.

Stepping forward, I hugged Analeise tightly.

"I owe you so much," I whispered into her ear. "Thank you." Behind me stood my two bewildered friends, probably wondering where all the jealously, all the envy had gone.

Smiling, I sent Jason a message: "Hey, wasn't it you who said all things come together for those who love?"

Jason, shaking his head, sent back, "Uh, no. That must have been something you heard elsewhere. Quite profound. Quite."

***

Looking back to the large tree where I had first spotted Thomas and Hannah, I once again noticed Ava, that darling little girl I had watched dancing earlier. Thomas and Hannah were gone, but another man was there with her. They were bent over, intently studying some flowers. The man picked a blossom, gently placing it behind Ava's ear. He then picked Ava up and danced in circles with her, making Ava throw her head back and giggle when he turned her faster and faster. The music stopped then and Ava and her dance partner stopped too, trying to shake off the dizziness from their twirling dance. Bending down, Ava's guardian gently stood her on her two little legs. Straightening back up, he turned to see us watching them. His face registered alarm, and whirling around, he took large strides in the opposite direction. I gasped aloud and grabbed Jason's arm.

Jason smiled at me. "It is your family reunion, Lil, so you should have known he'd be here.

"It's okay, Lil," Sky said, and nudged me forward.

"Is it, Sky?" I replied with no small amount of trepidation. I wasn't so sure. Given all the angst between he and I, I wasn't sure I was ready to face Dad. My heart took over. Quickly kissing Sam on the cheek, I stepped into the air and went after him.

***

Rising above the dancing crowd, I joined the mass of people floating in different directions above our party and quickly accelerated. Peering ahead of me, looking for that one figure I knew to be my father, I spotted him at least a half mile in front of me. Why had he left so quickly? Why didn't Dad want to see me?

The sky was darkening up ahead, and the crowds of people were thinning. Never had I been this far away from what had become my stomping grounds in Heaven. I slowed as I approached a massive arched gate, and descended to the grass below. A man, with a flowing white beard and matching robe, sat at a desk to the left of the gateway. Three people queued before him, waiting for him to check something in the large book in front of him. I quietly lined up behind the last person, listening closely to see where these people were going, what this path led to. From where I stood, I could see where the gate-keeper had written a familiar name: Garrison Hunt. A check mark was next to it. He was obviously checking people back in. But why?

"Were you successful in your mission, Mr. Talbot?" queried the gate-keeper.

"I'm not sure," Mr. Talbot, stooped in discouragement, responded sadly. "I slipped the life insurance policy on the kitchen table, but I don't know when she'll ever go back home to find it."

The gate-keeper spoke softly as he patted the sad soul on the back. The man gave a half-smile and nodded, looking somewhat consoled. The powerful gate swung open, and he walked through.

I was getting nervous. Only two people were ahead of me. Without my name in this guy's book, I knew I wouldn't be getting in. Looking on each side of the gate, I noticed a twenty-five foot high white marble wall stretching for miles on each side. Duh. Why weren't people just floating over the wall instead of going through this intimidating gate; or better yet, barging head first through the wall? I knew the answer, of course. Heaven was organized. There were protocols for everything. I looked at the gate-keeper again. He was engrossed in a conversation with a weary-looking woman. Quickly, I stepped out of line and retreated several yards. Then, with no one really paying attention to a brazen teenager, I moved quickly, travelling parallel to the wall for almost a half mile. And then, I floated up and over! Ta-Duh!

Of course, due to the delay, I could no longer see Dad ahead. I sped forward, covering several miles in just a few seconds. I slowed, confused now if I should have even gone after him. Maybe he didn't want me with him at all. I turned to go back and stopped in my tracks. I was totally disoriented. Before me were miles and miles of flat, park-like terrain. Where was East? West? North or South? None of this area looked familiar, and no one was anywhere close to even ask. Lost! Completely.

Night never came to Heaven, but for whatever reason it felt darker here, and gone was the light, fragrant air of Heaven. In this place, the air was damp and very cold, actually. I reached my hand up to feel it; it had taken on an actual consistency. I rubbed my fingers together: Greasy. As I walked, it felt like sludge clinging to my feet, weighing me down. For the first time since I had arrived in Heaven, I felt a pull far stronger than gravity back on earth.

I rounded a large outcropping of grey rock, brown water cascading down from the dark hills above, and swoosh, the ground disappeared from under my feet. Panicked, I realized that I wasn't falling as much as I was being sucked downwards, towards a dense, dirty fog. Coming from all directions around me, and hurling downwards with me, was an endless stream of souls. Barely able to see them in the dim light, I more-so heard them and felt their presence. Telepathically, I knew I was among murderers, drug dealers, rapists, and thieves. A disgusting smell engulfed me, and I writhed and struggled to get to the surface. No matter how much I fought it, the misery in this space pulled me farther downward. Life-giving light dimmed, and then disappeared as I tumbled towards the ground below me, covered with hordes of dark, disembodied spirits. No one glowed here.

Finally making contact with the spongy ground, I cowered behind a dead tree, its limbs barren and lifeless. A battle was playing out before me. The thousands of spirits here were pummeling each other with their fists; to no avail, of course. Their blows just passed through their target. But that futility just made them angrier. They spewed foul, vulgar profanity at one another, each of their mouths and minds a cesspool of filthiness. All of the negative energy of hate, anger and fear seemed to have collected here, and now my own fear was adding to it.

Sensing a dirty energy behind me, I turned to see a disheveled, wrinkled woman approaching. Her dark eyes penetrated mine. She reeked of hate and rage. I backed against the tree.

She faced me. "Whore!" she screamed.

Terrified, I stepped around the trunk of the tree to keep my distance from her.

"Such a worthless daughter you are! You ruined my life, Mazy. You're the reason I'm stuck here with these horrible people! I hate you! I HATE YOU!"

Whoever, and wherever Mazy was, I pitied her. Feeling myself withering under this spirit's barbs, I dropped to my knees and hugged the trunk of the tree.

What had I learned in class about these unevolved spirits? I looked up to see Mazy's mother raising her arms above me, her hands doubled into fists. I was about to get the beating of my life.

"Think, Lilly!"

A calm, feminine voice came into my mind: 'Wrap yourself in a veil of light.'

Squeezing my eyes tightly shut, I visualized myself surrounded by a thin veil of shimmering golden light, separating me from this spirit and her tirade. Why did she hate Mazy? Why was she here? Why were any of these spirits on this battlefield? Could they not float up and out of the violence and hatred around them? Could I?

Panicking, I stood and backed away from the tree, not daring to turn my back on her.

"Don't touch me; stay away," I commanded.

Drawing all my energy around me, I stretched my hands above me, reaching and clawing upward through the darkness, willing myself to get to the light above. And then, a strong, warm hand reached down and grabbed my own. Pulled to higher ground, I was quickly enveloped in the strong and familiar arms of my father. I clung to him, too traumatized to speak.

"It's referred to as Outer Darkness. You're safe now, Lilly."

To forgive is to set a prisoner free

And discover that

The prisoner was you.

– Lewis B. Smedes

CHAPTER TWENTY-TWO

With my head pressed against his chest, I could not contain the emotion. How long had it been since I had heard his voice? I thought back to the last time I had seen my father alive. He had come home drunk. Again. Mom had finally lost it. She didn't want to have any more fighting, to hear any more vulgar name-calling. And I? I was just so tired of being afraid of him, of always waiting for the next shoe to drop. We were done. Amazingly, Dad somehow knew that. He got himself up and out the door that night, announcing that he was leaving and would never come back. And, of course, he hadn't.

And now, here he was. We found a park bench among some tall pines, and I sought protection nestled by his side, his strong arm around me. There we sat, each of us silent as we tried to absorb the reality of once again being together. A beautiful twilight had come to Heaven, and multi-colored lights, much like the Northern Lights back on earth, were dancing through the trees.

After the longest time, I leaned back and looked up at Dad's face. He looked younger than I had ever remembered him. His face, which at one time was consistently covered with dust, sweat and a day's whiskers, was now clean, smooth, and fragrant. His eyes, which had been dulled by alcohol, were crystal clear and penetrating. Dad had always had startling, light blue eyes. Those eyes were now smiling down upon me.

"Why did you leave the party, Dad? Why didn't you at least say hello?"

"Lilly," he spoke softly. "Lilly, it was your party. You were having such a great time. I didn't want my presence there upsetting you. I have so much to explain, so much to do to make things up to you. It may take forever. Thank God, sweetheart, we have forever."

"Dad, don't. . . ."

"No, Lil," Dad interrupted, gently pulling me to him. "Let me say this, please. I was so self-absorbed, so intent on stuffing my own pain, that I was oblivious to the pain I was causing you and your mother. But I am here now, sweetie. I promise I'm going to become the father you always wanted, the father you always deserved."

Even the nightingales had stopped their singing; there was nothing to interrupt Dad's confessional.

***

"Joe and I had been in the field all morning trying to get the baler running again. Your mother and I never stopped at his house, we never asked for his help, so that morning he had jumped at the chance to come out and help me. Still, I said little to him. Any talk was just about how to get that complicated machine going again."

"At some point, I sat down in the shade of the tractor to rest, and took a swig of water from my canteen. While trying to cool off, I sat and watched Joe. He had started up the motor to see if our repairs were going to hold, but then I could see he was about to break an inviolate law: He reached into the baler, with the power train running. My pulse started beating in my throat. It was Joe's decision to take this risk, I rationalized, and so I just sat there, watching. Twice I saw the chain almost grab his sleeve, but Joe was intent on watching the hay feed into the baler. By this time, Lil, my heart was racing, my mouth like cotton. I knew I should stand up, stride over and turn the key off, shutting down the whole contraption. But I didn't. I just didn't. 'Almost,' I said to myself. 'He's almost done checking it, and then I'll be back on the job.'"

At this point, Dad–unable to go on–buried his face in his hands. I said nothing, as he tried to talk through ragged breaths.

"Sure enough. The chain grabbed the sleeve of his shirt, and he jerked back, trying to free himself. I had about two seconds to get to the key and turn the power train off, but I couldn't seem to move. It wasn't as though I made a conscious decision to just sit there, and watch my brother be dragged into the machine. But I didn't make a decision to get up and pull him out of its' teeth, either. Lil, I wasn't thinking I would let him die. I wasn't thinking I could save him. I was simply a spectator, watching the tragedy unfold in front me, not really thinking at all."

Dad turned to study the horror on my face. I couldn't say anything. Uncle Joe had done some rotten things, but how could anyone not act to save his own brother? Then, I knew I had done it again! I had accidently projected my private thoughts out to Dad.

"Don't you think I have asked myself that a thousand times, Lilly? Do you not think I have tried to come to grips with who I was that day in the field? I have felt so much excruciating remorse! I. . .I have been in agony, wondering if I could ever forgive myself, wondering if Joe would ever forgive me; wondering if God could love me still."

At this, Dad stopped talking, and studied his hands for the longest time. I sat, unmoving on the bench, wishing that I could somehow sink in to it. I hadn't been ready for this reunion, nor this conversation. Perhaps better to just get it over with. Where was Sam when I needed him?

"Lil, bottom-line, Joe had done the unthinkable, the unforgiveable. In my mind, no one could sink lower. Animals function on a higher plain than that. He may not have deserved to die, but did he deserve to live? I know now that was not my call. I know now that I should have done everything, risk my own life even, to save his."

"And then, I made matters even worse. I drank all the more to shut out what I'd done, and in doing so, I shut out the two people who mean more to me than life itself."

Quietly now, Dad turned to face me full on. His demeanor had changed radically, his anguish yielding to a calm and a peace that enveloped him, me, the entire grove.

"I'm still working on forgiving myself. But Lil, I know. . .I know that God loves me still. And, Lilly, He loves Joe every bit as much as He loves you and me."

I tried to have that last part sink in. Okay; admittedly, I could be strong-willed, sarcastic, jealous, and shallow, but

JOE got equal portions of love? How did that work? In MY world, that was not FAIR! The abuser was loved as much as the abused? The reckless driver was loved as much as the dead passengers?

"So, Dad, you're saying it is, ultimately, perfectly fine that Helena did me in, because–once here–there is no penalty? And Joe! Are you saying that he is basically getting away with his crimes, too? After-all, according to you, he is loved equally!" I held up my hands to balance an imaginary scale, exasperated with the glaring injustice of it all.

"He is loved equally, Lil. But getting away with his crimes? No, I would not say that. But you decide for yourself."

Dad stood, took my hand, and gently pulled me off the bench.

"Where are we going, Dad?"

"We, Lilly, are going to go see Joe."

"See Uncle Joe," I cried! "Where is he?"

"Well, I would say he's in Spirit Prison, Lil. Joe, however, would probably say he's in Hell."

***

Lesson learned. This time we went through the gate, not over the wall.

The structure we were rapidly approaching looked like it stretched for miles from our left to our right, and the top of it totally disappeared into the atmosphere above. Its roughly hewn grey stones gave the appearance of an ancient medieval castle, minus the turrets and the draw bridge. There were small square windows every few feet, yet there were no bars on any of them.

"Dad, can't this wait for another day?" I implored him telepathically.

"Lilly, I wish it could. But if by any chance you are not staying, it is critical that we do this, and the sooner, the better."

"What do you mean not staying? Of course I'm staying." My stomach lurched at the thought.

We had reached the entrance to the spirit prison. I expected there to be locks and bars on the 30-foot tall wooden door, but there was not so much as a door knob on its surface. The door swung freely in both directions, and we effortlessly pushed our way through into an inner courtyard.

"This place is huge, Dad!"

In front of us were hundreds of separate buildings, much like New York's skyscrapers back on Earth, but these buildings dwarfed anything a human could build.

"There are several areas to Spirit Prison, Lil. As you can see, the prison could house even more spirits than our Spirit World."

Moving closer to the first building in our path, I saw that it was made up of endless rows of transparent cubicles, stacked one on top of another, their columns climbing upwards into a winter-grey inversion as far as I could see. Each cubicle held one lone spirit. From where I stood, it appeared that nothing stopped the occupants from moving freely in and out of their cells, perhaps even drifting down to where we stood below them. But yet, they remained where they were, no one glancing down at us, all of them oblivious to their audience.

"Why are they staying here, Dad? I don't see anything preventing them from leaving?"

"Remember, Lilly, when we die we take our negative traits, our darkness with us." Dad turned and made a wide sweep with his arm, gesturing towards the myriad of people stacked on top of one another. "Once the residents here decide to set them down, they can leave."

I looked at Dad, rather dubiously.

"It couldn't be that simple."

"Well, it is almost that simple, Lil."

Before I could pester him for details, Dad took my hand. We drifted upwards and, picking a random floor, started down a long, narrow walkway. I was reminded of a movie I had seen once back on earth that featured a guy in a state penitentiary. To my left was a row of cells, each occupied by a lone soul, but without bars or guards. To my right was a drop-off, void of any railing. Stopping, I peered over the edge to the ground below. We were up at least 100 stories.

Even spirits can get dizzy. Steering clear of the edge, I hurried to keep up with Dad.

Trying hard not to stare at the spirits as we passed, I almost zipped past a familiar face. Stopping short, I backed up to take a closer look. Quigg! He was leaning against the wall opposite a large screen, his arms folded, his one leg crossed at the ankle. It wasn't quite a large-screen TV mounted there. It was more of a projected image, but I could not see the source of the projection. I could not understand why anyone would be interested in television up here, until I recognized the images as Quigg's girlfriend, Danni. Quigg was so engrossed as to what was happening on the screen, he didn't even notice us.

I moved closer. Danni was sitting in a classroom, staring into space. The scene quickly changed then, to a scene of an older woman standing at a kitchen sink, peeling potatoes. Where had I seen this woman before? She looked vaguely familiar. The scene switched again to Danni. Now she was walking down the main hall of my high school back on earth.

And then it dawned on me! "This is real time! This is happening right now, on earth."

The feeling of nostalgia, of longing to be back there with Danni–even with a backpack of books weighing me down–came upon me so intensely that tears sprang to my eyes. That was my life! Danni was still living my life!

Dad touched my shoulder. He had come back to retrieve me. I realized then that the older woman standing at the sink was Quigg's mother. I remembered meeting her the night of his viewing.

I stepped up to the threshold of his cell. "Quigg?" My voice came out in a whisper. "Quigg? Do you remember me? I'm Lilly, a friend of Danni's."

Quigg, startled from his reverie, looked at me with immediate recognition.

"Lilly, what are you doing here?"

"Well, I died, Quigg. I was, uh, killed in a car accident."

"Oh, Lil, it's great to see you."

Dad stood back as I passed over the threshold into Quigg's cubicle. Quigg and I exchanged hugs.

"What I mean, Lil, is what are YOU doing in Spirit Prison?"

"My dad and I came to visit a relative."

"Did he commit suicide too? Is he in this wing?"

I was confused; I didn't know Spirit Prison was divided into wings. "No, Quigg, he. . ."

"Oh, that's good," Quigg interrupted. Turning to the screen, we both watched as Danni left the school and walked out, alone, into a pelting rain. She seemed oblivious as to how quickly she was getting drenched. It was so apparent that she was zoned out on the life that was going on around her.

"In this wing, Lilly, we get to watch over those we left behind, and sometimes we are even sent back to try to help."

I nodded, remembering that awful party Sky and I invaded in our attempts to find Alli.

"My mother–Danni–they don't look too good, do they?"

Quigg looked down at the floor. Before I could think of anything to help him feel better, he continued.

"Were you at my funeral, Lilly?"

"Uh, no, Quigg, I wasn't." I had been to way too many funerals, and just couldn't handle another one.

Acknowledging my dad with a brief nod his way, Quigg struggled on. "Well, my dad was there, standing by my coffin. He greeted all my family and friends as they came by to pay their respects. My two best friends were there, Cole and Gee, and Dad was trying to make them feel better, telling them that I was at peace.

"I tried to scream, 'No, Dad! Don't tell them that! I'm not at peace!' But, of course, no one could hear me. Do you have any idea, Lilly, how many times I have followed Mom around the house, trying to explain? How many times I have said I was sorry?" Quigg shook his head in frustration. "I think she feels me when I'm there, but she can . . . Never. Hear. Me.

I stood there with absolutely no words to help Quigg

feel better. With nothing forthcoming, he continued.

"You know, Lilly, the very minute I arrived here I had all recollection back. In my Life Review, I saw my life back on earth, the beginning and the end. Not the way I ended it, but the way it was supposed to end. The realization of lost opportunities, of missed memories. . ."

Quigg's voice trailed off, and he stood, shaking his head slowly, unable to express the extent of his regret.

"Do you want to see this, Lil?"

Before I could answer, the image on the screen was changed to a little boy, playing with his toys, in a sandbox, on a bright summer day. Behind him was a much older Danni, laughing and talking.

"Quigg, he loves his truck, doesn't he? You couldn't have given him a better birthday present."

I frowned, puzzled.

Quigg answered flatly. "I was to be Danni's husband." Gesturing towards the screen, he continued. "He was to be our son, Lil. Life was going to get much better for me, with just a little time, a little patience. This, this is far worse than anything I experienced when I was alive. Where's the peace? Where's the better place?"

Not all of Heaven is nice, is it, Lilly? You wouldn't think that people would feel sorrow and anguish in Heaven, would you?"

Doubling up his fist, he hit the wall, but his hand

passed through unscathed. "Too bad we can't tell 'em back on earth, huh, Lil?"

Tears filling my eyes, I looked at the floor, not trusting my own voice. "What would you tell them, Quigg?"

"That death is final, Lil. That death is so very final."

Tears rolled down my cheeks. My heart ached for Quigg, but the selfish part of me just wanted to leave, to get away from all the consequences playing out on the screen before him. Nothing I could say would change anything.

Dad and I hugged Quigg goodbye and rose swiftly upwards, streaking past floors of cubicles at lightening speed.

Dad looked sideways at me and nodded reassuringly. "Don't worry, sweetheart. Quigg will have that peace, he'll know happiness again. But simply, if we don't create it, Lil, it is not ours to take." That was all Dad had to say.

***

Too quickly, Dad and I were standing in another cubicle, almost identical to Quigg's, but there were no images projecting onto the wall. I immediately felt another presence close behind me in the grey, barren cell. I did not need to turn and look at who stood there, for I already knew. It was Joe. Suddenly, such excruciating pain and overwhelming remorse washed over me that I was almost knocked to my knees. And then it was gone. I realized that, for whatever reason, I was allowed to feel what Joe was feeling.

Choking back emotion, Joe tried to speak.

"Lilly, Garrison, thank you for coming. I've waited so long, Lilly, for this chance. I. . ." His voice died out, and turning to finally look at him, I saw that Joe had sunk to his knees on the floor. His chest was heaving, and racked, gasping sobs came from deep within him.

"I have been cut off, Lilly. I have been cut off from God's light. Where He is, I cannot go, not for a very, very long time."

Clenching my fists, I spun around to face Dad. "And what is that to me?" I projected to him. My face was turning red, pressure building up between my temples. Joe's actions had put him here. What could I possibly do about it?

Putting his finger to his lips, Dad prompted me to wait, to not speak quite yet.

"The pain inflicted on you and others by my own despicable behavior hangs like a large, cold albatross around my neck, Lilly. I cannot free myself from it, I cannot escape it. It is always there; ALWAYS. And it reeks, and stinks, and binds me. I cannot lie down; I cannot stand straight. I am weighed down and left tethered to this spot, unable to move, to go forward. I am stuck, Lilly; hopelessly, hopelessly stuck. I, who should have been your protector, betrayed you in the worst way. I ask your forgiveness, Lilly."

Relaxing my fists, I took a deep, slow breath. I could not bring myself to look at the stooped, withered man before me, but I felt the contempt and anger fading somewhat. In their place came the beginnings of compassion for this man who had abused and betrayed our family on so many levels. But that time, that life, seemed now so long ago. The weight in my chest started to lift.

"Dad, what am I supposed to SAY?" I ran my fingers through my hair, totally overwhelmed. This was all too deep for me, and I was feeling way in over my head. Why had he ever brought me here?

Gesturing to the empty cubicle next to Joe's, Dad answered me.

"See that room, Lilly? Until Joe forgave me for allowing him to die that day in the hayfield, I was stuck there. Until you can forgive him for abusing you, HE will be stuck here."

"What!" I exclaimed out loud, feeling my face blush red again. "I thought Joe was relegated to this dank little cell for what he had done to ME! But now you're saying Joe is trapped here because I haven't forgiven HIM yet?"

I slumped against the wall. This stuff was way beyond Heaven 101, and I was going to flunk mastering this concept, for sure!

Dad put his arm around me and pulled me to him. Looking down at my face, he spoke quietly. "Each of us has a role in this forgiveness thing, Lil. Without forgiving Joe, your progress will come to a standstill. Nor can he leave here until you forgive him."

Dad stooped down, pulled Joe to his feet, and embraced his brother.

Joe smiled weakly at Dad, and then stepping back to let us pass, he looked at me and dropped his gaze. His voice was barely audible. "Lilly, I will do my best to make it up to you; I promise I will."

My words came out, flat and defeated. "And from Hell you are going to do that, Uncle Joe? Yeah, right! How will you make it up to me, now that I am dead, too?"

Joe said nothing.

Taking one last, long look at Joe, I followed Dad out of Joe's cell, and floated down to the ground.

"Can we go now, Dad? I get why you brought me here, but I can't be compelled to forgive just because I should."

"You're right, Lilly; and I'm not asking that of you. I brought you here to give Joe a chance to ask you for your forgiveness. That's all."

"So, can we go now?" I wasn't above begging. I hated this place! It was cold and grey and the despair surrounding all these spirits was sucking all light right out of me. I would rather have my spirit be vaporized into nothingness than have to live one minute in this self-imposed prison.

***

Instantaneously, Dad and I were in a vast field of wild flowers, sitting among them high upon a hill. I looked down at the peaceful countryside below, complete with a shimmering lake positioned perfectly in the middle of it. Everything here was warmth and light and peace. Only the song of a meadow lark interrupted the stillness.

Turning my head to the right and left, I surveyed the beautiful view before me. The perfect quiet was in sharp contrast to the howls that had surrounded me in Outer Darkness. Pulling my knees to my chest, I buried my face in my robe and tried to purge my mind of the scenes and sounds before they were indelibly etched in my mind forever. Dad put his arm around me, pulling me close. Taking a deep breath, he tried to help me make sense of it.

"Ultimately, Lilly, each of us chooses where we will live. God does not force His will upon us. We choose for ourselves, Heaven or Hell."

Wow, there was that free will thing again. I had experienced the best, and I had witnessed the very worst, both in the same realm, in this place called the Spirit World.

Looking out over the vast lake below us, Dad gave me a squeeze and stood up, gazing out over the shimmering lake. "Water seeks its own level, Lil."

I could not bring myself to ask Dad which level I was bound for. Could I eventually forgive Joe? Probably. But Helena?

Pulling me to my feet, Dad turned me to face a figure gliding quickly towards us. It was Sam, my best friend, the love of my life. I waved eagerly and started forward to go meet him. Dad's voice stopped me in my tracks.

"Come see me, won't you, Lil?" Dad's voice cracked with emotion.

"Where are you going, Dad?"

"Back to Spirit Prison, sweetheart."

"But why? Joe forgave you! I forgive you!" I rushed to embrace him but Dad stopped me at arm's length.

"And someday, I will finally forgive myself. It's a process, Lil. God gives us all the time we need, and remember, God's plan is perfect."

Tears sprang to his eyes, but before I could respond, my father was gone.

The best and most beautiful things

Cannot be seen or touched –

They must be felt with the heart.

– Helen Keller

CHAPTER TWENTY-THREE

Hey, Lilly, I've come to tempt you."

Sam's timing couldn't have been better. Only Sam could take my mind off of Dad and his parting comment. He wrapped his strong arms around my shoulders and pulled me tightly to him. Looking up into his green eyes that always seemed to penetrate my soul, I once again felt safe and protected. The chilling memories of outer darkness and Spirit Prison were quickly pushed to the back of my mind.

"You've always tempted me," I replied, not able to control the huge smile spreading across my face.

"Oh, really? Then I have been successful, as tempting you is what I have set out to do." Bending down, Sam planted one of his best kisses on me. Then he stood back and looked at me from head to toe.

"You, Lillybug, are looking mighty fine."

I looked down at my robe and turned to see as much of my backside as I could.

"You, Lil, are nothing short of radiant!"

"I am?"

"Can't you tell that your robe is shimmering?"

"It is?"

Shaking his head, Sam only said, "Lil, do you know what 'obtuse' means?

I looked at him blankly.

Sam threw his hands in the air, obviously giving up. "You, girl, have no sense of who you are and what you are becoming!"

Then shifting to a whole new conversation, Sam offered up his plan. "Pack your bags, babe, because we are off for a good time!"

"Where are we going, Sam?" I pulled back, thinking back to the 'tour' Dad and I had just returned from.

"Hey, not to worry, Lilly-Bug! We're going planet hopping!"

Placing my hand in his, he simply said, "Helam."

Instantly, we were in the blackness of space. The freedom of movement–to slow down, to speed up–was exhilarating. We could go where-ever we wanted.

"This is the ultimate ride, isn't it?" Sam smiled at me and held my hand tighter.

I smiled back. "It's great to be alive."

Poof! In an instant we were there, where-ever 'there' was! Standing on a street corner, I got the distinct impression that Sam and I were in a city much like London, England, plopped somewhere smack in the middle of the Earth's 19th century. A young couple approached us. I quickly moved to the other side of Sam. No way was I going to let another stranger pass right through me. A horse-drawn carriage rattled by us, jostling its occupants as it traveled over uneven stones.

Sending his thoughts telepathically, Sam explained. "No, Lilybug, this isn't England. The country is Pahoran, on the planet, Helam. This town is called Melek. And, even though it's been around as long as earth, by technology's standards this world is less advanced than earth. It has another few hundred years before people will be walking down the street with earphones stuffed in their ears."

We floated across the street and entered a small, cozy bakery. The aromas filled the crowded shop and I longed to taste the orange frosted, muffin-like treat sitting out on a counter inches in front of me. Customers were ordering a variety of goodies from the harried, big busted woman behind the counter. I gave a longing glance at Sam as I reached for a goodie.

"No, Lil! Someone might have a heart attack if they see a cake floating off the plate into mid-air."

Sam took my hand and–leaving temptation behind–we lifted above the shopping district, quickly traveling to the countryside. High on a hill, we sat on a large boulder and looked over the vast expanse in front of us. Sam pointed to a field below us. Grazing there were animals I had never seen before. They had the hide of a giraffe, but the size and features of a horse. How weird was this?

Sam explained. "That's a marlion. They require no breaking, no training. You could climb on him right now and ride bareback. It's one smooth ride."

Sam looked around. "What you don't want to come across on this planet is a bitbun. They look just like a cute little lop-eared rabbit back on Earth. But they are vicious. Bitbuns leap–high–." Sam measured six feet from the ground with his hand. "And the last thing you'll see are their teeth. They'll go for your jugular before you know what hit you."

Hastily, I tried to stand up on the rock–distancing myself from the ground–momentarily forgetting that I was dead, and invisible, and that I no longer had a jugular. Sam laughed and pulled me down by him.

"They are not around here, Lil. They live in higher elevations."

Relaxing, I leaned back on the rock and sighed. Looking up, I did not see the familiar blue I expected, but instead, an indigo sky. It contrasted beautifully with the pink-leafed trees and the yellow grass surrounding us.

"Wow!" I shook my head in disbelief that Helam, Selsia, and Earth could look so different from one another.

The breeze carried a sweet smell towards us and, looking around, I saw a grove of trees, their boughs heavy with fruit. Glancing over at Sam, he gestured toward them.

"Hey, go for it!"

Gliding to the nearest tree and looking around to make sure no one could see a fruit moving under its own power, I picked an oval, walnut size fruit with a fuzzy rose-colored skin. Biting into it, my mouth puckered as a thick purple liquid full of seeds oozed down my chin. Spitting it out, I madly rubbed my tongue on my gown, trying to remove the horrible taste. Looking over at Sam, he was doubled over, laughing. Taking aim, I pitched the fruit directly at his head. It barely missed him. Drats!

"Hey, watch it!"

"You set me up! You knew I would eat one, didn't you?" I walked to where Sam stood and pushed him backwards. "You rat!"

"Don't be mad, Lil! I made the same mistake the first time I came here. They kind of taste like a mixture of puréed grubs and vinegar, don't ya think?"

Dropping into the grass, Sam grabbed my hand and pulled me down next to him. Closing my eyes, I focused on the warmth of the multiple suns high in this world's heavens. Realizing I was lying in grass that smelled strongly of lilacs, I inhaled deeply. Mom's favorite flowers; her favorite scent. Did she have any idea of the wonderful things that awaited her on this side of the veil? How I wish I could share some of this with her.

"Did you ever study the universe in one of your school classes, Lil?"

"Yeah, in Mr. Adamson's Astronomy class. Why?"

"What do you remember learning?"

"Well," I replied, straining to remember if I had retained anything at all, "he spent a lot of time talking to us about the Ultra Deep Field the Hubble telescope had found. I remember his saying that there were a hundred billion galaxies, with hundreds of billions of stars in each galaxy. I pretty much sat there having a brain cramp. I couldn't comprehend it."

"Look up, Lil."

I rolled onto my back and looked into the sky above.

"OH. MY. WORD."

Beyond the multiple suns shining down on us was a

scene so unbelievable that I gasped. Overhead were planets on top of planets, with stars racing towards us, and then away. I suppose they had always been there, but only now, when it was called to my attention, were they so very vivid, and so very close, suspended there in space, all in their various orbits.

Streaming into my mind came a scripture out of nowhere. I spoke it out loud: " '*For behold, there are many worlds that have passed away by the word of my power. And there are many that now stand, and innumerable are they unto man; but all things are numbered unto me, for they are mine and I know them.*' "

We said nothing for several minutes, both of us subdued by the reality of all that was orbiting above our heads.

Pointing off to the right, Sam squinted, studying the sky until he got his bearings. "There it is! There's earth."

Leaning up on one elbow, I looked in the direction of where he was pointing, and could barely make out the pinpoint where every person I had known and loved had lived. Every event I knew of, whether it had been a local concert, a state-wide disaster, or a world war, had happened there, on that tiny fly-speck of a planet.

"It is kind of laughable, isn't it, Lil, how self important we all were?"

We lay in silence for a time, lost in our own thoughts about the lives we had lived on that speck of dust.

"What did you learn on earth, Lil? I mean, about yourself?"

I paused, deep in thought. "Hmmmmm. I learned I could handle some hard things, when I first lost Dad, and then Jason." I gave a rueful laugh. "I didn't learn how important it is to hang out with friends who would make me better than I was. Not that Sky didn't try to show me what a train wreck it would be if I stuck with Alex."

I rolled over, wrapping my leg around Sam's torso. He continued to study the planets overhead while I studied him. Mom would most certainly approve of this guy. My finger traced the dimple on Sam's cheek.

"So what would you do differently, Lil, if you could do it all over?"

"Oh, that's an easy one, Sam. Before I ever went to earth, I would have campaigned hard to be on earth the same time you were. I see no point in our going down at different times, do you?"

"YOU made that decision, Lil! Don't you remember?" I looked at him stunned.

"I did?"

"Of course you did!" There wasn't much opportunity to become a professional dancer during the 1800's, if you recall correctly, and you were all about dancing. You lived and breathed it! And think about it! You wouldn't have known Jason, or Sky, or. . ." Sam paused, his whole demeanor changing. ". . . Or Luke."

The mention of Luke brought me up short. I had not thought about Luke for one nano-second upon my return from Sky's and my assignment. How could I do that? I had been so caught up in my new life, this new world where I only had eyes for Sam, that I had not given Luke a thought.

Guilt flooded over me. I had mentally assigned Luke to be Mom's guardian and off I had gone, never thinking for a moment since how Luke was doing, or what he was feeling. Was he okay? He had now lost his little brother, Landry, and his three best friends. How had he stood it? Did he cave, as I had done? I had to admit it. Luke deserved more from me. Until Sam, no one had loved me better than Luke.

Feeling very serious for some inexplicable reason, I turned over and stared intently at the darkening sky. "You know what, Sam?"

"What, Lillybug?"

"Exploring these new worlds and now, lying here by you with the suns shining down on us will go down in history as my all-time favorite day."

Sam started to speak and I put my finger to his lips. "And you need to know, Sam, that I'm sorry if it seemed that dance was my priority over you. You are my priority and I will never leave you again. There is nothing and no one that would separate me from you."

I waited for a response from him, but there was nothing forthcoming. Sam just looked a little distracted, and then quickly standing up, said, "Daylight's burning, Lil."

I laughed at that expression which only applied to the living and to those worlds that marked time. Here neither applied, but I let Sam pull me to my feet.

The Past is a foreign country.

They do things differently there.

– Author unknown.

CHAPTER TWENTY-FOUR

And it was Jason and Sky there to greet us when Sam and I stepped back through the portal.

"Whoa! That was perfect timing, guys! I was just coming to summon you! Are you ready, Lil?"

"For what, Jason?"

"For your Life Review."

"NO WAY!" I quickly backed away from Jason's outstretched hand.

"Lilly! Must you? Why must you be so. . .so oppositional?" Sky stood there, hands on hips, looking at me with mock indignation.

"Why now?" I protested.

Jason took a deep breath and started again. "You've been flying under the radar for a long time now, Lil. The gig is up!"

"Besides. . ." Sky wrinkled her nose and pointed to my orientation robe, "how else are you going to get rid of that thing?"

***

We approached a three-story building, the walls of which were pure alabaster. Wide stairs, full of many people coming and going, led to two twenty-foot tall doors, their solid glass panes shimmering in the sunlight. Reflecting back to me were images of all my friends who had come along to give me moral support: Sam, Sky, Jason, and Analeise. They all paused on the top stair.

"Okay, Lilly; we stop here. Only those who are scheduled for their life review go in," Jason said.

"Did you bring money for popcorn and a diet Coke?" Sky asked innocently.

"Aren't you the funny one, Sky." The stress in my voice was, no doubt, obvious to everyone.

"Lil, it's okay." Sam tried to reassure me by pulling

me to him and hugging me tightly. "What are you so uptight about? It's not like you were an ax murderer back on earth." He dropped my hand, and pulling the door open, he bowed, his arm making a sweeping gesture. "And in you go, Madame."

I stepped forward, but paused to look back at my retreating friends.

"We'll see you back at our park when you're done," Jason yelled.

Turning, I saw a digital sign in front of me, flashing names and destinations:

Lilly Hunt, Room 209.

Wanting to stall as long as possible, I took the stairs one-by-one while everyone else floated quickly past me. I put my head down and avoided everyone's gaze.

"Why am I so scared?" I asked myself quietly. Then, knowing I no more had the luxury of self-denial, I answered my own question: "More efficient than the subtle hint of a dream, my life story will not lie. "

***

I reached for the doorknob to Room #209, but then froze. Do I knock? Do I just walk in? Have I already lost points for being late? I tapped lightly on the door.

"Come in," a deep voice responded.

I turned the knob and, leaning heavily against the

thick oak door, entered a vast chamber. Dark wood paneling wrapped the perimeter, interrupted by several large stained glass windows. Sunlight streamed into the room, creating a kaleidoscope of colors that filled the whole expanse. The ceiling was at least 40 feet high, dwarfing the twelve men and women who sat behind a semi-circular desk at the front of the room. Between me and the panel was one lone straight-back chair on a foot-high riser. I carefully closed the door behind me and turned to see that all eyes were on me. My voice echoed in the cavernous room.

"Hi." It came out in a squeak.

"Hello, Miss Hunt," they all answered in unison.

The man sitting in the middle of the panel had a warm, alto voice. It reassured me somewhat, and I gave him a tentative smile.

"My name is Mr. Montague. "We've been waiting for you."

"You've been waiting for me? Is that a good thing or a bad thing?" My voice shook. I was a nervous wreck.

The panel members looked at one another and smiled. Consulting some papers in front of him, Mr. Montague continued.

"Lilly. . . May I call you Lilly?"

I nodded.

"I see you've come for your life review."

Taking a deep breath, I tried to compose myself. "Yes,

I am staying, definitely staying." Lifting my chin, I set my jaw in rigid resolve.

"Staying?" Mr. Montague looked up from his papers. "Why wouldn't you be staying?"

All my fears came flooding out. "For a long time now I haven't known if I am coming or going. The last time I saw my body I was languishing in a hospital, still alive–barely–but I was looking pretty hammered. If I'm still breathing back on earth, I don't know why my spirit crossed over. It all could be a mistake my being here, but I hope not. Could someone tell me what I'm doing, please? Was it my time to die?"

There was a brief silence before groups of two and three people started consulting with one another in low whispers. Mr. Montague, drumming his pencil on the desk, looked back and forth at his paperwork and then at me.

A different man, with grey hair and a full beard, spoke up. "In my experience, everyone appearing before this panel has always known they were staying. Highly unusual." He clucked his tongue.

One of the women in the middle of the panel addressed me. "People do, at times, arrive in the Spirit World prematurely, Lilly; but that doesn't happen often. Heaven doesn't make many mistakes. Maybe one in a million."

Another woman, sitting at one end of the panel, interjected. "Ms. Hunt, how do you know your body is being kept alive?"

My mouth dry, my voice shaking, I tried again. "My friend, Sky, and I were sent back on a mission–I guess that was what it was–and I was trying to find my mom and I saw me." Pulling at my robe, I barged on. "So, if I'm on your list, showing I should be here, shouldn't I have been issued a different robe?"

They all sat, blinking–momentarily stunned at my grievance–which I had ended with more of an accusation than a question. Going for broke, I continued.

"Is it possible for an occasional spirit–take me for instance–to slip through the cracks here? Was my guide, Jason, given incomplete instructions concerning me?"

There was silence. I searched their faces. My hint at their incompetence didn't seem to faze them.

Mr. Montague, holding up a paper with names listed in a column down the page, took control. His voice reverberated off the walls.

"The fact that your name appears here on the roster, Miss Hunt–scheduled for a life review–would indicate that your death was not premature."

I backed up several steps. I was losing points. Fast.

"As to the issue surrounding your orientation robe, we will have to investigate that matter further." Mr. Montague's countenance then softened, and he suddenly did not sound so much like an important authority figure as he did a grandfather-type. He spoke softly. "Lilly, what do YOU want?"

"I want to stay."

"Why?"

"Because Sam and Sky and Dad and Jason are here. I'll miss Mom and Luke, but I can't leave Sam, not again!" I lowered my head, tears rolling down my cheeks.

They sat quietly, listening to my every word. Nodding. Finally, Mr. Montague, laying down his pen, spoke as the deciding authority.

"Well, then, Lilly, let's proceed."

Behind me a large screen was descending, and my chair, on its own power, slowly rotated so that I faced the screen square on. The lights dimmed.

Mr. Montague's deep voice boomed, as he spoke with power: 'PETACH'.

Upon hearing the word, I felt the strangest sensation. It was like a lid at the top of my head popped open, exposing my brain. Then, from deep inside my brain there was an unwinding. A thin, delicate thread rose from the crown of my head, drawn through the air to the large screen in front of me. Upon contact, large images burst onto the screen, full of radiant colors and life, for all eyes to see. I gripped the edge of my seat with both hands. This was freaky!

The images flashed across the screen in rapid fire, but yet I was seeing, feeling, hearing, smelling each scene as though I was once again living it. And not only was I feeling again my own emotions in each of these millions of moments, but I also–this time around–felt the emotion of the other people in each scene of my life. Voices swarmed around me, but I could distinctly make out what every last person was thinking and saying.

Nothing could have pulled my eyes from the screen. I was transfixed.

Here I was, truly back at the beginning:

Being born caesarean, the complications leaving my mom and dad unable to have any more children. The doctor shook his head, his forehead wrinkled with concern as he talked with Mom and Dad.

Whoa! This was weird, knowing what the doctor was thinking and feeling: Worry, concern, thoughts of a lawsuit.

Age Three: Stooping down to pick up pretty rocks off the gravel road in front of our ranch, I look up just in time to see a neighbor boy, Brian, barreling down on me on his rusty blue bike. I had totally forgotten being run over by a bike, but yet, here it was.

Age Five: Now I am tracing the alphabet very carefully on my double-ruled paper, looking up at the whiteboard as my kindergarten teacher, Mrs. Holmes, prints a large capital A and then a B.

More images blaze across the screen. . .

Losing my two front teeth, batting a ball through a plate glass window, being the lead in my elementary school play.

Age Nine: There is Dad, walking me to the corral to show me my own horse, Raven.

Age Thirteen: I am in junior high. For whatever random reason, Helena has intimidated the entire eighth grade into not talking to me. Totally ostracized for two weeks, I am walking the halls, saying "hi", trying to talk to those who had been my friends. They walk by me like I am invisible. Only back then, I wasn't.

Age Fourteen: At Gibb's party. His parents are gone for the weekend, and Gibb and I are in his parents' walk-in closet. Gibb is giving me my first French kiss. What a KISS! I float home.

Age Fifteen: My house. Jason, Luke, Sky and I furiously bail water out the front door, horrified at how we let our water fight get out of hand.

Age Sixteen: I am in my Algebra II class. Paige, the girl that everyone seems to harass, is struggling to answer a question that is so-o-o-o obvious. Mr. Hurst tries to encourage her, saying, "Paige, you know this! It's simple."

I say, louder than I mean to: "SHE'S simple!" Everyone hears. Everyone laughs.

Paige goes home, picks on her little brother, calls him a loser and a freak, dumping all her hurt on him. But it doesn't stop there. Crying, he runs outside, sees their little puppy, and kicks it across the lawn.

Next, I am learning to drive. Mr. Stoddard, my drivers' ed teacher, sits to my right, two of my compatriots are strapped–or trapped–in the backseat. I am approaching a narrow bridge on a country road. Quickly approaching from the opposite direction is a large diesel truck.

"Lilly, the bridge is too narrow to pass," Mr. Stoddard squeaks between gritted teeth. "Either speed up and get over it first, or slow way down, and let him pass."

I speed up. I panic. I slam on my breaks.

"SPEED UP, Lilly! NO, WAIT! SLOW DOWN!"

I go for it!

The two vehicles reach the bridge simultaneously. With no more than an inch to spare between us, we pass each other! My two backseat passengers–pasty white and curled in a fetal position–let loose with various colorful expletives.

Everything I said, did or thought, from the time I was born until I left earth was recorded in my subconscious–or my hard drive–just as Jason had said. Except. . .I had been abused by Joe sometime between the ages of three and five. Why was there nothing here about Joe and what he had to done to me?

Unbelievable how many images, how many memories for such a short life of eighteen years! But I had lived every day of those eighteen years and every day was filled with countless minutes of countless acts. The Good. The Bad. The Ugly.

Now I was getting a little defensive.

But, honestly, what did they expect? I was only a teenager. I wasn't perfect! Was anybody? Were THEY? Folding my arms, I slumped down in my chair, copping a bit of an attitude. How could I be judged when I wasn't even a legal adult?

And WHERE was that scoreboard? Displayed on a Jumbo-tron, with all eyes to see, should be:

'Shared her crayons: 1 point!'

'Took Sophie for a longer walk: 3 points!'

'Lied and told Sky she didn't look fat in her new pants: 5 points!'

Or would that be MINUS 5 points? W h a t e v e r.

Age 18: My birthday party. Luke is asking me to dance. Helena is dancing on her imaginary pole in front of Alex.

It's the next morning now. I stomp out of the kitchen, not able to get away from Carl fast enough. I see Mom's face. She's devastated by what has just happened.

Yuk, Diego's party.

I shudder. How naive we were to mess with the underworld.

A New Year: Now, at the side of the road, waiting for Helena to pick me up for dance practice.

I inhaled deeply! Here it was. The morning of the accident. Sliding to the front of the chair, I leaned forward, watching intently, bracing myself as I relived the consequences of Helena's crazy driving.

I hand her the phone. She makes a smart comment to Sky. I unbuckle my seatbelt.

Gasping, my hand flew to my mouth.

"STOP! STOP!" Turning back to the panel, I yelled again. "Stop it!"

The lights went up. The screen faded. The whirling in my head paused.

"I mean, go back; just a couple of seconds. Please. Play that part again."

"Which part, Lilly? " Mr. Montague asks.

"The part from where I unbuckle my seatbelt."

The lights dim.

I climb in the backseat. I hand my phone to Helena. She turns to Sky and laughs. I reach for the buckle on my seatbelt.

And, there it is; I had seen it right the first time.

"Stop!" I stood up as the lights came on. I felt weak. Black spots danced in front of my eyes. Was I going to faint right there? I grabbed the back of the chair for support, and turning to the panel, I tried to speak. Nothing came out.

"Lilly?"

The room's spinning.

The first woman addressed me again.

"Your life review is not quite done, Ms. Hunt. There's more. Are you alright?"

"No." With tears streaming down my cheeks, I back towards the door, shaking my head furiously.

"I can't. . . . I can't watch anymore."

If you judge people,

You have no time to love them.

—Mother Teresa

CHAPTER TWENTY-FIVE

Slamming into the heavy door with my shoulder, I pushed it open. I took the stairs two at a time, not caring that other spirits had to veer out of my way to prevent a head-on. Pushing through the outer door into the brilliant sunlight, I was immediately blinded by the brightness.

Just outside the door stood a lone figure. Sky. I was so thankful Sam wasn't here to see this. I could not bear to see the disappointment on his face when he learned the truth.

"Lilly? Are you okay?"

"No, no; please say it didn't happen; it didn't happen that way. . ." Shock trapped the words in my throat.

"Lilly! I'm sorry! I. . ." Sky was struggling to talk.

"You KNEW, Sky! All this time, you knew!"

Tears filled my eyes, making it hard for me to see. I groped for the nearby banister and sank down on the stairs. Burying my face in my lap, I tried to face even one of the implications of what I had just seen and heard. All it took was one short video clip to kick me out of my self-denial.

Sky sat down beside me, attempting to wrap her arms around my shoulder. I pushed her away.

"Sky, you had to have seen it in your own life review. You saw me try to get my phone back. You saw me lose my balance and grab the wheel. The car spun and flipped because of me. I did it! I DID IT!"

"Lil, it was an accident!"

"Skylar, stop lying for me. I've lied enough for both of us. We both know! It's my fault you are dead. It's my fault Helena–who I've blamed non-stop–is dead. I killed MYSELF!" I laughed ruefully, astounded at the irony of it all.

"Sky, I took away all our dreams. Why don't you hate me?"

"Because I knew it was my time to come home, Lilly. My Life Review showed me that. If it hadn't been the car accident, I would have exited from life some other way. Lil, I'm so sorry. I don't. . . . ."

"Who else knows, Sky? Who knows? Does Sam? Does Jason?"

"Sam doesn't know anything; there's no reason why he would. I think Jason suspects."

"Why? Because he knows what a total idiot I am?"

"No. Of course not! Jason was assigned to be your Guide, and Guides are told of special circumstances around a spirit's arrival back to the Spirit World."

Hugging my knees, I rocked back and forth on the stair, shaking at the enormity of it, the inescapable consequences of one stupid mistake.

"Sky, our turn is over! Any chance for me to go back to fix it, to make it right, is gone!"

I wanted to run, to hide, but where? Everything and everyone was so glowingly obvious here that there was no place to hide, no hole to fall in!

Gently, Sky tried to point out the obvious.

"Sometime, Lil, you will have to go back and finish your review. It's kind of a requirement, a policy here, to see it through."

Standing, I brushed the wrinkles from my ugly, ugly robe.

"I will never go back, Sky. Never. There's too much guilt; too much judgment."

"Lilly, how do you know they were judging you? Don't you think it was YOU judging you? Have you met anyone here who tried to put a guilt trip on you! In the Spirit World, there is no humiliation or shame."

Then a new horror occurred to me, my eyes like saucers with the implications of it.

"My dream, Sky! My dream! It showed me what was in store for me had I lived." I was up on my feet, pacing back and forth, definitely nearing hysteria.

"What dream, Lilly? I don't know what you're talking about!"

"Thank God I'm dead! If I had lived, I would have been arrested, tried, sent away for manslaughter! Can't you just see it, Sky? Lilly Hunt, doing hard time!"

Sky found her voice. "Lilly, get a grip! Quit borrowing trouble! You're not there! You're here!"

"But what do I DO with this H E R E, Sky? It's Spirit Prison, for sure!"

"Lil, I. . ."

I cut her off. "Hey, maybe I can room with my Uncle Joe, but–then again–he didn't KILL anyone, so he is in a much nicer wing than where I will be stuck."

My mind went back to our visit in Joe's cell. And to think, I had felt so smug: 'Should I forgive him? Should I not? Hmmmm.'

I sank back onto the stairs and hid my face, my shame,

in my lap. Such a mess-up I was! Couldn't I just evaporate into nothingness? Couldn't I just cease, altogether, to BE?

Hearing my thoughts, Sky spoke softly. "No, Lil. The only way around this is through. We do live forever. And this can be fixed; all of it. This can go away."

Before I could argue, Sky stood and took my hand, saying only, "Come with me."

I was too done in to fight her. I just allowed myself to be led.

***

Sitting on their couch, my 'support group'–Lillie and Teancum–waited patiently for me to feel like talking.

I didn't think Grandma, particularly, could help me with this debacle. As far as I could tell, Grandma Lillie was about perfect.

"Oh, you're so wrong!"

I looked up, startled! She had heard my thoughts.

Teancum took my hand. "Lilly, do you remember how I died?"

My mind went back to the day I first got to the Spirit World. When Teancum had given me that bear hug, I had instantly seen much of his own life flash before me, but not how it ended.

"No, I don't . . ."

"Well, let your grandmother and I remind you of the

events that led up to that day."

"Remind me?"

"Why, yes, sweetheart. You were there," Grandma said, patting my knee. "You were Grandpa's Guardian Angel."

"WHAT! I was assigned to be Grandpa's Guardian Angel?"

"You were a guardian angel to many before you went to earth, Lilly, and a very capable one, at that." Grandma's eyes caught mine, and the deep pools of blue registered pure and unconditional love for me, her granddaughter.

"You'll see, Lilly. You can see yourself in action." Chuckling, Grandpa raised his arm. With the palm of his right hand about two feet from my face, at eye level, I realized it had become a screen.

"PETACH!"

***

It is spring. Through an old screen door sunshine and crisp clean air stream inside the tiny, clapboard house. As Grandpa's guardian angel, I take a position in the corner, by the wood stove. At a small wooden table sit Great Grandpa and Great Grandma. Lillie is holding a teeny, newborn baby up to her breast, and he is eagerly nursing. That little bundle is Grandpa Benjamin, my father's father.

"I figure we have til nightfall tomorrow, Lillie, and then these wood floors could be under water. I will have to get you and the baby out tomorrow if we can't get control of it today."

"Teak, I'm too weak to walk. I lost too much blood, I don't know how. . ."

"Darlin, I'll get Ammon and we'll carry ya to his house. Hell, I'll take the door off the hinges and use it as a stretcher if I have to. But time's a wasting and I've got a hundred sandbags to fill."

"You gotta stay here with us and get some rest, Teak. You've been up almost two nights straight fighting this run off."

"Can't, Lil. Everyone else been up building dams, too."

For the rest of that day, and into the night, I am out, in the dark, watching a dozen ranchers working along with my great grandpa. It is a cold but calm evening, but close by is the roar of fast moving water cresting the banks of the Lewis Fork. The unseasonly warm temperatures have melted the snowpack prematurely, quickly turning the rivers and canals into rushing torrents of ice-cold water. They are filled to capacity, overflowing in many places. The water flows relentlessly over miles of range, drowning newborn calves and washing away precious topsoil. Moving oil lanterns from place to place, the ranchers shovel furiously, filling sandbags, setting canvas dams, everything they can think of to divert the water off their land and keep it out of their homes.

Three a.m. comes and, having saved the ranch house from the water, Teancum–muddy and soaking wet–turns towards home. I follow closely behind, hearing the water sloshing in his boots, hearing his teeth chatter in the early morning hours.

Once again taking my place in front of the coal stove, I watch over them as they sleep. Teancum, Lillie and Benjamin, all in a little more than a single bed.

"Teak. Teak." Lillie, talking in low tones, is shaking her husband's shoulder.

"Teak. I am feeling real sick. Please, get me something to calm my stomach."

Nothing.

Lillie leans up on one elbow and brushes her hair away from her eyes. My grandmother is pale and shaking; tired and irritable.

"Teak, wake up! I swear you need more sleep than this new-born baby!"

Grandpa hears her this time and arises from the bed to tend to her and the baby. He rocks his baby son, keeps him content, and puts coal in the stove. Lillie sleeps.

Morning comes quickly and they change places. Lillie is up, fixing oatmeal. Teancum is stretched diagonally across the bed, dead to the world.

There is a knock at the door.

"Good morning, Mrs. Hunt. Sorry to bother you this early in the mornin', but is your husband home?"

"Yes," Grandma says in a whisper. "But he is resting. He's been fightin the flood waters for days."

"Well, our foreman sent us to fetch Teak. We need to go up Blodgett Canyon for a few days to fell a stand of trees. It's good money, Mrs. Hunt."

"What's a day's wages?"

"Three bucks a day, Mrs. Hunt. But if Teak can't go, we can ask down the road."

By the stove, I can see Grandma's face clearly. There is a battle going on inside her. Lillie turns away from the door and looks long at Teancum. Then she turns back to the men. Their little house is barren except for a bed, a table, two chairs, a wash basin and a stove. Above the stove are three narrow shelves filled with mostly empty canning jars. She looks at the exhausted man stretched across the bed. There is, indeed, a battle going on inside grandma, and necessity wins.

"Teak, Teak, honey, they've come to take you to fell trees."

***

Standing somewhere in the Bitterroot forest, I inhale deeply, smelling the fresh scent of pine. We are in the lower elevations, where the snowpack has retreated, leaving the ground soggy and difficult to move through.

One of the men, the designated faller, makes an undercut on the side of the tree that will fall to the ground. This faller is an expert. He can always drop a tree right where he wants it. Except today. Grandpa and some other men, the buckers, are cutting trunks of other trees into shorter lengths.

"T I M B E R R R."

Grandpa and the others look up to see the tree striking another one close by, making the second snap in two, like a matchstick. The massive tree teeters, indecisive only for a fleeting second, before its free-fall spells disaster for the loggers below. Down it comes. Men scramble every which way. Grandpa is slower; he tries to move away, stumbles over a branch in his path, and sinks to his knees. He looks up, understanding instantly that he is a dead man.

I break all rules as his assigned guardian angel. I don't care that today is his day to die. I sprint from the shadows to try to get to him, to shove him out of harm's way. I am too late. The trunk of the tree lands squarely across his back. S N A P. His body sinks two feet into the wet ground, the branches totally obscuring him. The logging crew is at the tree in mere seconds, frantically trying to get to him. But it was only Grandpa's body that remained there. I had already reached down to where he lay, waiting for his spirit to rise so we could be on our way.

Grandpa straightened, looking around to see what might be tethering him to the earth. Nothing could. Pausing to look back at his body one last time and to bid a silent farewell to his comrades–all furiously trying to rescue him–he takes my outstretched hand. Recognizing me, he smiles and I lead him home.

***

Grandma Lillie reached up, took grandpa's hand and closed it into a fist, ending the scene. Sky and I had been so engrossed, it took a few seconds to get oriented. We sat back and exchanged looks. Wow!

Grandma was looking directly at me. "On one hand, I remember Teak being so exhausted that morning. On the other hand, we mightily needed the $12.00. And I made the decision. I woke him, and he went."

"Lilly, I've told your grandma a thousand times none of it was her fault. It was my ti. . ."

"Ssshhh, Pa, I'm telling this story." Grandma put her finger to his lips. "I never saw him alive again, Lilly."

I felt so sad, so sorry for Grandma, but I had no words to comfort her.

"Don't you think I carried the weight of unbelievable regret, Lilly? Don't you think it was my fault he died?"

Grandpa slapped his knee in frustration. "Now, dag-nab-it, there you go again, Ma!"

I jumped into the fray. "Grandma, Grandpa is right. That wasn't your fault. It was an accident and. . .and, it was his designated time!"

Sky stood and, walking into the kitchen, mouthed to me, "Yeah, accidents ARE accidents."

Grandma studied her hands lying loosely in her lap, and then–sighing deeply–continued.

"I grieved for the longest time. I grieved for my dear son who would grow up with no father, for the wasted years I could not spend with Teancum. How very long it took me to forgive myself."

I didn't have the perspective there that I do from this side of the veil, Lilly." Grandma shrugged and reached out to take my hand. "All we can do is ask those we have hurt to forgive us, to please forgive us, and whether they do or don't becomes their issue. The crux is if we can forgive ourselves. So, you go ahead and grieve, Lilly, for a time. Somehow, grieving shuts a door on the past."

An infinite God can give all of Himself to each of His children.

He does not distribute Himself that each may have a part, but to each one He gives

All of Himself.

As fully as if there were no others.

–A. W. Tozer

CHAPTER TWENTY-SIX

Grandma was right, of course, I had to go find Helena. I stood now where several paths converged. Grandpa had said to take the farthest path to my right. I could be gliding along with the crowd above me, but I needed to walk, slowly. I needed to process.

I would grovel, beg, cajole, bargain with, do whatever it took to try to make it up to Helena for the accident, and for all the hatred and blame I had heaped on her.

A scene flashed through my mind, a scene I had just

recently lived. There I was with Dad, in Joe's cell. Joe was almost groveling at MY feet, pleading for my forgiveness. What had I said?

"Think, Lilly," I muttered under my breath. And then the words were there, playing back in my head: "And how are you going to make it up to me, Joe? From Hell, no less, and now that I am dead, too?"

And what had I told Dad?

"I can't be compelled to forgive just because someone asks me to!"

And there it was. Why should Helena forgive me? Hell would freeze over first, and beyond that, when would I ever be able to forgive myself? I would hopelessly, helplessly be stuck. Forever. My despair weighed like a stone in my heart, too heavy to carry, to even breathe around.

The path weaved through orchards of blossoming cherry trees. At some points there were slight hills to climb, just to level out on the other side. As I walked, fewer and fewer people were above or on the path with me.

Turning, I looked back. The hill on which my grandparent's home sat had shrunk into the distance long ago. How far had I walked? Eight, ten miles? By choosing the slow mode, I was postponing the inevitable. Even though my feet felt weighed down by cement blocks, I could not bring myself to lift into the air and glide.

Ahead of me was a lone figure, a guy, on whom I was

slowly gaining. Getting closer, I broke into a jog.

"Passing on your left," I called out. I was in no mood for chit-chat.

"Hello! In a hurry?"

I broke my pace and slowed, speaking over my shoulder.

"Yeah, kind of."

"How about I just pick up the pace, then, and we can walk together for a bit?"

"Dang," I muttered under my breath. How was I going to lose this guy?"

"Sure," I said with zero enthusiasm.

"Where are you headed?"

"To meet a friend. Well, no, not a friend, really. A. . . a person I need to talk to."

"Do you have a name?"

"It's Lilly." Double Dang. It wasn't like we were going to become fast friends or anything.

"Nice to meet you, Lilly. I'm Jesse."

Looking down at the path, I didn't respond. I didn't care that his name was Jesse.

"Lilly, are you okay?"

There was that lump again, the lump making it impossible to talk around. I shook my head no.

"I'm a good listener, Lilly. Try me."

I felt like I was carrying a backpack of rocks, and how I

longed to set it down. I glanced over at this guy's face and noted the relaxed way he walked. He looked nice enough; didn't seem like an uptight kind of guy. Sometimes it was good to unload with a stranger. And anyway, our paths would never cross again.

"Well, okay, I didn't mean to kill my best friend and my worst enemy, but yeah, I did, and my life review showed me that. And ever since I got here, I've been ranting and raving over what a mess-up Helena was, blaming the accident all on her, too cowardly to own my part in it."

I looked at Jesse. He was studying the ground as we walked, listening intently.

"So where do you think I am going now, Jesse?"

Before he could answer, I carried on. "I am going to find Helena and some how, some way, make it up to her. I'll do anything for her forgiveness." My voice died out. What was the point of finishing? I knew the end. After all, I'd had no intention of showing her any mercy, before I learned the truth.

"You're struggling aren't you, Lilly?"

I looked at him and nodded, my tears blurring out his face and the path we were on.

Jesse smiled warmly, and putting one arm around my shoulders, hugged me.

I looked at my walking companion more closely. Reddish brown hair. Mustache. Short beard. A nose too big for his face, but his wide smile and great blue eyes made up for it. I liked him. I did.

"Well, yeah, I am struggling. About Helena, she and I have been oil and water forever."

Jesse studied me for several seconds. "Do you think it's possible that you got the brunt of all the hard stuff that was going on in Helena's life?"

Helena? Hard stuff? Unless having to decide between Mazatlan or Puerto Vallarta for spring break constituted a hard life, I highly doubted it.

I conceded a bit. "Maybe."

Jesse looked at me, nodding his head.

"Lilly, when we don't feel good about ourselves, others pay. But when you, yourself, are hurting, it's easy to lose sight of that fact."

Our pace slowed, and we walked in silence for several minutes. A beautiful twilight had come to the Spirit World. Soft light radiated through the trees, the color of the bushes and plants fading to dim pastels. A mourning dove in the top of a nearby tree sang a comforting solo.

"Well, then, what do I do from here?"

Jesse stopped walking and faced me. "Does God love himself, Lilly?"

What a strange question. I had never thought about it. I wrinkled my face, thinking it through.

"Well, He is perfect, so yeah, why wouldn't He?"

"Good, Lilly. And, does He see himself worthy of that love?"

"Well. . . He has done some awesome things, so yes," I replied

"That is why He can love others. All others."

My brain's CPU was slowly processing this as I carried on my inner dialogue:

–If I see myself worthy of love, and I can love myself, then I can love every one. Even the Helenas; even me, a killer.

–So, the conclusion is. . . I didn't like the answer I was getting. I didn't like it because I knew I couldn't do it.

I turned to Jesse and stated flatly: "So I have to love myself in order to be able to love."

Taking a deep breath, I shook my head in resignation. I could never forgive myself, and if I couldn't do that, then loving Lilly Hunt was a real stretch.

"How can I forgive myself, Jesse, with what I've done? I'm such a mess! And how will I be punished for it? How many years in Spirit Prison?"

"It was an accident, Lilly. You did not intend that outcome. Don't you think He knows your heart? And He doesn't punish. People do that to themselves.

***

"There once was a village potter," Jesse smiled at me,

drawing me into his story. "He was known far and wide for throwing beautiful pots. He was such a master potter that he could create an incredible bowl or pitcher in very little time. But one day, he decided to slow down, take his time. Using his best clays, he created a true masterpiece. It was a perfect pitcher, perfectly weighted and proportioned, with a graceful pouring spout and a delicate but strong handle. He applied a dramatic glaze, creating a gorgeous red patina after it was fired. Of all his work, this was his best, his favorite. He vowed he would never sell it, and he put it in his shop window where all the passersby could stop and admire the faultless work of art.

"One day, when a customer came into the shop a gust of wind caught the door, slamming it hard against its frame. The pitcher toppled from its shelf to the floor and broke into a hundred pieces. It was a real mess."

Jesse laughed and gently pushed me off the path. "Isn't that what you called yourself? A 'real mess'?"

I pushed him back and felt the load of rocks lighten.

"Well, Lilly, the customer was mortified and offered to pay for it, but the potter declined. The potter simply knelt and gingerly, tenderly picked up each and every last shard, no matter how small. Late that night, after the shops were all closed for the evening, the potter laid out all the pieces onto his work table and carefully, meticulously glued the pitcher back together. It was the wee hours of the morning before he was done and he lovingly placed it in a protected place at the front of his shop.

" 'What a shame,' a customer said the following day when she saw his masterpiece all cracked and glued back together.' You could have asked much for the pitcher when it was perfect; but now, it is broken. . .' she shook her head. 'It is worthless, no?'

" 'Not so,' said the potter. 'Come tomorrow, just before sunrise, and you will see for yourself.'

"His customer, curious to know what a rising sun could possibly have to do with a patched-up pitcher arrived at his door just before dawn.

" 'Now watch,' the potter said. The shop window, facing to the East, caught the first rays of the rising sun. The sun beams flooded the old shop, and directly in their path was the potter's masterpiece. Shining through the cracks in the pitcher, the light danced on the walls of the shop, reflecting back a kaleidoscope of shapes and colors. The customer stood breathless, awed at the sight before her.

" 'It is beautiful. I will buy it. What do you want for it?'

"' Aaah, it is not for sale,' the potter replied. 'The cracks let the light of the sun in. I will leave it here for all to enjoy.' "

***

We walked quietly for a few minutes and then my eyes widened as the light clicked on. I put my hand on his arm.

"Am I that pitcher, Jesse?"

"All of our Father's children are that pitcher, Lilly. And if you can hang onto the truth of that, you'll feel more peace should you go back."

I stopped mid-step. How could he have possibly known that going back was even an option?

"Oh, I'm not going back, Jesse. There's no reason to. Sam, Dad, Jason, Sky, dancing, even, are all here. Why should I go back? What does it matter?"

Jesse's eyes locked with mine. "It matters, Lilly. It very much matters to many, many others. But you have your free will. Heaven is all about love, and love does not force."

Jesse slowed and stopped at another crossroad. He pointed to a far-away hill.

"I go this way, Lilly."

"And I'm going that way." I smiled shyly, pointing in the opposite direction. We'd had such a brief encounter, yet we'd shared so much. I liked this man, Jesse. He was so easy to talk to.

He extended his hand to shake mine, but impulsively I stepped forward to give him a big hug. Suddenly, I was enveloped in his complete embrace. My miniscule glow blended with Jesse's into just one big, white orb. How, I knew not, but his countenance changed, now shining brighter than the noonday sun. Pulling back, I realized that his hair, once red, was now whiter than snow. And his blue eyes, now like flames of fire, penetrated mine. From the middle of my soul I knew that standing before me was the Being Mom had always talked to. Standing before me was the Being I had seldom talked to–Christ. I was overwhelmed by His love for me. It was palpable.

Christ held me at arm's length and with a deep, penetrating gaze, spoke to my heart:

"You are precious to me."

I gasped. Those words, that voice! It had been He! It was Christ who had come that awful day to my uncle's house.

***

The little attic window is open. An ivory eyelet curtain waves gently in the summer breeze. Through the window a brilliant light comes, filling the room. But it is not just light spilling into the room. It is a man, a man made of light.

He kneels down; we are eye-to-eye. He looks at me, with his beautiful blue eyes. "You precious child; you precious, precious child."

My spirit lifts up and out, separating from my body. He stands and, lifting me up, I wrap my arms tightly around

His neck. He carries me away, away from the room, away from the ranch for a time, protecting me as much as possible from what would come next.

***

And now, He was here to help me again. In His arms, I know. I know that I am forgiven. Feeling how perfectly and completely He loves me, I realize that to not forgive myself would be like flinging His gift to me back in His face.

"Did I not come to you, then, Lilly? And will I not always come when you need me?"

Giving me another long embrace, Christ stepped back and once again pointed to that far-away hill.

"You are greatly loved, Lilly. Remember, it's the cracks that let the light of the Son in."

And then, He–my Lord–was gone.

An Unexamined Life

Is Not Worth Living.

– Socrates

CHAPTER TWENTY-SEVEN

My eyes followed him until He was out of sight.

The meadow in which I stood was aglow, and I wondered how it was that He had left some of His light with me. I twirled, and the light swirled around me, brightening the path several yards ahead of me.

"Wow, you were always beautiful, but now, you're stunning!"

Sam! I turned to see him approaching quickly from behind me, a big grin on his handsome face.

"Sam, I met Him! I was with Him, Sam!" I grabbed Sam's shoulders with both hands, and dropping my voice to a whisper and pointing to the ground where we stood, I exclaimed, "He was right here!"

Sam grabbed me around the waist, and picking me up, spun me around. "I know, I know, Lil! Isn't He incredible, Lilly? When I met Him, I knew I would never be the same, nor will you. Look at your robe, Lil. Your robe is made of light!"

***

Sam and I searched high and low for Helena, just to be told that Helena was last seen in what was referred to as "The In-Between." It would take an explanation from Jason for me to grasp what the 'in-between' was. We found Jason, in one of those rare moments without Analeise. He and Sky were indulging in white chocolate, macadamia cheesecake on the patio of Sky's favorite café.

Sky pointed her cake-laden fork at me. "Remember me describing the tunnel I passed through between the earth and here?

"Well, yeah. So?"

"That's the 'In-Between,'" Jason replied. "I suppose Helena, for whatever reason, decided to stay close to the earth plane."

"But why? Why would Helena, once seeing how glorious the Spirit World is, choose to go back?"

Jason shrugged. "Maybe she thinks she has some sort of unfinished business with someone on earth."

I shuddered. Somehow that was worrying.

"Like what?" I needed some reassurance that Helena was at least acting rational.

Sky spoke up. "I can understand that. Maybe, because her death was so sudden and unexpected. . ." She looked at me sideways, mouthing the word S-O-R-R-Y. . . "Helena wants to somehow comfort her family."

"Being a spirit," Jason expounded, "means, though, that her thoughts and feelings are magnified–like ours are here. Earthbound spirits can be pretty determined to get what they're going after."

My vibes were yelling: DANGER! DANGER! I tried to get a grip and swallow the fear settling in my throat. Where was this weird reaction coming from? I wasn't returning to earth, so I certainly wouldn't be bumping into her there! And some day she would be back here. Then I would find her, and I would most surely do anything and everything to make amends.

"So, what now, Lil?" Jason asked.

"So, now it's back to finish my Life Review." I said this feeling absolutely no dread. After my talk with Christ, I saw my life, and all its foibles, for what it was: A series of soul lessons.

"Would you all be so kind to accompany me to the steps of the theatre once again? I need to see when the next showing is in Room 209."

***

"We left off at the. . ." Mr. Montague consulted his notes.

"The accident," I offered.

"Well, yes, that. So, we'll start from there."

Once again, in a voice of authority, Mr. Montague made the command, "PETACH."

And once again a lid at the parietal part of my skull popped open, and an unwinding began.

I hated it, but–there on the large screen before me–I watched it all:

We roll, Sky is thrown. But this time I notice a detail I hadn't seen before. Sky's spirit leaves her body before she ever hits the wind shield. And then Sky, after checking out her own lifeless form on the ground, takes off into a wide conduit that opens up directly over her. I realized Sky had never felt a thing.

Helena and I, however, are lifted into the back of an ambulance. Helena dies on the way, never regaining consciousness. I, alone, reach the hospital alive.

Before me now is the hospital room, and there I am in

my coma. Mom hovers over me for several weeks, and there, too, is Luke. I had no idea that he was there almost as much as Mom, singing to me, telling me his silly jokes, holding my hand.

I come to and start feeling better until I hear about Sky and Helena, and then I pop the pills. Stupid!

Dr. Kimball looks at my red-hot leg and tells me to gear up for more surgery. Afterwards, I'm wheeled back to my room.

An alarm blares. I look to the screen to see a flat line moving horizontally across the monitor. A nurse slams open the heavy door and runs to my bed. Looking at me, she pushes another button and a programmed voice blares through the halls of the hospital:

'Code Blue! Code Blue!'

She runs to the hall and yells down the corridor, 'Crash Cart! STAT!'

I turn to look at the panel. They are still staring above my head at the screen. Come on, this movie should be ending any minute now. After-all, this was a life review, not a death review. Did I have to sit through the funeral, too?

I turn just in time to see me being wheeled back into surgery. The doctor is telling those around the operating table that he's not able to repair my ruptured spleen. It will have to be removed.

Now in the ICU, Dr. Kimball is telling Mom that I almost bled out. They can only hope that my kidneys won't shut down because the shock usually kills a person.

"Shock. Shock," I whisper under my breath. So that is what killed me.

Now back to my regular room, with machines still circling my bed.

Enter Luke now, backing in end first, with McDonalds for their midnight snack. Luke, bending over and picking up a scrabble piece.

Now, Mom and Luke having their heart-to-heart talk. That is where I had said that I was outta there, for good, and I had come back to Heaven to stay.

So, I must have breathed my last breath right after this, right? Again, I turn in my chair to watch Mr. Montague.

"Uh, excuse me, Mr. Montague?"

The lights go up.

"Do I have to sit through my funeral? I would rather not, if that's okay?" I certainly didn't want to see Mom and Luke feeling sad.

The panel–all of them–sat there mute, staring at me.

Mr. Montague cleared his throat. "Well, yes, Ms. Hunt. None of us are going to be sitting through your funeral, because. . ." He looked to his right and left and got a universal nod from his associates. "Because, there hasn't been a funeral; at least, not yet."

"What!" My temples bulging, my face bright red, I shot

to my feet. "What are you saying? I'm NOT dead?"

"No, Ms. Hunt." Consulting his papers, Mr. Montague continued. "There has not been a cessation of heartbeat and there is measurable electrical activity in your brain. No, you are not dead."

I wasn't getting my head around this. "Do you mean I am still in that stupid hospital bed, after all this time?"

"Ms, Hunt, from the time your spirit left your body until right this very moment has been. . . ." He checked a watch on his wrist. . ."Has been, in Earth time, only forty-eight hours. Two days, Lilly."

Two days? HOW was this possible? Two days were. . . I struggled to find the words to describe this anomaly. . . Two days were just a pitiful, paltry piece of time. How could that be? I had lived a life-time here, a wonderful, magical lifetime.

"You have a decision to make, Lilly."

I sank into the chair, covering my face with my hands.

"I already made my decision," I whispered under my breath. Why were they making this so hard?

"Excuse me? We didn't hear you, Lilly."

I sat up and looked at the panel. Speaking louder, I repeated. "What decision do I have to make?" The question came out flat. Looking down at my hands, weak in my lap, I shook my head ruefully. All this time. ALL this time flitting around Heaven. And I was never dead.

A third woman, with striking features and raven black hair, spoke very slowly.

"You know, Lilly dear, your returning here was indeed premature, and it is not yet your time. But we certainly will not make your decision for you. It is your choice. We will not intervene."

What was the right thing to do? Did it even matter? Of course, it did. Christ had taught me that. Everything matters. The thought of leaving this magnificent world was almost unbearable. Just as I was discovering who I really was, the Lilly who could forgive and love, I would have to return to a world that was seriously lacking in both.

"But there will be consequences either way, won't there?" I addressed the panel once more.

"Ms. Hunt, there are always consequences," Mr. Montague replied gently.

Ms. Ravenhair took a turn now. "The unknown is always scary. You know what awaits you here. But going back?" She nodded her head in understanding.

Mr. Montague took over. "But then again, Lilly, we panel members who have been here for a long, long time, have come to realize that everything seems to happen for a reason. Nevertheless, we know this has been hard for you. And because of that, Lilly, we'd like to give you an overview of what awaits you back home should you choose to go back."

He again referred to his notes, reading each line carefully. "Going back into your body may be excruciating, painful."

Looking at the alarm on my face, he hurried on. "But you will heal. . . . ."

"How much will I heal? Enough to be a dancer?"

Long pause.

"We can't tell you that, Lilly. That is not something you can know."

I swallowed back. "Understood. Go on."

Mr. Montague continued. "All the skills you regained upon returning here will leave you: The ability to levitate. . ."

He went on, listing all of the many, incredible things my spirit had relearned to do, and that were now being stripped from me: No more thought travel, no more telepathy–and just as I had finally mastered it. No more dancing all night with Sam, sans the blisters and aching muscles. No more eating the incredible food with no thought of calories or fat content. No more verbal sparring with Sophie. No more passing through walls. A foreboding came over me. I was relinquishing everything magical.

"You may remember all or some of your experiences here, Lilly, or you may not. A power higher than us determines what memories are key to take back with you. We do not know what will remain and what will leave your conscious mind."

Not remember meeting Christ? Not remember finding Sam? Not remember spending time with Dad, Sky, and Jason? Not remember my grandparents? I slumped into the chair. I would not choose to go back. Not ever.

"This all seems a little daunting, I know, Lilly."

Mr. Montague flipped through more pages, quickly scanning over the words.

"There are a lot of wonderful reasons to go back, Ms. Hunt. There will be many lives impacted if you are not a part of those lives. Mostly, Lilly, if you choose to learn from life's lessons, you will fulfill the specific mission assigned you. You are not to worry about what your mission is. It will be done according to its time."

Mr. Montague closed the folder firmly and set it aside. He sat back in his chair and, with the other members of the panel, waited.

Gripping the sides of the chair, I rocked back and forth, studying the warm yellow glow of the alabaster floor beneath me.

Stay. Sam. I could never leave Sam.

Go. There was a reason it was not my time to be here, and it mattered.

Stay. Dad and I had just found each other again. We needed to make up for so much lost time.

Go. Maybe I really couldn't be at peace knowing I had

not finished.

One lone tear rolled down my cheek. It clung tenaciously to my chin for as long as it could, and then–resolved to the inevitable–fell down, down, down to the hard, cold, alabaster floor.

I may not have gone

Where I intended to go, but

I think I have ended up where I needed to be.

– Douglas

CHAPTER TWENTY-EIGHT

If I was going, then that was that. Absolutely no goodbyes, for I knew that if I so much as looked into Sam's eyes, all resolve would disappear. I would just go and be done with it. I hoped everyone would understand. Here, in Heaven, I had learned that I could do many hard things, but saying goodbye–to Sam, Sky, everyone–was not one I could do.

Streaking above the crowds, I searched for the exact spot in which I had entered the Spirit World. The day was not unlike the first day I had arrived here. Then and now, the warmth, the fragrant air, the soft breeze, the glorious blue of the sky all spoke to where I was. This was indeed Heaven, and I was leaving it. The veil was before me, stretching from one horizon to the other. And unlike when I first arrived, it would no longer move beyond my grasp. Oh, how I wished it would.

I slowed as I reached my portal. Obviously, there were no secrets in Heaven, for before me stood a few of the precious people who made up my identity, my life. They were here now, to send me off. This would make it s-o-o-o very much harder. Sam was at my side, wrapping his arms tightly around my waist.

Dad stepped forward, his jaw set, resolute, struggling not to cry.

"Lilly, you and your mom no longer have to worry about money. It's been taken care of. Remember what I'm telling you; you'll see."

I stared at Dad. How could Dad have possibly taken care of our money worries from Heaven?

Dad smiled a big smile and embraced me. "The healing for guilt is forgiveness, sweetheart, and you are looking at a free man."

"I am looking at my hero, Dad. I love you."

Dad motioned for Jason and Analeise to step forward. Jason gave me one of his bear hugs and kissed my cheek.

"Be good, and don't hurry back! And oh, ya, tell Luke hello for me!"

I felt Sam's arm tighten around my waist at the mention of Luke's name. I looked up at him, but he stared straight ahead.

"Sam? What's. . ."

Something small and furry was working its way between my legs. Looking down, my eyes met the deep, brown eyes of my beloved Sophie. Her tail was wagging furiously as I bent down and picked up her wiggling torso. Burying her wet nose in my neck, she covered my face with her tongue.

"Remember, Sophie-girl, you're my favorite."

Sky took Sophie from me and, in her classic way, tried to lighten the mood. "You'd better be able to see dead people!"

"I'll do my best, Sky. I promise!"

"Guess what new assignment I have recently been given?" Sky was looking rather smug.

"Gossip columnist? Gatekeeper? Party Planner? I give! What?"

"Wellllllll. . . . ." Sky was doing a masterful job of building the suspense. "There are many angels assigned to help us on earth, as you well know. I applied to be your Guardian Angel, but Grandpa Teancum already hogged THAT job. So, I have been assigned to be one of your Teachers!"

"One of my teachers? I'm thinking, Sky, that I have pretty much learned how Heaven works."

"Not Heaven, duh! EARTH! How to navigate around back on earth!" Sky squealed with delight. "Oh, the possibilities! I can help with directions–you know how you get lost! And tests! When you're taking tests I can. . . . ."

"Alright, already! I get it!" Stepping back, I let my fears take over again. "And just how are you going to do this, Sky? How will I know it's you and that you're around, if I really can't see dead people?"

"SYNCRONOCITY, Girl! When you think its coincidence, it will be so much more than coincidence! When it just 'pops' into your head to look in the couch cushion for your keys; when you take a wrong turn and pass by the perfect apartment in New York, and you see the 'FOR RENT' sign, that will be me! If it seems like a weird occurrence, MY fingerprints will be all over it."

She was beaming! Never doubting, always confident, full of enthusiasm and light! That was Skylar.

Every one and every thing faded away, and all I saw before me was the face that I had studied, and kissed, and cradled in my hands. Sam's face.

"I cannot do this, Sam. I simply cannot do this." I pressed my face against his chest as tears streamed down my cheeks. "I am going to tell them I'm staying."

"Sssshhh, Lilly. This is just for a short time, Lil. We can

do this." Sam lifted my chin. "Look at me, Lillybug. You need to remember this! When you return for real, there will be only one question. Here's that question: How much did you love in your life? If you go back, you will have a whole life time to practice love. And," Sam said, with a wide smile, "when you die, look out, because, oh boy, are we going to live!"

"Will you stay close to me? What if you forget me?"

Sam shook his head, giving me an incredulous look.

"Lilly, you're talking to Sam, remember? Lilly, I am bound to you by all the memories we shared before we ever went down. I have all the memories of us since you've been back. These are the ties that bind, Lil. These are ties that only the powers of Heaven could break. And I am so deeply grateful that you and I have had each other for so very long." Running his hands through my hair, Sam kissed the top of my head, my face, my mouth.

"Oh, Lillybug, If I can petition the powers that be, I promise I'll be close, to protect you, to protect those you love. Always. When a breeze brushes your cheek and tousles your hair, know that I am right there, whispering your name. My love for you is eternal."

I took Sam by the shoulders and talked inches from his face. "You talk of memories, but I may not have those memories, Sam! I may not remember you for the next seventy or more years of my earth life! It could be 'Sam Who?'

Don't you get it?"

Sam moved away and held me at arm's length. I saw the determination, heard the strength behind his voice as his eyes penetrated mine.

"Oh, I get it, Lilly; I do. There's a lot of 'ya, buts', and 'what if's'. But you and I, Lil. . ." Sam's voice cracked, betraying his tough exterior. "We will trust. You and I will leave it to Heaven."

Sam stepped forward, and finding an opening in the veil, parted it.

Time was up. I could no longer cling to my life here. Tears flowing, I grasped the veil. With quivering lips I whispered, "Earth" and–not looking back–I stepped through.

***

Voila! I was levitating only inches below the ceiling, in a corner of Room 430. The bathroom light, casting a sliver of light to the cot where Mom lay, was the only illumination. From my vantage point, I could see a familiar figure in the hospital bed, under a blanket.

I was terrified. 'Excruciating pain' Mr. Montague had said. My body looked so beaten up, so heavy and stinky. And here I was in spirit, light, airy, and smelling like fresh heavenly flowers.

But I had made a commitment, and before I lost all nerve, I had to do this. I had to rejoin my body.

"Not so fast!"

I spun around. In the opposite corner of the room another spirit levitated just below the ceiling. Helena.

"Helena! What are you doing here? Sam and I looked and looked for you. I wanted to. . ."

"You didn't find me, obviously, being as I am here in your hospital room, Lilly. I've been here, with your dear mother, waiting for you. You certainly took your time."

My mind was racing. Dirty energy swirled around Helena. Fearful and angry emotions poured from her, leaving her mouth and face distorted. What had Jason said about spirits who choose to stay in the In-Between? I remembered it wasn't good. And now, even after having experienced the peace, love, and the perspective of the Spirit World, Helena was still choosing to be Helena.

Trying to hang on to all my own newly learned lessons, I gently, but firmly, tried again. "Okay, Helena, let's be straight up. Why are you here?"

"The question is, Lilly, why are YOU here? You caused the accident! You should be dead and your body buried in the cold ground. But no, you actually have a body to come back to. You still get to live! You still get to dance! Where's MY body, Lilly?"

Venom dripped from every word. Her eyes drilled into mine. Did she really expect an answer? She waited.

"I. . . . your body is. . . Helena, I am so, so sorry. Please forgive me. Please! I would do anything. . . ."

"Anything? ANYTHING, Lilly? Are you saying you would do anything to make it up to me?"

Tears sprang to my eyes. I would; I most certainly would. I wanted to hug Helena, look into her eyes and tell her how sorry I was. Love and compassion flowed from me to her. At one time I was convinced she was a literal spawn of Satan, but now I loved her as I loved Sky.

"I will if I can, Helena. I'm not sure how to. . . ."

I was cut off instantly.

"Oh, but I do, Lilly! I know how you can make it up to me!" Helena turned and pointed to my body. "That's how!"

I was dumbstruck. What was she asking? I looked from Helena to the three-dimensional me in the bed. I looked back to Helena.

"You can't be serious, Helena. You want to enter MY body?"

"How sorry are you, Lilly? Didn't you say you would do anything? How else are you going to even remotely make this up to me? You are the only one out of the three of us who even got a choice. I want your body. I wasn't ready to die, and I want it. Now!"

There was that question again; the very one Sky and I had deliberated over on Selsia. Can a spirit have the use of two bodies? Can a spirit give her body to another spirit? I knew I had a stewardship over my body. I shook my head. I didn't think I could do this.

Helena intercepted my thoughts.

"No one can stop you, Lilly! It's YOUR body! You want forgiveness from me? Well, this is how you're going to get my forgiveness. Period!"

I was processing the pro's and con's here: Without my body, I would need to return to Heaven, and then I could be with Sam. Without my broken, physical body, I could dance in Heaven all I wanted. And, without Helena's forgiveness, I could not progress.

Those were three powerful reasons to just turn my body over to her.

Mom stirred in the cot below, tucking her blanket under her chin before she once again lapsed into a sound sleep.

Mom! Certainly Mom would be able to tell that it wasn't me in there! Helena was even witchier than I. Mom would think I had constant PMS.

I looked at my greasy hair, my stinky body–much in need of a bath–and then back to Helena. I shook my head in frustration. She wanted to be back on Earth so badly and I wanted to be back in Heaven so badly. What was I missing?

"Why do you want my body so badly, Helena? What is keeping you here?"

Helena's face froze. She stared, unblinking, into space,

seeing something I could not see. There was only one way I could know. In an instant I was at Helena's side, tightly embracing her.

Images flew through my mind, hundreds within a matter of seconds: Helena as a child, being picked up and held by her mother; Helena as an adolescent, staring at a pile of smoking cinders.

Helena shoved me away so forcefully I bounced against the opposite wall.

"Get away from me! Stay out of my head," she screamed.

I was stunned, not only by the force of her anger towards me, but of what I had managed to see.

He who cannot forgive

Breaks the bridge

Over which he, himself,

Must pass

—George Herbert

CHAPTER TWENTY-NINE

Everyone knew that Helena lived with her father and a stepmother and had quit asking her a long time ago where her mother was. But because Helena climbed on a plane every month and flew to California by herself, it was assumed she was visiting her mother. I certainly hadn't cared enough to ask. But now, I knew. No one could make up this stuff. Life really could be stranger, and sadder, than fiction:

Loss # 1: Helena's father left her mother–and Helena–

for another woman.

Loss # 2: Helena's and her mother's home burned to the ground in one of those infamous California wildfires.

Loss # 3: Helena's mother, only thirty-three, suffered a debilitating brain hemorrhage, never to recover. Helena was barely eleven.

Loss # 4: Helena moved to Montana with her father and step-mother, leaving her mother in a care center in California.

What had Christ asked me about getting the brunt of Helena's 'hard stuff'? He had patiently and lovingly waited for me to care enough about Helena to discover the truth.

My heart ached. I so very much wanted to hug her, to tell her that we could meet on common ground.

"Oh, Helena, I get it! I get it now! I know all about loss. We throw up walls, we strike back, we try to hurt like we've been hurt." I moved towards her, my arms reaching out to her, but then I stopped short, not sure what she would do.

"Can't you set it down, Helena? You and I, we aren't broken. We don't need to be fixed. We just need to be healed."

Helena's eyes, staring past me, were deep pools of fear and grief. "Who will take care of her? Mother won't know where I've gone. She'll think I've abandoned her, too; and I haven't, I haven't."

I was seeing a Helena that she had allowed no one to see. She looked liked a lost, heartbroken child. For a moment, she softened, her posture sagging. Helena looked so very tired, worn out from carrying her own backpack of rocks for so very long.

Where was Skylar at a time like this! Wasn't she supposed to be my Official Teacher!

"I'm right here." Sky was at my side.

I looked at my lateral self again and then at Helena.

Turning to Sky, I said, "I am going to give Helena my body. I know there will be some kind of consequence, but I need to do this."

"Lil, it's not that easy; it's gonna get complicated. . ." Sky shook her head.

I sensed a motion below me. Through the heavy hospital door came another spirit. But this spirit was different. It was a little girl. She looked about three years old, with blue eyes and honey-blonde hair. Walking on tip-toe, she spun and bounced and flounced into the room. She stopped at the cot, studying Mom's face for a moment before she bent over and kissed her lightly on the cheek. She then got in two more twirls before climbing onto the bed right beside me. Pressing her little body into my side, she lay there as though waiting for me to awake.

"Well, it's certainly getting crowded in here." I nudged Sky and pointed towards the bed.

"What are you talking about?" Sky looked clueless.

"That little girl on the bed by me!"

Sky stared at the bed.

"You can't see her? She's right there! Look HARDER!" Why was Sky choosing now to be difficult?

"I am looking, Lilly! There's no one there!"

"Well, then, what IS going on here?" I threw up my hands in total frustration.

"I know you hate it when I do this, Lilly, but it appears you need to have your memory refreshed from Heaven 560. When you see something no else sees, what is that called?"

"An hallucination? A mirage?" I was in no mood to take an oral quiz with Helena having a melt-down across the ceiling from me.

"Try a VISION," Sky prompted. "Now I would think that if you are seeing something no one else can see, you might want to ask yourself 'why'. Why would it be important for Heaven to send you a vision?"

Sky had a point there. This was getting heavy duty. Who was this child and why was she here? I studied her some more and then the epiphany came in the words of Christ.

'For others, your going back will very much matter.'

I gasped, and turning back to the little girl on my bed, I studied her every feature: Round face, big eyes. My eyes.

Now I was resolute.

I projected to Sky. "I understand now, in part, why I was to return."

"Helena. . ."

I took a deep breath, bracing myself for the verbal assault that most certainly would come my way. Drawing strength from Sky's presence, I started again. "Helena, I don't think I can do that. As much as I want to make everything up to you, I don't think I can just hand over my body."

Helena's whole demeanor hardened. Any softness, any yielding was gone in an instant. She spit out her response.

"I WILL get even! You thought I made your life miserable before! You could at least SEE me then! Then I didn't have the. . . the. . . should we say 'freedom of expression' that I have now? And oh, do I know how to use it! I'll be your worst nightmare."

Helena threw her head back in a maniacal laugh. "I will make The Sixth Sense look like a Disney movie! You'll see dead people, alright! Lots of them!

"When you feel someone is watching you, and you turn to see no one there, it will be me!

"When your bedroom door creaks in the night, it will be me behind it.

"When a bookcase falls over, it will be me. Will you be under it? Gosh, Lil, I don't know." Helena shrugged her shoulders in mock concern.

Sky, temporarily spellbound at Helena's performance, looked sideways at me. She found a sniveling, trembling spirit. Helena's unrelenting rant was draining the life force right out of me.

"LILLY! Get a grip! Helena and all other earthbound ghosts thrive on fear energy. The more fear you have, the more strength you give her! Do Not Give Her Your Power!"

Helena was there, in front of me, inches from my face.

"You're going to wish you'd died in the accident, Lil. Really."

And then POOF! She was gone. I think.

***

I entered through the top of my head. Freezing, my teeth started chattering. Reaching for the covers, I realized my arms, my hands, were stiff, heavy as lead. I winced as a dull, thudding pain came flooding into my conscious mind.

How quickly I had forgotten cold and pain when on the other side of the veil, where neither had existed, and where I was able to do anything, to go anywhere. I was now imprisoned in a heavy blob of clay. Not having been encased in skin for the longest time, I felt like a stuffed sausage. Hating the sensation of my entire body making contact with the stiff sheets on the bed, I tried to levitate above them. No go.

Having drooled in my sleep, my matted, tangled hair was now stuck to the side of my face. Swallowing back my saliva, I became aware of the revolting taste in my mouth. No doubt my breath smelled like rotten gym socks. To sum it up, my body was disgusting. I wanted no part of it. I kept my eyes shut, trying to block out all sensations of my body, trying to will myself to once again pass through the portal at the top of my head, and leave this room, this world. Nothing happened. I was trapped. The sound of my heart beating heavily in my chest confirmed it.

Lub-dub. Lub-dub. Inhale. Exhale. Lub-dub. Lub-dub.

Why had I exchanged a spirit of light for a body of blood and bones? How quickly I had forgotten that blood spills out and bones break. A heavy blanket of depression settled over me.

"Jesse, Sam, I can't do this. Please let me come home; please, let me. . . ."

"Lilly, sssssh. We are going home, sweetheart. Dr. Kimball said you will be released really soon now. They have finally fixed everything."

It was Mom's voice. Now there were other voices, farther from me.

"I'm here, Lilly." This was Sky's voice. "Remember how

fast you and I could get to Earth and back? I'll stay close. Promise! And watch for those synchronicities, okay? Don't you just love that word?"

"Is she awake?"

"Yes," Mom said, responding to someone. "I was resting and I heard her talking. She so wants to go home."

I felt a warm hand touching my arm.

"Hey, Lilly. Can you hear us? It was Luke's voice, talking louder now. "Earth calling Lilly!"

"Luke? Mom?" I opened my eyes to see two huge smiles inches from my face.

"We're here, Lil! You had some complications. The last few days have been a tad rough, sweetie, but you're on the mend now. Soon, you and I can actually go home." I could tell Mom was crying behind her smile.

"Yeah, Lilly, we're going to break out of this place and go have some fun." Luke squeezed my hand.

"Is Sky still here?" My words came out in a slur. Sky must have been in the room. I had heard her voice. Something about how fast we'd gotten here. Where? Where was here?

I slowly turned my head, and tried to lift it to look around the room. So heavy. So very heavy. I moved the fingers of my right hand. A strong hand grasped mine. So tired. So very tired. Closing my eyes, I had just one request before sleep took me.

"Don't let go of my hand, Sam. Promise you won't let go of my hand."

Dwell in Possibilities

– Emily Dickinson

CHAPTER THIRTY

From my wheel chair parked directly in front of the window, I felt the warmth of the sun on my face. Outside my hospital window, a Chinook wind had blessed Missoula with an early spring day. The branches of a tree, with teeny buds starting to appear, waved to me in the breeze. A clear blue sky made the perfect backdrop. It had been almost two weeks since I had awakened from my last surgery. I felt rested. The deep-down, bone tired was gone. Enough strength had returned to enable me to sit up, to even swing my injured leg–heavy in a cast–over the side of the bed, and with help, practice using crutches. I ate like a horse. Everything Luke brought me, I devoured. I knew I was finally on the upswing. I was healing quickly now. Healing, and changing.

Somehow, I knew I was different. From the time of the accident until now was a little more than two months, but I felt old; at least older. It was hard to get my head around it.

The parking lot outside my window was filling up with cars, probably visitors coming to see a special someone who played a key part in their dance. This was a new perspective for me, certainly not one I had entertained before the accident. But then, lying in bed days on end had given me a lot of time to think. The accident, and almost dying, had made me realize that life was not at all as I had perceived it. There were many dancers, many styles of dances, with innumerable dances being performed simultaneously on the stage of life. And who was to say that one dancer was any better than another? No longer did I think it was just my stage. It was everyone's stage, and we were all just inexperienced dancers bumping up against each other, and–for the most part–trying to get our steps down, and trying to do our best. That was all. And that was enough.

And now, today, I was to learn a new dance. Soon I would be out in that fresh March air, being wheeled to that parking lot. Today we were going home.

Turning from the window, I rolled my chair towards the bathroom where Mom was combing her hair. Mom had been very thorough in answering all my questions. I had barely remembered the infection that had settled into my ankle bone, causing me to have more surgery. From there everything was a blank until I woke up to see Mom and Luke hovering inches above my face, reassuring me that soon this day would come.

Mom told me that the surgery to take care of the osteomylitis had gone well. But, in the middle of that night, when the nurse had come in to check on me, I was not responsive; simply, I was bleeding to death. Back to surgery to discover and remove a damaged spleen. Once again seeing me hooked up to a bunch of machines, Mom's faith–for the first time ever–had started to falter, she said. Mom started planning my funeral. But two days later, I rallied, and she threw my funeral notes away.

Having to be on major antibiotics for a couple of weeks made me loiter in the hospital longer, but now I had been given the green light. As Luke had said, 'we were breaking out.' Once home, I would soon graduate to a walking cast and–when it came off–the doctors would see how well my ankle had healed. I wasn't going to think about it. That day would come soon enough.

There was a day, however, that couldn't come too soon

for Alli or for me. She had stopped by just yesterday. Seeing Alli made me miss Sky that much more. We clung to each other and cried.

But Alli had some news to share with me. It had taken the past twenty-four hours for me to come to grips with that news. Alex, Missing In Action–at least from my life–was being charged with attempted rape. His court date was coming up. Alli thought I would be so mad at her. But no, now that my head had stopped spinning, I admired her guts in going after the scumbag. There were no witnesses, so it would be her word against his.

"You were right, Sky." I whispered. "You knew all along who and what Alex was." Yes, indeed, if Sky were here, she would have loved to hear my admission. A lot.

Mom, what are we waiting for?"

Throwing her comb in her make-up bag, Mom turned to me and smiled. "I've got everything boxed up and ready to be hauled to the car, Lil. We're just waiting for staff to help us to the elevator with all this stuff."

Mom waved her arms at all the boxes piled on her cot, all filled with magazines, flower vases, the old journals she had shared with me, stacks of cards and letters from my friends, even dead roses that had dried nicely enough to keep. She squeezed in between them and let go a deep sigh.

How I loved Mom. What a strong woman she was. Not

only had she endured my roller coaster ride, but she also had to accept the fact that her boyfriend, Carl, had just up and disappeared on her. No note; no call; nothing. Mom was devastated, I was ecstatic; and Luke, looking like he knew more than he let on, wasn't talking.

"Lil, may I share something with you?"

I knew that look. At one time I would have tuned Mom out. Not anymore. I was all too thankful to be alive, so thankful to hang out with my Mom, even.

"I don't want you worrying about all the expense of this little adventure you have had, Lil. I just want you to focus on getting all the way better."

"How can I not worry, Mom, it must have cost a fort. . . ." I was immediately cut off.

"Yes, it has cost a small fortune, Lil. But, miraculously, we seem to have fallen into a small fortune."

I gave her a side-long glance. I couldn't have heard her right.

"When you were back in the ICU, I fell asleep in one of the recliners there. I had a dream, Lil. A most incredible dream."

My eyes were glued to Mom's face, waiting for further explanation. For some reason, her dreams were starting to have credibility with me.

"Your father came to me. I couldn't tell where we were, or what I was doing. He was just 'there' in my dream, looking and sounding just like Garrison."

I studied Mom. Whenever she talked about Dad, she looked years younger; there was love in her eyes, in her voice, the way she said his name.

"He said the strangest thing. He said, 'Lilly's Uncle Joe has something for her.'"

"Something for me? That's weird." I screwed up my face. "My Uncle Joe died when I was so young. I barely remember him."

Mom looked at me with a strained expression and kept going.

"Your dad told me to find the old watch fob in one of his dresser drawers, because on the chain was a small metal key. I rummaged through his drawers and finally found the watch. It was pretty hammered with the glass face cracked, the lid too bent to latch, but yes, there was a tiny key."

"A key? What for?" My heart started racing.

"Garrison told me to borrow a ladder tall enough to climb into the loft of the barn, because the stairs were rotting through. So I had Luke bring over a ladder and lean it up against the loft. Luke must have thought I had gone over the edge, but I said nothing about the dream.

"I hadn't been up there in the longest time. There was some old ranch stuff that, gosh, must have belonged to your great grandfather, Teancum. Garrison told me to look over by the window, by some beams. Wedged between two beams was a metal lock box. The key fit perfectly."

I had almost forgotten to breathe. A hospital bed could have fallen through the ceiling from the floor above us and I wouldn't have noticed.

"And?"

"Lilly, you wouldn't believe it. In the box were stacks of stock certificates, wrapped with rubber bands. When I lifted some of the bundles, the rubber bands were so old and brittle they fell away."

I swallowed hard, waiting for the rest of the story.

"I thought Joe had hoarded his money. I was wrong," Mom said, still incredulous. "Every cent he had ever made, he invested. All the time he was eating our cattle's oats, your Uncle Joe was getting richer and richer. And who knew? Who knew?"

I shook my head, my eyes wide, my mouth gaping open. This was truly incredible.

"Lilly, your father–after he told me about the ladder, the loft, and the metal box–just said, 'tell Lilly it's from Uncle Joe. She'll understand.'"

Mom looked at me, expecting something.

Looking at her wide-eyed, I threw my hands into the air. I didn't understand. Not at all.

"Lil, sweetie, we don't have to worry about moving off the ranch; you don't have to worry about having money for

New York, or. . ." she hesitated. "Or, if you decide you want to go to college, instead."

The door to our room opened. In strutted two muscle-bound orderlies, ready to help us get everything down to the car.

Mom jumped up and reached for her winter coat off the bed. Something fell from her coat pocket and rolled across the floor, stopping under the footrest of my wheelchair. I bent and picked it up.

"Oh, dang it! Is that a button off my coat, Lil?"
I looked at Mom's coat. No buttons missing there. I turned it over in my hand. "Well, it's a button with a little flower on it, but where it belongs . . ."

Suddenly, the room spun. With flashes, images:

> Sky, handing me this very button, telling me to 'focus, focus;'
>
> Jason–standing in the middle of a paradise–laughing at a story;
>
> A petite blonde lady, covering me with an afghan;
>
> A long path filled with light, a light brighter than the sun;
>
> Dad, hugging me and telling me to remember, to try hard to remember;

And Sky, again, saying something about
fingerprints and staying close by.

Mom gave one of the orderlies the keys to our car and they started packing boxes out the door. Turning back to me, she looked alarmed.

"Lilly, are you okay? Do you feel alright?"

"Mom, Mom, I. . . ." I closed my eyes tightly, trying with everything I had to hang onto those precious, precious images.

It was so hard to know where to even begin. I felt my mind had been hurled down a long, long tunnel, a tunnel that held at the very end of it many of my favorite people. And they were alive! They all were so very ALIVE!!

In a whisper, I finally answered. "I think I've had an exceptional experience, Mom."

"I don't know if you'd call a bad accident and an endless hospital stay exceptional, but you've certainly had a wild ride."

I clutched the button tightly in my hand. Little did she know.

***

I was wheeled out into an unseasonably warm day. As Mom slowly drove, I stared out the window in true wonderment. All the trees and buildings and cars and people! After looking at white walls for weeks and weeks, this was almost sensory overload. I gripped the edge of the seat.

Mom studied my face, perhaps worried that a panic attack may be coming on. "Are you sure this can't wait, Lilly? Why are you so intent on stopping at the cemetery today?"

"Maybe it's closure, Mom. I just don't want to go home and start a different life until I say goodbye to Sky."

Mom nodded, and struggled to find her voice. "I understand, sweetheart." Fumbling in her purse, Mom found her cell phone and handed it to me. "If Luke is late picking you up, here's my phone. Call him, because I'll be in my district meeting."

The Taylor cemetery was an old country cemetery. It sat up on a prominent hill above the town, among the fields and irrigation canals. Large, established trees–pines, maples, and quaking aspens–framed the cemetery, as well as providing shade among the headstones. The cemetery was mostly filled with settlers of the Bitterroot, and many of their descendants. My own family was here: Benjamin and Rachel; Teancum and Lilly. Dad, Uncle Joe, and Jason were buried here, as well.

Mom had told me that Helena was buried in the same cemetery as Landry; in the larger, city cemetery just outside town.

Mom turned off the road into the narrow opening between two chain link fences, our tires crunching the gravel as we slowed and made our way to the second section of graves.

Being so far out in the country, there was little traffic to disturb the robins, singing their first songs of spring from the trees. This morning we had the whole cemetery to ourselves.

I had always liked coming here with Mom each Memorial Day. We came with metal cans filled with lilacs, tulips and daffodils–pussy willow branches interspersed among them–all fruits of Mom's beautiful yard. There was no denying there was a special feeling to this place, a sense of peace and calm. All was well here.

"Sky is up here on the right, Lil. Unfortunately, her grave isn't right by the road, but it's not too far in, so I'll help you with your crutches. And here's the car blanket to sit on. It's certainly a perfect day to get outside and breathe some fresh air. There's not so much as a breeze."

I didn't answer. The lump was back, and as always, I couldn't talk around it.

Mom put the car in park. "Here we are."

Opening my door, I swung my cast around and stood up, using the door for support. Mom got my crutches and slowly we made our way to where Sky lay. Her headstone was already in place:

Skylar Vidal

April 6, 1990 – January 3, 2008

Daughter – Sister – Friend – Dancer

Mom spread the blanket out to the side of the stone, and helped me get comfortable. Reminding me to use the phone for anything, she got back in her car and slowly drove away.

I pulled the button from my jacket pocket and held it to my lips. I didn't know how, or why, but this was my connection; my link to Sky, to Dad, to Jason. I made it a point to talk out loud.

"Sky, are you close? Wow! You could be sitting right on this very blanket with me. I know you wouldn't want me sad. I know you are happy in that glorious, spectacular place, but how am I going to go on here, on earth, without you and Jason and Dad? How do I do that, Sky?" I smiled. "You . . ., you who always had all the answers when we were growing up, never told me how to do that."

The limbs from a nearby tree gently swayed as a slight breeze passed through, messing with my hair.

My thoughts were interrupted by an ancient Volkswagen bug pulling into the cemetery. Slowly making its way past me, I could see a middle-aged woman obviously trying to get her bearings. She came to a four-way stop to my right and sat there for a minute, her car sputtering out an irregular beat.

The driver turned in front of me and slowly rolled away, having obviously found what she was looking for. My eyes fell to her personalized license plate:

Montana – Big Sky Country
L I L L Y B U G

Lillybug! L I L L Y B U G! Who had called me that? I saw a miniature me running around through all the rooms of my mind, almost frantic to grab hold of another piece of memory, a five-second vignette that would tell me who had called me that name. Someone did. Someone wonderful! I counted the letters. 1-2-3-4-5-6-7-8. License plates here could only have seven figures. There were eight on that license. I squeezed my eyes shut, trying to close out everything else, to focus, to give every brain cell I had to remembering. The breeze carried the fragrance of lilacs and new spring grass, and I took in a deep breath.

"Think, Lilly, think! There was something about lilacs and grass, I was lying with someone. . . ."

There was a crunch of tires on gravel behind me. The sound of the motor told me this was Luke's car.

Poof! It was gone. The delicate thread of a precious memory floated gently away in the wind. I could not hang onto the who, or what, or when.

I hastily wiped away my tears. I did not want Luke to see me once again being a bawl baby. I would show him just how together I was now. I placed the button in the deepest pocket of my jacket and checked again to make sure it would stay. That was my tie to all of it, to everything I had experienced somewhere else, somewhere far from here. Perhaps–over time–holding that button could bring it all back. Reaching for my crutches, I pulled myself to standing. I grabbed the blanket and, shaking the leaves and grass off of it, threw it over my shoulder.

I looked to the heavens. "Sky, I'm leaving now, and I'm not going to look back. My life now is out there in the future, up ahead where this wonderful world will take me. I love you, Sky. I love you."

Luke stopped and stepped out of his car, waving hello with a huge smile on his face.

I smiled back. Taking long, strong strides on my crutches, I pointed myself toward his car. Luke–Luke with the honey blonde hair–had come to take me home.

EPILOGUE

I hated driving in the city. Every time I got within the city limits it seemed I grew a target on my back. Particularly harrowing was the high-rise construction beam that missed my car by inches. But then, the missing manhole cover right in my path scored high on the terror scale, as well. Mom said I either had nine lives or my guardian angel was working over-time.

Now, inching my way down the narrow side street, looking to my right and left, I found myself praying to that guardian angel to help me find an empty parking space. Parking spaces were at a premium in this city, which is why I had set out early for the audition. I allowed myself an extra hour in case I had to park several blocks away and then hoof it.

Amazingly, a car pulled out just up the street and, thanking my angel for such good fortune, I sped up, making sure no interloper would come out of nowhere and steal it before my eyes. I was able to parallel park on the second try, which is no small feat for me. I turned off the engine, slid down into the seat and took a deep breath. What do I do with a whole hour? Reaching for my case, I flipped through my cds until I found one of my favorites. I slipped it in and hit the 'next' button until I found No. 6. It's amazing about music. I could hear a certain song and memories–complete with smells and emotions–would all come flooding back. This song reminded me vividly of my 18th birthday. I closed my eyes and remembered.

A horn honked and I jumped! Grabbing my phone I checked the time! Yikes! Where had the time gone? Thank heavens I was close to the school.

"Please, please, don't let me miss this audition." I looked up to the sky.

Luke had left work early and promised he would meet me there. This was big! A professional career in dance rested on this final performance. The time had been put in; the talent was there; the drive was there. Ava would pull this off, and her father and I would be there to cheer her on.

THE END

ODE

Intimations of Immortality from Recollections of Early Childhood

Our birth is but a sleep and a forgetting:

The Soul that rises with us, our Life's Star,

Hath had elsewhere its setting,

And cometh from afar:

Not in entire forgetfulness,

And not in utter nakedness,

But trailing clouds of glory do we come

From God, who is our home.

– William Wordsworth, 1770-1850

ABOUT THE AUTHOR

Victoria Fielding is a mother of six, an educator, and a writer. She is currently the academic director of a residential treatment center for troubled teens at the base of the Rocky Mountains. It is there that she works with some of the best kids in the world. Victoria has had a life-long career in public and private education, having taught all ages, but mostly high-energy teens (and she still has her sense of humor–amazing!). As a classroom facilitator, she has trained professionals in the use of various software packages. Also, she was the state director for Kaplan, a national test prep company.

Victoria has lived a full and abundant life. Her life experience provides much of the background for this novel. Victoria is also mindful of all her ancestors, some of whom play a role in A Piece of Time. Her great, great grandmother, Sarah suffered many losses and struggled immensely while walking 1200 miles across the western plains; Lillie–who loved Teancum dearly–really did misplace her button, which became a fob for her father-in-law's watch; the farm house does exist, as well as the attic bedroom and the card-table gone mad. Lastly, departed loved-ones have indeed returned to warn, to reassure, and to inspire the discovery of a golden find in a barn loft.

Victoria's real claim to fame is her family of six awesome kids, their spouses, her two grand-daughters, and all of her other grandchildren waiting to take their turn on earth. When she isn't working with kids or playing with her grand-kids, Victoria loves to hike, garden, write, dance, scrapbook, and eat chocolate (yes, she's addicted to chocolate).

It is Victoria's sincere hope that when the last page has been read and the book cover closed, you will recall all the times YOU have been prompted, directed, warned, and comforted. WHO are your guardian angels?

Victoria welcomes comments. She can be contacted at her website www.victoriafielding.com. Victoria is available for speaking engagements at book clubs, etc.

For the story behind the story,
log on to victoriafielding.com to listen to a FREE audio interview with the author.